DYING TO BE LOVED

BY: ERICA COLEMAN

To Stephani
My CT Friend
Thank you so much
for supporting my dream.
Enjoy & spread the word.

Love

Moving Forward Publications
P.O. Box 35124
Detroit, MI 48235
www.ericacoleman.com
www.dyingtobelovedthebook.com

Author: Erica Coleman
Library of Congress Number
ISBN: 978-0-9850193-0-3
Editing Contribution: Dr. Natasha @ www.firstediting.com
Cover Photography/Design: Jay Rizee of TVJ Photography
Cover Models: David Taylor and Leah Turner
Copyright © 2011 by Erica Coleman

This is a work of fiction. Names, characters, places, incidents and themes are a product of the author's imagination or are being used fictiously. Any resemblance to actual persons, business establishments, events, or locales is purely coincidental.

Printed in the United States of America

To My Loves

Thanks for your continued encouragement and support throughout the writing process. You know who you are, because you believed in me even when I questioned my own ability. I thank you

Acknowledgements

"Dreams. Declare them Early"

I always knew that I would write a book someday. I started a few but just didn't know when or how I would finish one. But that's the funny thing about life. Every step along the way is a mystery waiting to be revealed. I'm glad I was finally unveiled. God is amazing.

I want to give thanks to God but in a different way. I want to give thanks to the man above for delivering me and enabling me to share my gift with the world. Writing this book was truly an amazing journey. A journey of learning the importance of love, life and the things that give you a reason to keep moving forward.

I could not have done this without the one person that not only believed in me, but motivated and pushed me daily to deliver because you wanted to see it done. My special friend, I thank you. You really mean more to me than you know. It's not every day that someone enters your life and wants the best for you with no expectations. I thank you for being the magic behind the words, inspiring me and serving your purpose.

Special thanks to the "Lucky Seven" (Dayna, Lisa B., Olivia, Iesha, Larry, Vasterie and Isaac). Thanks for the great feedback and reassurance that my gift is good enough to share with others.

To the lovely, beautiful and talented models: David, Leah, Tabitha, Whitney, Tiffany, Andrew, Devon, Ciara and Darius, I thank you so much for helping me make the book come alive. To Conrad thanks for being an awesome friend and opening your doors to me. To Mz. Tish of Divine Women and Jay Rizee of TVJ Photography, your amazing work speaks for itself. To my sisters Iesha and Olivia for being my wings on the set, I love you.

To my BFF, I love you lots. I told you all those stories would be put to use one day. Special thanks to my Mom. Whom I know is gonna be my biggest cheerleader. Your support and answering questions without asking why during the book writing process really helped me develop my characters.

To the lovely Lisa Banks, it was you that declared that my book would be a success even before it was written-and it is so. I love you and thanks for your all your help with making this book come alive and your continuing to be my mouthpiece ☺

To my REO family, that didn't bother me or complain about my early morning closed door sessions when I was in the office getting down. Thanks for supporting and encouraging me to get the job done.

To all my Y.B.I.F. Bookclub ladies, even though I waited to the last moment to share the book's finish with you, I was always inspired by your feedback during sessions about your likes and dislikes of other authors.

I would like to give special thanks to my son for loving to go to daycare everyday, which allowed me to write this book during the early morning hours you were there. I would have never been able to do it with you at home. I love you DJ.

To my friends and family that love and support me on every journey. I love you.

Guess what yall? It's official. I'm an author now. I declared it early and now it is done. Praise God.

DYING TO BE LOVED

"There's a voice that cries out in the silence, searching for a heart that will love him…" -Forever Jones

Prologue

"Lord, I come to you today in hope of receiving a listening ear. I want to thank you for your mercy, your grace, your favor and loving kindness. I want to say thank you for keeping me under your wings and showering me with all the blessings that you have seen fit for my life and circumstances. I promise to continue to be thankful, loyal and faithful to you Lord. I will continue to listen to your voice as you guide me daily. Lord please continue to guide me, as I know that my journey is not over but just beginning. Lord, as you may already know, I am not here to ask you for material possessions, as such things come and go. Today, I'm asking for your help in making my foundation stronger. I've surpassed so many hurdles, and I've accomplished goals that I couldn't have imagined I would.

However today, I feel that my foundation is weak and I'm looking forward to making it a solid one with your help, Lord. At this point, I don't know what I'm doing wrong because I work hard daily. Every day, I try to work on myself in areas of parenting, career, goal setting, finances and forgiveness, and even love. I know that you are thinking, *Love?* But yes, love. I'm willing to try this again because I'm ready. Yes Lord, maybe that's it—love. I'm going to try it again…. Amen."

****

"Hey man, I mean God. Or Heavenly father whatever they call you. As you know, I don't do this often. I'm here today because my mother won her bet for me to come to church with her. I said that I would come on Tuesday, not thinking that there was actually going to be a prayer service on a Tuesday. Go figure! Well, she got me and she's kneeling right here next to me, watching me pray. I know this may be funny, right, because I'm supposed to be praying, but I don't even know where to start. There's a lot going on in my life right now and I just wanna ask you—why me? I did everything right. I graduated from high school and college and I even got a good job right afterwards. So, why me? Why did everything have to come crashing down for no reason. First, I lost my job and then my house and I have five kids to take care of. I've never admitted this to anyone, but I'm struggling. Struggling to make it, struggling to provide, and struggling to hold on to all the things that make me a man.

My mom keeps saying that things will get better and that I just need to pray about it. I have kids to take care of and this isn't helping. Man you know what, I'm just ready to give up. But I can't! So lord if you can hear me please help me. Yeah, that's right please help me."

"Father can you hear me, we need your love today.

I know that you are listening, you hear me everyday

Father please hear us……...and we will be okay"

Father we need you to heal families today"

Kyndal

"Honey, I'm dying and I only have five months to live," were the words Michael chose to tell me that he was dying.

The memories of that night still give me nightmares. I find myself waking up in cold sweats, reaching for him, only to find no one there. My friends say that I just need to get over it. But how do you get over the love of your life? He was everything I ever wanted in a husband—rich, successful, well groomed, smart and connected. Not to mention the fact that he absolutely adored me.

When I first met Michael, I was immediately attracted to his charm and his affluent lifestyle. He was a successful doctor who appeared much younger than his 44 years. Aside from the huge age gap, my family and friends loved him. Still, 18 years had never stood in my way before. At the age of 26, I knew what I wanted and I wanted to live the good life. I was always told that the more aged the wine the finer it was. That is exactly what Michael was, my fine wine.

On our first date, Michael told me that he was going to finally start living his dreams. He said that I was his dream girl and that he wanted to make sure that I always had whatever I wanted, no matter the cost. We experienced many "first times" together. We travelled the world within the first six months of us dating. Six months later, we were engaged to be married. We were in love.

I just knew that, in Michael, God had finally answered my prayers for a dream husband. However, six weeks before the wedding, he dropped a huge bomb on me.

There I was, standing in front of the mirror with my beautiful wedding dress that we'd spent over $10,000 on. It had just arrived from Paris and I wanted to see myself in it one last time before the wedding. My mother said that she was on her way over to help me with it.

I wasn't expecting Michael to come home from his appointments until later that evening. So when he walked into our bedroom I was totally surprised.

"Michael, what are you doing here?" I questioned, frantically trying to stuff the dress in the closet so that he would not see it and ruin my surprise on the big day.

He glanced at the dress still in my hands, noting how beautiful it was. Then, with a serious expression on his face, he announced that he had something to tell me.

That was when he told me that he was dying of cancer and was in his last stages. At first, I was in complete shock and denial. I never saw the signs. How could he be dying? He looked fine. He was on a few meds, but I didn't think it was anything major. We had been having so much fun in the past months, mostly travelling, so he couldn't have been seeing a doctor regularly.

For the last two months of his life, I didn't want to do anything with him because I couldn't fathom the thought of me losing everything that we shared.

"How could he do this to me?" I would ask myself repeatedly, even after he passed away.

I couldn't stop thinking about him and all the memorable moments we shared. I would never stop thinking about him.

"Kyndal, Kyndal!" my mom yelled as she pushed my bedroom door open.

"I've been calling your name for the last ten minutes. What are you doing in here?"

Before I could respond, she looked down at the photo of Michael and me in Paris that I was holding.

She shook her head and I slid the picture into the last bag I was carrying to the car.

"Mom, can you give me a few more minutes?"

"Baby, the longer you hold on, the harder it will be to let go," she said, as she turned to leave. "We'll be waiting for you in the truck. Everything is packed and ready to go, Kyndal. We're just waiting on you."

"Okay mom, I'll be right down," I said.

It was hard to believe that I was losing everything I had come to love during the last two years so quickly.

Our mansion was repossessed by the bank, as Michael had taken out a reverse mortgage and I could not afford to pay the outstanding $200,000 in order to keep it. Now I was being forced to move on with my life with almost nothing.

I took one last look at the huge empty bedroom that contained so many good memories before closing the door.

I walked as slowly as I could down the spiral staircase leading to the front door, trying to savor the good memories our home held—all the wonderful parties, dinners, love making and pure fun. When I finally reached the bottom, I didn't want to look back, so instead, I looked up and said "Michael please walk with me. I really need you."

Kent

These last five months have been pure hell. First, I lost my job and then I find out that I have two babies on the way. What the hell could I have done to someone to deserve this? I know that I haven't always lived a good life, but how was I to know that being young and having fun would catch up with me like this?

Fuck'n women! They've always been my biggest addiction. They come so easily, I just can't seem to resist them. My Pops tried to warn me, but that obviously didn't do me any good. Hell, he was the reason I loved women so much.

When I was younger, he would bring pretty women around all the time. My Pops is what many may call a player. He has always been smooth with the ladies. There was never a time that I can remember that he had only one woman. He said that he had what he liked to call a '90 day love contract', which stipulated that, after 90 days of fun and unrestricted sex, he could either take it to the next level with the woman in question or leave her. During my childhood, he mostly chose to leave them. I vowed that I would never be like him, but over the last two years, I've noticed that his ways are slowly becoming mine.

I've always tried hard to please the woman I was with, but after being with so many that were either confused or just plain dumb, I realized that all they really wanted was somebody to come and lay down next to them at night, and I was happy to be that man.

I've been told on many occasions that I am extremely handsome. But I don't let that get to me. I really don't have to do much to capture their attention. I'm not much of a talker or charmer. I just say 'hello' and smile, and they're hooked. This damn smile has gotten me into beds of many single and married women, which inevitably lead to too much trouble—including the loss of my job.

I'd been at my job for two years without sleeping with any of my female colleagues because I vowed not to mix business with pleasure. Still, she got to me. After two months of constantly trying to ignore my supervisor's flirting and sexual advances, I finally gave in. Stacey was the aggressive type. She knew what she wanted and did whatever was necessary to make it happen. At least, that was how she was with me.

And I always loved women that knew how to take control. Her being my boss didn't really bother me, as I felt that it was a win-win situation. In my view, she would get all the sex she wanted from me and I would eventually be promoted to a higher position.

Everything was going fine for the three months I'd been sexing her after work. She was happy with the 'no strings attached' theory. I never called her to have casual conversation nor stayed over at her place after our sex-capades. She was just a fuck! Who knew that she was telling other female employees about our sex life? I just figured that the other ladies were just as attracted to me as she had been. So about two weeks ago, I started sleeping with Krystal. Krystal was more of my type anyway. From the first time we went out, I knew that she wanted me in her bed, and I obliged, of course. It wasn't until I saw her laughing with another co-worker and Stacey that I sensed that something was up.

See that's the problem with women. They need to learn to keep they damn mouth shut! Always gotta brag to their girlfriends about what they got or what they're getting. Then their friends want exactly the same thing she's getting. And I do mean exactly.

Apparently, Krystal told another employee that I was amazing in bed and Stacey walked in on the tail end of the conversation. Krystal told Stacey that we went to dinner and afterwards I stayed the night at her place. Stacey was pissed and later confronted me about it. She didn't seem to be upset that I had slept with Krystal; she was more upset that I had taken her to dinner and stayed the night with her.

I used the little charm I had to win her over and agreed to spend the upcoming weekend with her. However, something came up and I couldn't make good on my promise. She got really upset and started demanding that I commit to her or else. Of course, I ignored her threats, and now I'm pissed off. She got so mad that I didn't want to take our relationship to the next level and got me fired.

Now, here I am, 30 years old with three kids and two on the way, with four different women and no job. Where do I go from here?

Kyndal

When we first pulled up to my new condo, I almost wanted to cry. There was nothing luxurious about this place. No gates, guards or gardens. Instead, there was a chain grocery store across the street and cement yards, and it appeared that the neighbors parked their vehicles in front of their homes instead of using the one-car attached garage.

I couldn't believe this is what they called a brownstone. This place looked nothing like the pictures I'd seen in the brochure that my sister had given me. She advised me that it was a "nice and cozy neighborhood", but this was a mess. I really felt that I was taking two steps back instead of moving forward.

"Walk with me Michael," I screamed before opening the door. "This is all your fault."

My mom must have felt my pain because she immediately walked up behind me and patted my back to soothe me. "I'm here for you, baby. Just relax."

As I walked around the 1200 square foot townhome, I realized that it wasn't so bad. The painters had actually done an excellent job with the color scheme. I loved my natural brown and red tints that covered the living and dining room walls. The kitchen had been completely remodeled with nice laminate countertops, because I couldn't afford granite. The master bedroom was small compared to at the one I had at the mansion, but I liked the sky blue paint color and the crown molding.

My mom could tell that I was a little happier, so she signaled for my brothers to start unloading the truck. I decided that I wouldn't fight it because I had nowhere else to go. I'd purchased this place with the very last of my savings without even looking at it.

My sister was a real estate agent so she told me it was a good deal since these townhomes were less than 10 years old and selling for $15,000 cash. I trusted my sister to handle it because I just didn't want to deal with anything after Michael's death. My family had since been taking care of all my responsibilities including my son, Noah.

"Noah?" I yelled. "Mom where's Noah?"

"Honey, you know that Noah left yesterday to stay with his grandmother for a few weeks. Please, don't tell me that you don't remember that conversation about him going to be with her while you spent some time getting used to your new place."

"Mom, I don't remember that conversation. I wouldn't have let Noah go, knowing that I would have to be in this new place all alone," I responded sadly.

"Kyndal, please don't start with the crying again. You really need to get your emotions in check, stop daydreaming and come back to reality. I'm going to be staying here with you for a few days, but you need to get used to the fact that you're going to be alone for a while."

I just stood there, looking at my mom. Had she lost her mind? She had some nerve talking to me like this. I was the one who just lost her fiancé. I was the one who was broke and had to revert to living in common places again. I was the one who had all my dreams stolen away from me nine months ago. Still angry, I decided it was best that I just walk away from her while I had the chance.

"Kyndal you know that I love you, but you have got to get a hold of yourself. It's been nine months. You've lost a lot, but you're going to lose your job and your son if you don't pull it together. Here's the number to a doctor friend of mine that will help you through these hard times. I told her you would give her a call on Monday at noon. Please use it," she said as she walked out of the bedroom.

Yes, she has really lost it. I can't believe that she thinks I need to speak with a therapist. There is nothing wrong with me. I'm just a little down in spirit, which is to be expected after you lose someone you love. Well I don't care what people think of me, I know that I don't need to speak to a therapist about anything.

I walked over to the master bath, which I found was quite small. I was even more disappointed to see that it had a shower instead of a nice Jacuzzi tub. Now, that was all the therapy I needed—a glass of wine and bubble bath. But, I guess, I would just have to deal with it for now. I grabbed a piece of toilet paper to wrap the card in and threw it in the trash.

"I'm not calling anyone," I said to myself as I closed the bathroom door. "She's the one that's losing it."

For the remainder of the evening, I decided that it was best that I stayed as a far away from my mom as possible, to avoid any arguments so I stayed in my room.

Ring. Ring. Ring. I looked down at my phone and didn't know if I should answer or let it ring. It was my best friend Gabrielle. She had been calling me for days, but I just didn't feel like talking to anyone.

"Hello," I finally made up my mind and answered.

"Hey girl! What's been going on with you? I've been calling you like crazy," she asked.

"I know, I've just been busy," I replied.

"Busy my ass," she replied. "You haven't been to work in six months. Hell you haven't even been out of the house in six months."

"I know, I just—"

"You've just lost your damn mind," she interrupted. "Girl, I'm on my way to come get you and take you out for lunch,"

"Umm I can't go to lunch," I replied.

"Well you are going today. I want to see your new place anyway," she demanded.

"It's not quite ready for visitors yet. That's why I can't go to lunch with you today. I have to get the house ready."

"Whatever, I already called mama and she told me that she has been unpacking all your things and doing everything else for you so you can save all the bull, Kyndal. I'm on my way, so you'd better be ready when I get there," she said before hanging up without waiting for my response.

Damn! I didn't feel like going anywhere, but I knew that Gabrielle wasn't going to let me stay in the house any longer once she got here.

Gabrielle was the kind of friend that didn't take no for an answer. She wouldn't allow you to "rot" by yourself, as she liked to call it. She was always there to listen to anyone's problems, even if it meant that your problem would be the highlight of her gossip session with her friends later that day. I knew that she was a trip, but I loved her like a sister anyway. She had been a part of my family for over 10 years and I really couldn't imagine my life without her. However, these last few months had been rough and I didn't want to talk to anyone, including her.

When Gabrielle arrived, I think my mom was happier to see her than I was. My mom loved Gabrielle.

"Kyndal," my mom called upstairs, "Gabby's here."

Before I could respond, I could hear her coming upstairs.

"Ooh girl, I love this place!" she exclaimed excitedly before giving me a hug. "I've missed you."

"I've missed you too," I responded while hugging her back.

"Well you look good, Ms. Beautiful," she said while flipping through my hair.

"Well you know that I have to keep myself beautiful on the outside, honey," I said as we laughed.

It felt good to laugh. It was at that moment that I was genuinely happy to see my friend.

We finally left the house and headed to J. Alexander's for lunch. This was our favorite spot, even though it was located outside the city. During lunch, we caught up on the events that had taken place in each of our lives over the past few months. Gabrielle told me a little of everyone's gossip, including her own.

She had been seeing this guy named Benjamin for about two years now. She felt that they needed to take their relationship to the next level; however, it appeared that he was not ready to commit to her so soon. As I listened to her, I found it very strange that, although they have been dating for two years now, I had yet to meet him. I also didn't like the fact that she sounded more sad than happy when she talked about her new love. Still, I loved her dearly, and as long as she said that she was happy, I was happy for her.

Once we finished lunch, we decided to do a little shopping. Now I always loved to shop, but since my funds were now restricted, I no longer enjoyed going into the stores as much as I had before. However, Gabrielle was on a spending spree. She grabbed a pair of BCBG pumps and a bag to match at Macy's. She also bought a gorgeous pair of gray Nine West pumps at Neiman's, which she gave to me.

"Girl, I wish I could spend money like this again," I said upon leaving the store.

"Oh you will have it all back in no time," she responded. "You just have to get back out there and do it like you did before Michael. Girl, you know that you're easy on the eyes," she concluded and we both laughed while getting into her car.

I loved Gabby and I just hoped that she was right about me getting my life back sooner than later.

Later that evening, when I returned home, I decided that it was time to talk to my mom about why she felt that I needed to speak with a therapist. Although I was still a little annoyed that she even brought this whole therapist thing up, I knew that she had to have a reason for feeling this way.

"Hey Ma," I said as I slid next to her.

"Hey baby," she replied as she covered my legs with her blanket.

"Why did you give me that card to call your 'doctor friend' yesterday?" I asked.

"Well Kyndal, you should know that I love you and I want nothing but the best for you. However, lately, I've been worried about the way you've been dealing with Michael's death. It's as if, when he died, he took a part of you with him. I'm scared that you are really losing yourself. My dear, you may not know it but, you are depressed."

"I'm not depressed mom. I'm just sad," I responded with tears in my eyes.

"Baby I'm your mother. You can trust and believe that I know what you are. I know the beautiful, loving, kind and smart child that I birthed and this ain't like her. You are depressed. And I'm scared that you may be on the verge of a mental breakdown if you don't speak with someone soon."

"Now mom, how can you say that?" I asked before getting up from the couch.

"I'm not saying this to hurt you. I am only trying to make you realize that you really do need help, Kyndal."

"I don't need help mom. And I think you're the one that's going crazy," I replied. "I'm done talking to you," I shouted as I ran upstairs to my room.

A few minutes later I heard my mom knock on my door. I didn't open it.

"Kyndal, I love you and I know what's best for you. Your mind is really fragile right now and I don't want to lose you to this thing you're going through right now. Don't you remember the vibrant person you were before Michael? Don't you remember the girl that was "about her money and business"? Don't you remember the kind of mother you used to be to your son? Don't you remember the friend you were to all your friends? It's as if you're losing everything because of this man's death. That's just not right and I won't let it happen to you. So, dammit, you need to wake the hell up because you ain't lost nothing that you didn't already have. If God felt that you two were meant to be then it would be done. But it's not, so you need to move on. So if you don't call Dr. Anderson tomorrow, I will have her come over here to see you personally. I love you Kyndal. Good night."

I almost couldn't believe that my mother felt that way. What hurt me the most was the realization that there was a little truth behind what she had said. I had been neglecting family, friends and work, but most importantly, my son.

I remained in bed for the rest of the night, crying and thinking about what my mom had said to me. I figured that even if I wasn't depressed, maybe it would be good for me to speak with Dr. Anderson. She could help me see how to get past the hurt of not moving forward with the life that I had planned with Michael.

Gabrielle

I really enjoyed myself with Kyndal yesterday. I've missed my friend over the last few months since she'd been going through the whole losing Michael ordeal. Still, I personally think she just needs to get over it and move on. I love Kyndal, but that girl has got some real issues when it comes to men. She can get whomever she wants, which she always does. Yet, once she gets them, she just either leaves them or chases them away. She's what I like to call a "confused li'l skinny bitch". You know the kind of girl that has everything but doesn't know what to do with it once she gets it.

If only my love life could be so easy or, better yet, as interesting as hers is, I would be fine. But no one has written a book that allows "Got it altogether thick chicks" to live happily ever after with Mr. Prince Charming. So that's why I have to deal with all the bull that I'm dealing with Mr. Benjamin.

Benjamin and I have been seriously dating for a little over two years now, and I often feel as if we are still at the first base. When I first met Benjamin, I didn't know what to think of him. He seemed to be a pretty nice guy, but the thing that I liked most about him was that he was white. Yes white. Kyndal always thought that I was crazy because I've always told her that I was going to marry and have kids with a white man. I don't know when this thought entered my head, but I just had a feeling that a white man would be a better fit for me.

I mean, as an engineer, I do work in corporate America with a plethora of white men. My chances of being with a black man that is on my level are slim to none. Not to mention the fact that I'm smart and probably more advanced than most black men would prefer. But that's just how I see it.

Now, back to Benjamin. Benjamin is not exactly the type of white guy that I would have preferred, but he likes me, and for right now, that's all that matters. I'm willing to deal with the fact that he has a minimum wage job and has to take care of eight kids with six baby mamas. His past has nothing to do with me because I'm gonna get exactly what I want from him, a ring and a baby, whether he knows it or not.

But, for right now, I have to convince him to spend more time with me instead of his boys, doing what they call "hanging on the block." I really love him and I know that he can be the man I want him to be, if he just lets go of his childish ways. He's 33 living the life of a 21-year-old. But I can convert him. I know I can.

Kent

"I'm sorry Kent. There's nothing that we can do for you at this point. Your records show that you were tardy regularly and consistently behind on your work. It seems that you should have been fired months ago, but your supervisor saved you. Once again, I'm sorry Kent."

I didn't want to hear any more so I just hung the phone up. I still couldn't believe that I'd been fired for no damn reason. Sure, I'd been late for work a few times, but everyone on that job comes in late. Oh well, I guess, I'll have to move on. I just hope that they hadn't used attendance as the reason I was being fired because I was definitely going to file for my unemployment. I'm sure that unemployment would hold me over for a little while until I find something else.

Who am I kidding? The little money that they send bi-weekly would only cover one of my bills and that's this mortgage on this condo that I'd paid too much for to begin with. That's what I get for screwing my real estate agent, Angela, in it the day we met here.

Angela is one of my current troubles. She is six months pregnant and continues to nag me every day about us being together. I told her from day one that I wasn't interested in a serious relationship, but for some reason, she felt that because she had a little money, she could change me. I'm still trying to figure out how the hell she got pregnant. We always used protection except the one time that she wanted to get freaky in the restaurant after her birthday dinner. I should have known that she was up to something because she didn't ask me for the condom as she usually did before we got down. She already had a kid and had repeatedly said that she wasn't having any more until she got married. That's why I can't understand why she waited three months to tell me that she was pregnant. Now she's trying to have this damn baby and I'm definitely not marrying her.

Ring. Ring. Ring. I looked down at my phone and it was Angela.

"Hey Ang, wassup?" I answered.

"What do you mean wassup? I've been trying to call you since this morning," she said.

"Well, I've been busy," I replied.

"Yeah, busy with one of your tramps," she retorted.

"Whatever Ang. I got a lot going on and I really don't feel like arguing with you. Did you want something?"

"Hell yeah, I want something. I want you Kent. Can you come over?" she asked seductively.

"No Ang, I told you that I was good on you," I replied. "I gotta go. I'll call you later."

"Kent!" she yelled. "Don't play with me. You know you not good on me. We are about to have a baby, so you might as well start spending some time with your new family and leave them other tramps alone."

"Family?" I laughed, "Ang, you are really tripping. I already told you that I'm not going to be with you. I don't even know if that baby is mine."

"Get the fuck on Kent! I hate you! You know that you were the only one I was with."

"I don't know shit. I only came over on Tuesdays and some Thursdays and we used protection 99% of the time. You mean to tell me that the one time we slipped up you got pregnant. "

"Yes that's exactly what happened, Kent. I can't believe that you think that I was sleeping with someone else. I was only with you. But it's good to know that I was right about me being your Tuesday and Thursday girl," she started to cry. "I love you Kent and I know that you want us to be a family. You just can't leave those tramps alone. When you get it together I'll be here waiting for you."

"Whatever Ang. I already told you how I feel and I'm going to make sure to get a test done when you have that baby. I already got enough kids," I said before hanging up the phone on her.

"Fuck her!" I yelled. I couldn't believe that I had let myself slip up like that with her. I never really liked her at all. She was a little on the bi-polar side. One minute, she was nice and the next, she was going off into one of her crazy rants.

But I guess she wasn't too much different from the other women I'd dealt with in the past. Why couldn't they just see our relationships for what they were—just sex. I never made any promises to any of them. I never had the relationship talk with them. I rarely took any of them out on dates. I was simply just laying pipe.

My life didn't have room for love and all the emotions that came with it. I'd tried that once, with my ex-fiancé, but that didn't work out. She cheated on me and lied to me about everything during most of our relationship. That is why, once that relationship was over, I vowed that I would never commit to another woman again. It's just much easier to have several women than to just love one. No strings attached.

Knock. Knock.

I went to the door and looked out the peephole to see who it was. It was Sasha, my daughter's mother, who was also currently pregnant by me. I opened the door.

"Hi Kent," she greeted me. Layla, my daughter, ran right past us straight to the refrigerator.

"Hi Sasha," I replied while letting her in.

"Come here Layla and give daddy some kisses," I yelled.

Layla just stood by the refrigerator smiling until I came to her side.

"Daddy can I please have some chocolate milk," she asked.

"Sure. Is chocolate milk the only reason you come to daddy's house?" I asked jokingly while grabbing a glass from the cabinet.

"No daddy, I come to play video games with you too," she said.

We all laughed while I poured some milk for her. As I glanced over at Sasha, I noticed that she had gotten much bigger since the last time I saw her. But I didn't comment. I just smiled.

"Why are you looking at me like that Kent?" she asked. I didn't respond.

"I know that I've gotten bigger; you don't have to say it. This baby is killing me. I don't think I'm gonna make it to nine months," she complained.

"You have to," I replied. "I don't want any premature babies. plus I'm not prepared for any early arrivals either."

"Well, you should already know that parents are never really prepared for babies when they arrive. But then again, you wouldn't know because you've never stayed with any of your babies' mothers," she said sadly before turning away.

I felt kind of bad in a way. But I wasn't going to console her because she brought this on herself. Sasha and I had always had a sexual relationship. Even after Layla was born, I never wanted to commit to her because I just wasn't feeling her like that. We had been friends since high school and had remained cool during our college years. Sasha was the girl that I knew would always be there. But I tried not to mislead her whenever we hooked up. That's why I couldn't understand why she was having this baby. She told me she was on birth control. Still, I am convinced that she was trying to trap me this time. But that wasn't going to work. I was happy where I was with Karen, my current girl.

"Ok Kent, well I guess, I'll call you after I leave the doctors appointment to let you know what we're having this time."

"Okay. I hope it's a boy because I have enough women in my life already," I joked.

"So true, so true," she replied. "And where is your 'li'l girlfriend' anyway?"

"She's at work," I replied.

"Hmph! Just hope she don't fall too deep in love with you and end up like the rest of us."

"Whatever Sasha. I'll call you when I'm ready to bring Layla back."

"I won't be home 'til late so call me around 8 o'clock I might stop by to get her."

"Oh no you won't," I quickly replied. "I'll drop her off to you."

"Oh I forgot, you still haven't told her about the baby. That's a damn shame, Kent. One day, you're gonna learn that all your lies and the way you treat women are going to catch up with you, as God is my witness."

"Bye Sasha, I haven't lied about anything to anybody," I replied, as I rushed her to the door.

"I see you're still using the 'Women never ask, so they don't need to know' theory. You need to grow the hell up Kent. You got three kids with another one on the way. Please grow the hell up!" she yelled before walking out the house.

I slammed the door shut, startling Layla. "Daddy why is mommy mad?" she asked.

"Because she's a woman," I replied before turning the television on.

"Daddy can we watch Dora," she asked.

"You know that you're daddy's girl, and you can watch whatever you want," I said.

As Layla watched television, I walked over to the kitchen to start dinner. I took out the lamb chops that I purchased earlier from the store, cut up a few potatoes and steamed the asparagus. I thought about how I was going to tell Karen that the baby that Sasha was carrying was mine and I had another potential baby on the way with Angela, the realtor. I still hadn't told Sasha that I was having another baby a month before she was due.

But what the hell, it wasn't my fault that women never ask questions.

Kyndal

"Hi Kyndal," Dr. Anderson answered. "Your mom tells me that you've been going through a very difficult time after the loss of your fiancé."

"Yes I have but I'm doing well now," I said.

"I see. If you wouldn't mind, please just tell me a little about how you felt after his passing."

"I believe that I felt as any other person would feel after losing someone they cared deeply about. I mean, I loved Michael and I wanted nothing but the best for our future. I didn't expect him to leave me so soon with nothing," I said, as I began to cry.

"You have every right to be sad about that, Kyndal. But just know that I'll be here for you if you ever feel as though you can't go on. I know that times like these can be extremely hard on a person, in particular if they are unprepared. I know that your mother cares deeply for you and she was very concerned when she called me. For this reason alone, I would like for you to agree to come in next Tuesday to my office so that we can discuss your feelings in private."

"Well, I don't think there is anything more that we need to discuss. I'm fine and my mom will be fine as well. Thank you so much for your time Dr. Anderson. Have a great day."

I immediately got up and walked over to the kitchen to grab a cup of coffee. Although I usually don't drink coffee, it was the only thing that I could think of to calm my nerves.

I can't believe that everyone thinks that I'm going crazy or that I am truly depressed. Maybe I do need to spend some time with Dr. Anderson to release some of this sadness. On second thought, I just need to get back to work, so that I can keep myself busy. I know that the people at the clinic miss me. Yeah that's what I'll do. I will go back to work.

"Hi Dr. Gordon. How are you?" I asked greeting her after I called the clinic.

"Hi Kyndal, I'm doing just fine. It's so good to hear your voice. How are things going for you? The girls miss you here," she replied.

"I'm doing fine but I'll be even better once I'm able to return to work. I miss helping the girls. But I knew that I couldn't be of much help while facing my own problems."

"I know Kyndal. That's exactly why we haven't bothered you. But we really need you back. You know that you have a way with the girls here at the crisis center. They need your friendly, caring spirit. Karen asks about you all the time."

"Oh wow, I really miss Karen. Is she doing okay with the baby and everything," I asked.

"Yes she's fine. Why don't you come see for yourself when you're ready?"

"As a matter of fact, I will do just that. How does tomorrow sound?"

"Tomorrow will be excellent," Dr. Gordon replied enthusiastically.

"Great! Tell everyone that I said 'hello' and I'll see you tomorrow. Thank you."

"No thank you, Kyndal."

The "Moving On" Crisis center had been a huge part of my life for the last three years. I knew that right after college I wanted to be able to give back to the young women that had lost track in my community. The center was designed for women who needed help moving on after some sort of life changing event occurred in their life.

I felt so connected to the women there because I knew that I would be helping them get their esteem and feelings of self-worth back. I knew firsthand how hard it was to not be able to let go of pain and to allow it to become a part of your life, instead of letting it go.

The more I thought about the clinic, the happier I became. I knew that I should be helping people instead of worrying about what was happening in my life. It was time for me to move on.

Gabrielle

"Benjamin, where have you been?" I yelled. "I've been waiting for you for the last hour."

"Baby, I ran into one of my homies that I haven't seen in a while and he wanted to blaze one."

"Blaze one huh?" I responded sarcastically. "I guess you couldn't have told him that you had plans and had to pick your woman up from work on time?"

"I figured that you wouldn't mind, baby. I was only 15 minutes late. Quit nagging me."

"Well, this is my car you are driving and I already told you what I thought about having your good for nothing friends in my car smoking."

"We weren't smoking inside the car, honey. We were standing outside," he replied.

"You must think that I'm a complete fool. I can smell it all over my car," I yelled as I looked into the backseat to see ashes on the floor mats."

"Your friends are trifling. They can't even put ashes in the ashtray?" I said.

"Baby quit tripping. Nobody was smoking in here, I promise," he replied.

"Well, we both know that your promises aren't worth nothing," I said.

The car remained silent as we headed to I-94. All I could think of was how I wanted to go home and take a bubble bath before sex. It had been over a week since Benjamin had even touched me. I was beginning to notice that we only had sex when I initiated it. When I asked him why we hadn't been having sex regularly, he would usually respond that he was tired and wanted to go home because he had to work the next day. Hell! I had to work too. But I also wanted to be held by my man at night too.

"Baby, are you spending the night?" I asked.

"Ummm, no baby, I was just going to drop you off and head back to the hood to kick it with the boys for a little while. I can come back later if you want me to."

"Ok baby. I guess I'll see you later. But do you think you can come in before 1 a.m. because I have to work in the morning and I want to play a little before the night is over," I said before I reached over to kiss him.

"Yeah baby, I'll try," he replied not kissing me back.

"Well, try hard Ben, try hard," I said closing the door.

I walked into my one bedroom luxury apartment, alone again.

This was an everyday routine with him. Pick me up and drop me off only to return in the late night hours or sometimes the next day, right before it was time for me to go to work. But for some reason, I love him. He accepts me for "the big girl" that I am. He tells me that he loves me too. I guess, he just doesn't know how to show it. But I'll teach him.

Ring. Ring.

"Hello," I answered.

"Hi Gabrielle, How are you?" Lauren, Benjamin's daughter, greeted me.

"I'm fine sweetie, How are you?"

"I'm good. I was just wondering if you would be able to help me with my project for school. It's due the day after tomorrow," she said.

"Have you asked your mom or dad yet?"

"Well, I know my dad has to work and my mom is busy so I just asked you,"

"Oh how thoughtful. Sure I can help you," I replied. "Tell li'l Ben to have his things together for soccer practice tomorrow," I said.

"Okay. See you tomorrow," she said before hanging up the phone.

I always found it strange that Benjamin's kids always felt the need to call me to help them with whatever they needed, but never said 'thank you' when I agreed to do so. Come to think of it, Benjamin never says 'thank you' either. I guess this is gonna be something else that I have to work on with them. They'll learn eventually.

When we first met, he told me that he had three children by his ex girlfriend. What he didn't tell me outright was that he had five other kids by five different women as well.

Since I've been with Benjamin, it seems as though I'm the one on child duty. Every day, I'm either running errands, doing homework, or taking the kids shopping for things. At times, it feels that I'm giving so much and not receiving anything in return. But I can't give up. I've invested too much time to let go. I'm going to get what I want from him.

Kyndal

"Welcome back, Kyndal," everyone cheered, as I walked into the office. The room was filled with balloons and people. I immediately started to blush because I could feel the warmth and love coming from everyone in the room.

"Kyndal, we're so happy to have you back," said Dr. Gordon.

I spent the first few hours circling the room, giving hugs to my fellow co-workers and clients, as I passed them by. I was happy to see the faces of some of my old clients that had graduated from the program and moved on to living much healthier and happy lives.

After lunch, Dr. Gordon came into the room and asked if I would like to see a client today and I agreed. As soon as Karen walked into the room, I was thrilled. Karen was one of my favorite clients, probably because she reminded me of myself. She was 24 years old, a recent graduate of WSU with plans of becoming a teacher. Karen was extremely optimistic with a very caring heart. She loved kids and spent much of her time volunteering as a tutor for reading programs throughout the city.

Karen came to the crisis center a little over a year ago after she had been raped by her college boyfriend. She spent several months trying to forget what had happened to her on the night that she and her best friend went to visit their ex-boyfriends. For months, she couldn't help but think about the pain. Still, she chose not to tell anyone about her ordeal. She felt that if she did share her experience, she would sound silly telling someone that her ex-boyfriend raped her. It wasn't until three months later that she found out that she was pregnant that she knew she had to do something.

When Karen came into the center, she felt as though her world had ended and she would be stuck forever with a memory of what happened to her that night. She told me that she didn't believe in abortions. Thus, she decided to have the baby but give it up for adoption once it was born. The adoptive parents were grateful and agreed to allow Karen quarterly visits. The baby had just had her first birthday and Karen was extremely happy to spend it with her.

"Hi Karen," I greeted her with a smile, as I walked to the other side of the desk to hug her.

"Hi, Ms. Kyndal," she said happily. "I've missed you."

"I've missed you too. You look great Karen," I noted. "How are you feeling?"

"I'm feeling fine actually," she responded. "I got to see Grace on her birthday and I just got a new job as a full-time teacher at Metropolis Elementary."

"Well, it's great to hear that you're moving right along, because you've come a very long way."

"I know Ms. Kyndal, and I thank you for all your help. I'm proud to say that this is actually going to be my last meeting with you. "

"Well, hearing that gives me great joy, Karen. I know that you will do well. But don't be afraid to call me if you ever need a friend."

"I won't, you'll be at the top my list. Thank you."

After she left, I knew that returning to work was the right decision. The rest of the day went by smoothly.

When I got home later that day, I told my mom that I would be fine without her. She agreed that I needed some time to myself before Noah joined me in our new home.

The night my mom left was the first night that I couldn't sleep at all, and also the first time I decided to use the sleeping pills my doctor prescribed shortly after Michael's death.

Kent

The lights were low. The aroma from the vanilla-scented candle filled the room. The dinner table was set for two. I poured another glass of wine for myself and looked at the clock. It was a 7:15 and Karen should be arriving any minute now.

It's been almost nine months since I first met Karen at a friend's birthday party. She seemed a bit reserved that night. She wasn't drinking or dancing during the party but she caught my eye. She was wearing a white, long flowing summer dress that showed off all her curves. She was very petite, but thick in all the right places. I walked over to her towards the end of the party and asked if she wanted to dance. She declined and immediately turned away from me. Any other man would have walked away, but I asked if she didn't mind me sitting next to her. She shook her head to indicate 'no', so I slid into the booth and complimented her on her dress. She smiled but still didn't turn to face me. It wasn't until her friend came over and introduced us that she finally looked me in the eyes. I smiled and complimented her pretty hazel brown eyes. Her friend said that Karen needed to go out on a date and that I should be the one to take her.

Even though she immediately refused, I said that I would like to take her, so her friend took my phone and put her number in my phonebook. Karen tried to snatch it away, but I wouldn't let her. She even said that she wouldn't answer my call.

Normally, I wouldn't have even attempted to call anyone that didn't respond to me the way I was used to, but I felt something with her. The first time I called, she didn't answer, so I left a message, which she never returned. The second time, she answered and asked me if I was crazy. I laughed and told her that I was just interested in getting to know her. She laughed and after we chatted for a few moments, we made plans to have lunch the following day. That day, a great friendship was formed between us. We spent a lot of time together, just hanging out. For the first five months, she would shy away from anything having to do with sex. I couldn't understand why she didn't want to have sex but I didn't pressure her because I was still handling my business elsewhere. I really enjoyed her company so I didn't mind the lack of sex. When we finally approached the topic of having sex three months ago, she asked me if she could trust me. I reassured her that she could. She said that she would only have sex with me if I would agree to be with her and only her. I was a little uneasy at first, but then I realized that she was different from the other women I'd dated in the past. So, I decided to give it a try and see if this would work.

The first time we slept together was a little strange because she seemed to be a little uneasy about the way I touched her. She always wanted to have sex with her clothes on and the lights off. I didn't mind because I liked it that way too. The only thing that had me puzzled was the fact that she never allowed me to see her naked. She said that she had some scars that she wasn't ready to reveal to me just yet, so I haven't fought her about it. I could tell that she wasn't a very sexual person, which was rather hard for me to accept, given that I love sex. Still, I really liked Karen, so I assumed that we would eventually find a way of dealing with it.

In a way, I'm glad that we built the friendship first because I feel that I can tell her anything. Having said that, I don't know how she is going to take the news about the babies.

"Hey baby," she said as she walked through the door smiling.

"Hey honey," I replied. "How was your day?"

"Well, I have some great news to tell you," she said.

"Oh really," I said while removing her jacket.

"Yes, but that can wait. It smells so good in here, baby," she added before kissing me.

"Well, I wanted to do something special for you tonight," I said, taking her hand and leading her to the dining table.

"Ooh I see," she said approvingly, as she sat down in her place. "All this for me, honey? I feel really special tonight."

"Well, you are special. Very special to me."

We enjoyed dinner and wine and she told me about her new job offer at Metropolis. I congratulated her and decided that I wouldn't tell her about the babies tonight because it just wasn't the right time.

Tonight was the very first night that she initiated sex between us. She started off by straddling me at the dinner table and kissing me with so much intensity that I felt as if I was with someone else. She had never shown any interest in sex before and the way she took control of my body sent me over the top before we had a chance to make it to the bedroom. I pleasured her right there on the table without reaching for the condom. She didn't object. She let me enter her as I had never entered her before, raw and rugged. I grabbed her waist and entered her from behind. She moved forward, so I pulled her back. She murmured 'stop', but I kept going. Before I knew it, I had reached my peak, but I managed to explode all over her backside, instead of inside of her. She hurriedly moved away from the table and ran into the bathroom to wash herself. Once she was done, she joined me in the bed and laid her head on my chest.

"Baby," she said.

"Yes baby," I replied.

"I think I've fallen in love with you,"

"Me too," I replied. "Me too."

Gabrielle

"Benjamin, why haven't you answered your phone all day? I've been trying to call you."

"I was sleep most of the day because I was tired from last night," he replied.

"Well, if you would come in at a decent hour, you wouldn't be so tired all the time. But that's not the reason that I'm calling you. I took Lauren to buy supplies for her school project yesterday and she said that she forgot to get the money from you, so I had to pay for it. Lil' Ben needed some new shoes for practice because the old ones were too small, so I picked those up for him before I took him to practice yesterday."

"Oh baby, good looking out."

"Good looking out? Why didn't you give them money for these things if you knew they needed them?" I asked.

"Because they didn't ask me. They knew that I would have told them to wait until their report cards came back today."

"Oh really? So now I'm at a loss, right?"

"You should've asked me first," he said.

"You never answer your phone when I call you," I retorted angrily, trying hard not to yell at work. "And their report cards came back yesterday. Although their grades were okay, I know that they could have done a lot better."

"Why haven't you tried to help them after school more?" I continued.

"My kids are real smart. They just get lazy sometimes. I'm just going to have to pull them from the other activities. That's all," Benjamin replied casually, as if not caring.

"I don't know why you would do that. That's the only time they get to leave the house and spend time with other kids. Maybe you should just try to help them out a little more."

"I do. And you don't have any kids, so please don't tell me what to do with mine," he said before hanging up the phone.

This was how most of our conversations ended. I tried to give him helpful advice about life and how to help the kids, but he always took it as if I was trying to insult him. For the two years I've known him, I have never seen him help them with homework or attend any of the parent teacher conferences. I've been trying my hardest to help them in my free time, but they refuse to listen to me. Lauren only calls me when she needs something or wants to go somewhere and Li'l Ben is just going with the flow. I know that I can't tell him how to raise his kids, but if they are going to be around me, they need to learn to respect me as more than just a 'go to girl'.

I picked up the phone to call Benjamin back. He didn't answer, as usual, so I sent him a text instead.

"Baby, I apologize for suggesting that you need to help your kids. I guess, I'll try to spend more time helping them out. I hope this doesn't change our dinner plans for tonight because I miss you and I really want to spend some alone time with you tonight. I love you Ben."

I waited for two hours for Ben to show up but he never did. I guess that's what I get for nagging him about things before its time for us to go out. I spent the rest of the night watching the HBO "Real Love" soft porn series. This was my favorite type of porn because the men showed a real interest in the women. They bought them flowers, kissed them and made love to them. I guess I'll experience this with Benjamin someday. Until then, I'll let this bullet go to work.

Kyndal

"Kyndal, we have a new client that has recently suffered the loss of a child. Her name is Melissa, she's 24 years old and claims to have no family. I know that you just got back from dealing with your loss, but most of the other counselors have a full caseload and I know that you will be a great fit for her. Do you think you can handle it?"

"Sure Dr. Gordon. No problem," I replied confidently.

"Are you sure?" she asked again.

"Yes Dr. Gordon, this is my job. I'm fully capable of handling all my clients just as I have done previously. There's no need to be concerned. You can send her in as soon as she's ready."

Dr. Gordon left the room. I grabbed my notepad and rearranged the flowers on my desk. Ten minutes later, a tomboyish looking girl walked in.

As she walked in, I stood up immediately and walked towards her with a broad smile.

"Hi, you must be Melissa. My name is Kyndal and I will try to help you in dealing with your issues."

"Yeah that's me," she replied. She ignored my extended hand and walked straight to the window to look outside.

"Well, why don't you tell me why you're here today?" I prompted her as I walked back to my desk.

"I honestly don't know," she replied. "They tricked me into coming here. They said that I needed to talk to someone about my situation. Go figure."

"Can you tell me who 'they' are and what your 'situation' is?"

"My homies from the block. One of my home girls said I was in denial after losing that baby, I was carrying."

I paused for a moment because I couldn't believe what she had just said.

"What do you mean by 'that baby', Melissa? Was it your child you lost?"

"Well, it was my child for a month or so, but he gone now. So there's really nothing to talk about."

"Ok Melissa. How did the baby die?"

"That baby caught pneumonia and died at the hospital."

"Ok," I replied trying to remain calm and composed. "How did he catch pneumonia?"

"You see, now you getting too personal. You just gon' find a way to blame me too like everybody else."

"Melissa, I'm not here to judge you. I'm here to help you. I do understand that you might not be comfortable enough with me yet to reveal what happened to your baby. However, I'm here for you to talk to.
"

"Yeah, I think I better leave," she said, heading to the door.

"Melissa, I would love to talk with you whenever you're ready. Please take my card. Call me whenever you're ready."

She took my card and closed the door. I walked towards the door, opened it and stood in the hall to watch her leave the building. She walked towards Woodward Ave. and proceeded to cross the street. I watched her as she went inside the gas station on the corner of McNichols and then back out with a cigarette in her hand. She walked over to the bus stop and waited.

"Hmmm," I said to myself, as I watched her light her cigarette and take two puffs before stomping it to the ground. She must have wanted some type of help if she came here on her own by bus, I thought. I turned around and headed to Dr. Gordon's office.

"Hi Dr. Gordon," I greeted her as I peeked through her door.

"Hi Kyndal, May I help you with something?" she responded, as she looked up from some paperwork.

"Yes. Where did that client Melissa come from? Who referred her?"

"She didn't say that anyone referred her. She just said one of her friends told her about the center and she wanted to talk to someone."

"Oh well, that's strange, given that she didn't seem as though she wanted any help at all."

"Well Kyndal, you should know that most clients say that they don't really want help at first because it's hard to admit one's vulnerability. Once they get past the denial stage, they'll be more willing to accept the fact that they need help."

"I know. But she was a little different than any of my previous clients," I said.

"There are really no two cases alike when it comes to people we handle here in the crisis center, Kyndal."

"I know that everyone has their own issue and story, Dr. Gordon. I am also well aware that we're here to help in any way we can."

I left Dr. Gordon's office and returned to my desk. I wrote down a few notes on Melissa. I opened a new file for her on my laptop and named it "Melissa, the lost child".

 After I was done, I closed my laptop, gathered my things and headed to my car.

I was five minutes late when I reached the New Center Eatery to meet Gabrielle for lunch. As I walked into the restaurant, I realized that she wasn't there yet. I immediately picked up my phone to call her, she didn't answer, so I allowed the waitress to seat me at a table by the window. I pulled out my cell phone and proceeded to text her, because she knew that I hated waiting for people. The moment I pressed the 'send' button, she walked in and smiled at me.

"Hey psycho," she said. "I knew that you were going to be tripping because I wasn't here yet. Breathe girl, breathe," she teased, laughing.

"You know it," I replied, joining her in laughter.

"You look nice and refreshing today," she commented.

"Thank you," I replied. "I feel good too, now that I'm back to working with the girls."

"Well that's great. I'm glad that you're back to doing what you love and out of that house that you were trapped in for all those months."

"Girl, I was not trapped in the house. I just didn't want to be bothered. That's all."

The waitress took our orders and I was surprised to hear Gabrielle order a chicken salad instead of her usual—chicken and waffles.

"Girl, what's wrong with you?" I asked. "We are at a chicken and waffles spot and you order a salad. What the hell is going on?"

"You silly. I'm on a diet. Benjamin says that I eat too much meat and I need to get my body ready for the baby."

"Baby? Girl, what baby?"

"The baby we're going to make, silly!"

"Ok, so he's finally agreed to having a baby?"

"No. He's still saying that he doesn't want any more kids, because he has enough. But that doesn't have anything to do with me. I want him to give me my baby and he will."

"You're crazy. Why would you want to have a baby with someone that doesn't want one? That's stupid."

"It's not stupid. I want what I want. And you can't talk because you have your baby already."

"Yes I do. But trust me, it's no fun being a 'baby mama'. And weren't you the one telling me that you weren't having a baby until you got married because of how it would make you look to your co-workers. Don't let this little white boy make you look like a fool."

"Nobody's going to make me look like a fool. I love Benjamin and he will be my husband before I have the baby. Trust me. He just doesn't know it yet."

"Ok Ms. Know it All. I just don't want you to have to go through what I went through with Noah's dad. Sometimes, I wish I had never made that promise to God before I met him. Because, I can tell you, that pregnancy is miserable when you don't have someone there to support you."

"Well that's not going to be me because he's going to marry me and we're going to be happy with our baby," she objected, clearly offended. "How's my little Noah doing anyway?" she changed the subject.

"He's fine. He's at his grandmother's until Friday. I miss him so much now that mom is gone and I can't sleep at night."

"I may come over on Friday after I pick the kids up from school."

"You're the best stepmom without a ring I know. You're always with those kids," I said.

"I know. Benjamin doesn't seem to appreciate it though. Oh well—"

"There shouldn't be an 'oh well'," Kyndal interrupted, "He should be grateful because there are not many women like you out here willing to take care of someone else's kids and not complain about it."

"I never said that I didn't complain, I just wish he was more responsible and grateful."

"Hmph, and this is the man you want to have a child with. You really need to rethink that whole thing."

"I already thought about it. Please, let's just change the topic. When are you going to get your groove back?"

"What groove? I'm good."

"I don't think so. You seem a little uptight. You need somebody to work that ass out," Gabrielle noted, at which we both burst out laughing.

"Girl please. I don't want nobody near this until further notice. I got too many problems already."

"That's one of them," she said.

"I beg to differ. But you must be getting it in regularly now since you're teasing me, Dr. Ruth."

"No comment," she replied.

It was at that moment that I saw the sadness in Gabrielle's eyes even though she was still smiling. She had told me once before that Benjamin wasn't having sex with her regularly and always complained that he was tired or would change the subject whenever sex came up. I really wanted my friend to have the happiness that she deserved, but for some reason, she was holding on to the fantasy life that she wanted so badly with a white man. It wasn't always my place to keep repeating that he was showing sure signs of infidelity. It was obvious that he was lying to her and using her, and that he was breaking her down, slowly but surely. I loved her dearly, but I also knew that I could not make her see the truth. Sometimes people have to learn for themselves.

Kent

"What the fuck do you want now Angela?" I yelled into the phone.

"Why don't you answer your phone at night when I call, Kent?"

"What are you talking about? Maybe because I'm asleep."

"Don't fucking play with me, Kent. I know that that little tramp of yours is living with you."

"What tramp? Angela you're crazy."

"You damn right, I'm crazy Kent. I'm crazy because I love you. I really miss you, Kent. Can you come over tonight?"

"No I can't. I have other plans."

"Plans. What plans? Oh you're staying home playing house with that whore instead of coming to be with your real family."

"Real family? What real family?"

"Oh really? You don't remember the family that you spent the last nine months with. Kent we have a baby on the way so we need to get the house ready."

"That's not my problem, Angela," I said, now really frustrated with the conversation.

"It is your fucking problem! You're the reason I'm sitting here fat and ugly with your baby instead of living my life. You are going to take responsibility for what you did to me."

"I didn't do shit to you. You're the one that didn't want to use a condom that night. You probably did this shit on purpose. You know what, I'm done talking to you Angela! I might say something that I won't regret later."

"You already did. And if you don't get it together, you'll regret ever meeting me. You have two months to lose the whore or else."

I hung up the phone. Damn. How could I have fucked up like this again? But Angela's even more psychotic than my first son's mother. I hope that baby ain't mine, because I don't want to have to deal with her.

Ring. Ring. I looked down at the caller I.D., relieved to see that it was Karen.

"Hey babe, how are you today?"

"I'm fine honey, I really enjoyed last night."

"I did too. I loved the way you unleashed your wild side."

"There's a lot you don't know about me, but you'll find out in due time."

"In due time huh."

"Yes, in due time. But I called to ask you if you wanted me to bring dinner tonight. I have a taste for Chinese."

"Sure. If you don't mind. That'll save me some time because I have a few errands to run before it's too late."

"Ok honey, see you around 7:30."

"Ok babe. See you then."

"Oh honey, what did your manager say about you getting your job back?"

"I spoke with him yesterday and nothing has changed. It looks like I'm going to have to find something else, quickly."

"Awww! Sorry to hear that, baby. But I know that you'll find something soon."

"Thanks baby. I'll see you later."

"Alright honey. Have a good day."

Damn. I still had to find a way to tell Karen about the babies. I'm just going to have to do it tonight.

I grabbed my keys and headed for the door. I had agreed to pick the girls up from daycare today. That was also something I had to figure out how I was going to pay for. It cost $300 a week for both of them and I only had $2500 in my savings account. Now I really felt bad about my foolish spending habits for the years I worked at Delphi. I easily made $120,000 over the past two years, and have nothing to show for it, apart from this new loft and my truck. Now I don't even know how I will manage paying the note on both of those. I'll figure something out one way or another.

"Daddy," yelled Layla. "Can you take us to McDonalds to play today?"

"Yeah daddy! Let's go to McDonalds," Brittany chimed in.

"You know that daddy's girls can go wherever they want," I agreed.

"Yay! Yay!" they yelled as I fastened both of them in their car seats.

I headed towards the McDonalds on Mack and 75 so that I could drop Brittany off first once her mother got off work.

Brittany's mom, Taylor, and I grew up together in the same Rosedale Park neighborhood. We were actually best friends when we were in fifth grade. It wasn't until we were fifteen that we decided to be a couple. She was seeing another guy at her school at the time but she told me that she liked me more. I took her virginity shortly after and then we were inseparable. It was at the age of 16 that I could honestly say that I experienced my first love. I loved Taylor, however, her mother caught us having sex one day and refused to allow me to see her again. This was difficult because we went to different schools and she was not allowed to go out during the entire summer. At first, we tried our best to sneak around, but after a while, I got bored. I was becoming very popular at my high school and girls were pretty much throwing themselves at me. Of course, I wanted to be the man, so I slept with as many as I could that summer. Right before school started, someone told Taylor that I had been seen kissing one of their friends and she got mad at me. She stopped calling me as often and I barely got to see her except at the YMCA on the weekends. She was on the small league cheer team that I played ball for.

My love for Taylor never died and we continued to be friends throughout our college years. During my senior year of college, I proposed to her and she accepted. It wasn't until right before graduation that I found out from one of her friends that she had been sleeping with another guy at her school her entire senior year. I was heartbroken and vowed to never commit to another woman again. After we both graduated, we came back to the city, as planned.

Even though I was hurt, I still tried to make it work because I really loved her. It wasn't until I had to tell her that I was having a child with Sasha and Missy, a girl that I'd slept with twice in college, that she became really upset with me. She left me for two months. We eventually got back together after I explained to her that I was really hurt by what she did to me so I started fooling around with other women. She said that she understood and still wanted to marry me.

Eight months later, she found out that she was pregnant and wanted to have the baby. She moved in with me and we began to plan the wedding. However, after only three months, I found out from a mutual friend that she had started seeing Eric—the guy she cheated on me with in college—once again.

I called her late one night when she didn't return home. She didn't answer. So I stayed up to wait for her. When she arrived at six o'clock that morning, I asked if she had been with Eric and she blatantly said yes.

I couldn't believe it. She went on yelling at me for getting two women pregnant at the same time and then expecting her to marry me. She called me all kinds of names and weak bastards. She said that she hated me for ruining her life by cheating on her and embarrassing her. Finally, she said that she could never marry me and left.

At first, I was more hurt by the fact that she told me that she had cheated on me, but then the pain really started to sink in when I realized that she hated me. How could the only woman I truly ever loved say that she hates me after what she did to me?

I didn't leave the house all weekend because I couldn't focus on anything else. I kept seeing her face, hearing her screaming hateful things at me and not shedding one tear of remorse. I vowed to remember the pain so that I would never feel that way about another woman again.

Later I found out that she was pregnant, but there was no hope of us getting back together. Even after our daughter, Brittany, was born, I continued to ignore Taylor as much as I could. Our encounters were very strange at first but we had just begun to be friendly with one another at Brittany's 2nd birthday party a year ago.

"Hey Taylor," I said as she opened the front door.

"Hi Kent," she replied, kissing Brittany. "Thanks for saving me a trip."

"No problem," I replied. "You know how much I love my girls."

"Yeah, we know you love all the girls," she said, laughing.

"Anyway, I think I'll be picking them up from now on since I'm not working right now."

"Oh wow. They didn't give you your job back. That's crazy."

"Yeah it is. But life goes on."

"Well, let me know if you need anything," she offered sincerely.

"I'm good for now. I just have to get back out here and find something different, and fast, because daycare is expensive."

"Yes it is. And I'm not paying for it because I can't afford it."

"I know. I wouldn't put that burden on you."

"Brittany told me that Layla had a new little brother on the way."

"Yeah she does," I said looking away.

"Kent, please tell me that that baby isn't yours," she said softly.

I paused for a few moments before replying. "I wish I could."

"That's a damn shame Kent. A damn shame," she yelled before slamming the door in my face.

At least I had one woman out the way I still had three more to tell, including my mother.

****

"Hey Kent," yelled Sasha. "Can you go to the store to get some milk for Layla before you leave?"

"I guess so," I replied.

"Thank you and can you please bring me back some laundry detergent and garbage bags as well."

"Ok," I said as I headed towards the door.

"Take Layla with you so that I can be sure that you'll return."

"Whatever Sasha, I'll be right back."

"Please come right back," she yelled after me.

Layla followed me out the front door. "Daddy can I go with you please?"

"Sure baby, C'mon."

I turned on the radio to hear what Michael Baisden was talking about today. I heard a few callers give their opinions on the strange lovers they'd had in the past. Right as I was getting Layla out of the car, a blue G6 pulled up next to me. I turned to see who it was, instantly recognizing Angela.

"Oh so you playing house today huh?" she screamed.

"Angela, what the hell is wrong with you!?" I yelled.

"I told you that I wanted to see you today, didn't I? But I see that you're visiting all your tramps but me. So I thought I'd come and see you personally."

"Get the hell on Angela," I said trying to put Layla back into the car.

"Oh no, I'm not going anywhere," she said as she got out of the car. Her belly seemed huge on her small frame. She was short so I stood about a foot over her.

"I'm sorry. Did I upset the little one?" she asked sarcastically.

"You need to go home right now," I yelled. "Look at you out here, acting all ignorant. Why did I…"

"Why did you what Kent? Why did you ruin my fucking life?" she said looking as if she was going to start crying, "Or why did you lie to me about our future? Or better yet, why did you fuck me?"

"Yes, those are my exact feelings at this moment." I said turning away from her. "Please go home and do something to yourself Angela."

"Oh so now, I don't look good enough for you Kent. I'm carrying your baby and this is how you goin' to treat me."

"That's not my baby Angela," I said. "Please go and find your baby's real father and fuck with him."

I fastened Layla back into her car seat and pulled off. When I got back to Sasha's house, I opened the door and told Layla to tell her mom that I would bring the stuff back later. "Ok daddy," she said.

I got back into my truck and pulled off. On the way home, I kept looking in my rearview mirror for Angela. I couldn't believe that she was following me. She was really fuck'n crazy. When I got home, I checked the parking lot for her car and was relieved to notice that she was not there.

I walked into the house, dropped my keys on the bar and flopped down on the couch. How the hell did I get myself into this again?

Back at Sasha's House…

"Mommy, daddy said he's going to bring your stuff back later," said Layla.

"What?" she yelled getting up from her bed. "Where is he Layla?"

"He's gone," she replied.

Sasha shook her head in disbelief and picked up her cell phone to call Kent.

"Mommy, that Angela lady was yelling at daddy," she continued. Sasha put the phone down.

"Angela?" she asked. "What did she say?"

"She was using bad words, yelling at him and her tummy was big like yours," she said.

"What?" Sasha sat down on the bed in silence for a few moments before asking Layla "Was she pregnant like mommy?"

"Yes mommy, she was pregnant like you."

"I can't believe that Kent would do this to me again. Layla please go downstairs and play with your toys for a little while, I'll be down there in a minute."

She picked the phone back up to call Kent. When he didn't answer she grabbed her shoes and put Layla in the car. She tried to call him twice more but he still didn't answer. "Oh, you will answer the door, trust me!"

****

I looked up at the clock. It was almost 7:30. I had enough time to jump in the shower before Karen arrived. After the shower, as I looked down at the phone, I saw that Sasha had called three times. I made a note to call her back before the night was over because I knew she was upset with me for not bringing back her stuff from the store.

The doorbell rang.

"Hey baby," said Karen as she kissed me at the door.

"Hey baby, I missed you," I said as I closed the door.

"Oh really, well how about you kiss me the way I like, to show me how much," she said.

I pushed her up against the wall and slowly slid her dress down to her ankles. Right as I got on my knees, there was a pounding at the door.

"Who the hell? " I said as I stood up.

Karen grabbed her dress and ran towards the bedding area.

"Open the fucking door Kent!" yelled Sasha.

For a moment, I just stood by the door, frozen. Finally, I decided to open the door, knowing that she wasn't going to go away. As soon as I opened the door, she started yelling at me.

"You lying fucking bastard. You ain't shit. Why didn't you tell me that you had another baby on the way? Layla told me about Angela. How could you do this to me again?"

I was shocked. I didn't know what to say. Before I knew it, Karen was dressed and back in the living room.

"Kent?" she yelled.

"Oh, and look at you, still being the fucking whore you are! I hope that you don't end up like the rest of us," Sasha yelled at Karen.

"Excuse me," Karen said.

"Kent hasn't told you that this baby I'm carrying is his because he's such a little bitch. But here's one even better, his other girlfriend is pregnant too," she laughed.

"Kent?" Karen screamed.

"That baby ain't mine," I yelled.

"Which baby Kent?" Sasha yelled. "'Cause we both know you are the only loser I've slept with the past four years."

"Angela's baby isn't mine," I said.

"Whatever Kent? That's the same line you ran about K.J. and he looks just like you."

"Kent?" Karen yelled again, looking at me pleadingly.

"Yes, baby. I'm sorry I was going to tell you."

"Yeah he's sorry alright. Sorry that he hasn't grown up yet. Sorry that he can't keep his dick to himself. Sorry that he's such a fucking liar. And sorry that he will never be shit."

"Baby, I'm sorry," I said, turning to Karen.

Karen walked right past me through the front door.

Sasha immediately stepped in front of me, "I can't believe that you did this to me again, Kent. I really can't believe you."

"No, I can't believe you. We aren't together never have been. I can't believe that you came over to my fucking house to confront me about someone else's baby. That baby may not even be mine and you just ruined my relationship with Karen."

"Here you go, blaming me for your problems again. Someone else is always to blame for your immaturity Kent. I know that we're not together and probably never will be. But I do deserve some respect from you as the mother of your child. Why didn't you tell me Kent?"

Sasha started to cry. I felt bad for her, but I couldn't comfort her because she didn't deserve it after what she had just done.

"Where's Layla?" I asked.

"She's in the car," she grabbed some tissue from the box on the table. "I better go," she said without looking at me.

"Yeah, I think that you should leave now."

After she left, my head started spinning. I couldn't believe that all of this happened to me in one day.

"Karen?" I said to myself as I thought about how she must be feeling. I hoped that she was okay. I knew that I had to find a way to make it up to her.

Kent

I pulled up at Karen's place an hour later. I really hadn't thought about what I was going to say to her other than simply stating that I was sorry. Damn if it wasn't for Sasha showing up I would have been able to tell her in a way that she would understand. Oh well, nothing really happens that smoothly for me these days.

I tried calling her twice before I finally went to the door of her apartment. When she looked out and saw that it was me, she yelled at me to go away.

"Baby, I know I messed up really bad. But can you please open the door so that we can talk."

"Talk about what Kent? You weren't trying to talk to me about anything before."

"I just want a chance to explain what happened and then you can decide for yourself."

"Leave his ass alone girl," her neighbor yelled. "I'm sure he's a dog just like the rest of them."

I turned around to see the nosey old lady with glasses and rollers in her hair, standing in the doorway with her robe on. She snarled at me and before I could say anything, Karen opened the door.

"Come in Kent, "she said. "But you only have 10 minutes."

"I'm sorry Karen," I started to apologize, as I headed towards the couch.

"Please don't sit on my couch because you're definitely not welcome here. I just didn't want the neighbors to hear you."

"I see. Well where do I start?"

"Start at when you were going to tell me that you had two women pregnant and where and how you got them pregnant?"

"Sasha and I messed around in the earlier stages of our relationship. I haven't been with her since I've been with you. And Angela and I were just having sex."

"Angela," she said. "Isn't that your realtor?"

"Ummm yes," I said hanging my head low.

"Oh I see the phone calls that you were telling me about were not business-related at all. You've been screwing her all this time and playing me for a fool."

"No. I haven't slept with her in months."

"How many months Kent? Two or three? We've been together for nine and…"she started accusing me, before I cut her off.

"We didn't start sleeping together until three months ago."

"Oh so that's going to be your excuse! Just because I wasn't sleeping with you, you thought that it was okay for you to have sex with other women."

"No that's not what I'm saying. We were just friends, right? I didn't know that sleeping with other people was out of the question."

"Now that's just stupid!" she replied. "Get out of my house, Kent!"

"Ok Karen, I'll leave but I just want you to know that I really do care about you. I don't want to lose you over this foolishness."

"Foolishness? Are you crazy? You have not one but two kids on the way, and you already have three. What kind of relationship can we have? I'd be a fool to stay with you and accept all of this into my life after what I've been through. Get the hell out of my house Kent and don't ever come back!"

As I walked to the front door, I turned around to kiss her before I left.

"Baby, I love you," I said.

"You don't know what the hell love is Kent. Get out!"

As I walked to my car, I felt as if someone had just shot darts all around me, but the needle from Karen's words had just hit the bulls-eye.

"What the hell have I done?"

Ring. Ring. I looked down at my phone. Seeing that it was Angela, I decided not to answer.

I took the long way home so that I could sort out my thoughts. However, by the time I reached Lafayette, I knew that I didn't want to go home, so I called Pops.

"Hey son, what's going on?" he answered.

"Nothing much," I replied. "Where are you?"

"I'm down at Flood's having a few drinks. You should come down for a few."

"Alright," I said, "I'm right down the street. See you in a few."

My dad was probably the worst person to get advice from, but I needed someone to talk to.

Gabrielle

"Hi Bill, I hope that you got the reports that I emailed you last night about the part order."

"Yes, Gabrielle, I did receive them. However, I feel that many of these items are unnecessary because there will be some upgrades on the Chevy vehicles this year, in which a lot of these parts will just phase out."

"I can definitely understand what you're saying. However, these are the parts being used now, so the workers need them now. Any changes that will be made will take effect on the subsequent models and will not affect the design of this one. I have already forwarded the report to the appropriate parties for review and everyone has accepted except you."

"That's because I don't agree with you, Gabrielle."

"I understand. However, you need to address your recommendations directly with management. I'm just following my orders. So can you please accept this so that we can get the parts ordered on time? I don't want to have to tell John that you are the reason for the delay again."

"You know, it's hard working with you people," he said. "I don't understand why management has to correspond with me through you, rather than directly with me. They really have to work on restructuring levels here. There's no way I'm supposed to be taking orders from…"

"From what Bill? A woman?" I shouted, "Please don't finish your statement because I don't want to have to report this to John either. I will be expecting an acceptance shortly. So please follow up accordingly," I said before hanging up the phone.

This issue with Bill and the many 'Bill's at Lamco has been driving me crazy for quite some time now. They just can't seem to get over the fact that I'm a young, African American female engineer. I'm sure that they believe that Affirmative Action or equal opportunity employment has played a role in my being here, but I know that my hard work and dedication speak for itself. Since I've been here for the last three years,

I've noticed that the men like me when I'm helping them out with their work. Still, when it comes to me giving them direct orders, the level of respect is minimal. I don't care. I know that I'm here because I belong and I'll just have to keep on proving my value until they get a real understanding of me.

A few minutes later, I received an acceptance email from Bill along with a disclosure statement requesting a meeting with management to discuss recommendations for future part order handling. I laughed and closed the email.

"The nerve of these people, "I said to myself before getting up from my desk to leave for lunch.

I headed for the cafeteria and ordered a veggie wrap with a side salad. This whole dieting thing isn't for me, but the way Benjamin has been complaining about my weight lately has started to get to me. I mean, I was this size when he met me. I guess, he just wants his woman a little tighter in some areas, so I'm doing my due diligence.

I picked up my phone to call him. "Hey baby," I greeted him when he answered the phone.

"Hey," he replied. "What's up?"

"Nothing much, I just wanted to chat for a little while since I'm on my lunch break," I said.

"Oh lunch huh?" he laughed. "Let me guess what you're eating today. Tubby's steak and cheese with extra tubby sauce and those greasy curly fries."

"Ha ha. Very funny," I tried to sound amused, even though he hurt my feelings. "Actually, you'd be surprised that I'm eating a veggie wrap with a salad and water."

"I'd have to see it to believe it," he said.

I instantly got quiet as I found it hard to hide my hurt feelings. "Well, at least I'm not the only one with trust issues."

"Oh here we go," he replied. "What don't you trust me about now?"

"I looked through your phone last night while you were sleeping because the alert went off. I was rather shocked to see that you were on Facebook, chatting with naked girls."

"You didn't see nothing. And so what if I chat? It's not like I'm seeing any of them."

"How am I supposed to know that?" I asked.

"You're supposed to trust me, but you don't, so that's on you. You know what, I don't feel like talking to you anymore. Bye." He disconnected the phone before I had a chance to say anything. But that is what he always did whenever I found out some information about him.

Last night, after he came to the house around 12 am, I couldn't sleep. I got out of the bed and headed to the living room to watch "Real Love" again. Just as I was getting comfy, I heard the message alert going off on his phone. I reached into his jacket and took the cell phone out. He never locks his phone, so I was able to check it without any problems. The message was from Nikki and it read, "I had a good time with you last night. I hope that we can do it again sometime. Oh and I hope that I looked as good in person as you said I did online." I was really angry, but I wanted to see what the heifer looked like, so I clicked on the link and checked the picture out for myself. No this chick didn't have a picture of her ass tooted up in lingerie smiling. She wasn't that cute but she had a nice ass. She was a little smaller then I am, but I felt that I was more attractive. Moreover, any woman showing her ass on the internet is a hood rat in my book.

Intrigued, I continued to scroll through the messages in his inbox, noticing how he was complimenting these hood rat type women in every message. He rarely gave me compliments. I was truly hurt by what I had found but I didn't want to bring this to his attention, as I knew that I would only make him mad at me for snooping.

An hour later, I went back into the bedroom and watched him sleep. I knew that he liked to flirt with women, but I didn't have any evidence of him cheating on me. I finally fell asleep and decided not to mention it the next morning at breakfast.

"I don't know why I just did that," I reprimanded myself.

I cleaned my table and headed back upstairs to my workspace. Right before I reached my desk, I saw Bill. He glared at me, but I ignored it and just smiled. It wasn't my fault that I was in the position that he wanted. He was the type of white man that I knew how to handle. Too bad Benjamin doesn't fall into that category. But he too will learn.

Kyndal

"Kyndal, Melissa Graves is here to see you?" the secretary announced.

"Give me a few minutes," I replied. I hadn't seen Melissa since she rushed out of my office two weeks ago. She didn't call or schedule an appointment. I cleared my desk and headed to the lobby to meet her.

"Hi Melissa," I said cheerfully. "How are you today?"

"I'm good," she replied as we walked into my office.

I went back to my desk and took my seat. Instead of sitting down in the chair across from me she went straight to the window. "Melissa, you can sit here in this chair if you like."

"I'm straight. I don't wanna feel like I'm in therapy or nothing. I'm good," she said before laughing.

"Okay. How can I help you today?"

"I'm not sure that you can help me. I just wanted to come here to get something off my chest. You know."

"Well, I'm here to listen."

"I'm just pissed that I carried that damn baby for nine months and it just died on me."

I sat silently, waiting for her to continue.

"I mean, why couldn't it have died in the womb before I gave birth? Why did it have to wait to get here and make me grow attached and then just die on me? What kind of shit is that?"

She looked at me as if she wanted me to answer that question, but I didn't have an answer. "Melissa, we never know when or why people that we love die. All we can do is thank God for blessing us with their presence."

"That's bullshit!" she yelled. "God don't have nothing to do with this. My daddy is a pastor at a church, so I know all about the Holy Book. However, God has never saved me from all the bullshit I've had to deal with in my life. My daddy preaches about oh how great God is and how he will make everything right. Where the hell has he been the last three years of my life? Just when I thought that I was going to be able to do something good, it was taken away from me. If God is so great, why would he continue to hurt people like me?"

I sat in my seat, bewildered, staring at the girl standing across the room, dressed in men's clothing. I had dealt with many clients that questioned God's judgment, but none that spoke of Him so harshly.

"Melissa, I know that you are facing very trying times right now, and I know that it hurts. But talking about it will make it so much easier because you may be able to find a resolution behind God's plans for your future. Why don't you take some time to tell me about the past three years of your life and the experiences that caused you so much pain?"

"Hell no!" she refused flatly. "I don't need a therapist. I don't need anybody trying to read my mind only to tell me that I have problems with this or that. I know what I need. I just came here to release that. I'm out," she said as she headed to the door.

"Melissa, I know you don't want to talk about it. But just do me a favor and take this notepad to write a few things down as you think of them."

She took the small notepad and stuffed it into her jacket pocket and left. I went back to my desk and wrote down a few notes about things Melissa had said. As I reviewed my notes, I circled the comment that she questions God Judgment in red ink and closed the file.

I closed my eyes, bowed my head and spoke softly. "God I don't know why you felt the need to speak to me today. But I'm still hurting whenever I think about Michael's death. I loved him and I can't understand why you would take him away from me so soon. I don't understand how you could allow me to be so happy at one point and then feel the need to allow that happiness to cause me so much pain. I won't ask you why, God. But I can't understand why you chose me?"

****

The rest of the day moved slowly. I couldn't wait to get off work to pick Noah up from school. I promised to take him to the park if the weather was nice. Finally, by the time I picked him up, although the sun was still shining, the wind was strong, so I decided to take him to Chuck E' Cheese instead.

"Mommy, mommy when is the pizza coming?" he asked.

"It should be here shortly sweetie," I replied.

"Can I go play now mommy?" he asked.

"Sure but remember to wash your hands before you come back," I said.

He took off running. I reached in my purse and pulled out Iyanla Vanzant's book "In the Meantime" and began to read. Ten minutes later, two kids ran past me and almost knocked the pizza from the waitress's hand. I heard a man's voice call them back to the table from behind. I called Noah and told him to go to the bathroom to wash up. We ate the pizza and talked about his recent visit to the museum. He was so excited to learn about dinosaurs that he talked about them every day. Noah was very smart for a 3-year-old. I liked to call him 'my little old man' because he was really into science and Michael Jackson. He was such a character and the highlight of many of my days.

Once we left Chuck E Cheese's we headed to Target to do a little shopping. I noticed a dark grey Benz similar to Gabby's pulling out of the parking lot. I did a double take because once I noticed the little red scratch on the back, I knew that it was hers. But she wasn't driving it. It must've been Benjamin with a woman in the car with him. I pulled out my cell phone to call Gabrielle.

"Hey girl," she answered.

"Hey girl, where are you?" I asked.

"I'm at work waiting on parts to come in. What's up?"

"Nothing, I just thought I saw your car here at Target."

"Oh," she replied. "You probably did since Benjamin's driving it today."

"Yeah that's what I figured. But he had a woman in the car with him," I said softly.

"A woman!" she yelled. "Let me call him right now. I'll call you back."

"Ok," I said. She hung up before I could finish my sentence. I hoped that it was one of his daughters because I hated being the bearer of bad news.

"Come on Mommy, I need to get a new movie," Noah tried to get my attention.

"Okay baby, but none of that scary stuff," I joked. "I can hardly sleep at night as it is."

"The monsters scare you mommy?"

"No baby, I wish it was that simple."

After about an hour of browsing through the store, we paid for our things and headed home. I put Noah to bed in his room and went to the living room to relax on the sofa.

"The world is going crazy with all of this mindless reality TV," I said to myself.

I flicked through the channels until I reached a movie on Lifetime called "Amy's Disaster." I hoped that this would put me to bed since I hadn't been able to sleep without taking the sleeping pills for weeks. I didn't like the effect it was having on my body in the morning and I was beginning to have more nightmares that I couldn't seem to wake up from more often. Tonight would hopefully be the first night that I would be able to fall asleep without them.

After about 20 minutes of watching the crazed white girl stalk her boyfriend, I began to yawn. However, before I could get completely comfortable, my phone rang.

"Hey girl it's me," said Gabby in a low voice.

"Hey," I said tiredly.

"Girl, let me tell you what this scumbag told me happened today. He said that he had to take his sister's friend to Target after her car broke down on her. So that was him that you saw today and I guess that was her in the passenger seat. Did you get a good look at her? What did she look like?" she asked.

"Um, I don't know. All I saw was a female with light complexion as they pulled off."

"Oh," she said.

"So what are you going to do now?" I asked.

"Nothing. I guess he was telling the truth," she replied.

"Ok. Well I'm going to bed now. I'll call you in the morning," I said before hanging up the phone.

I tried to close my eyes, but that didn't work. I was too alert now to fall asleep.

"Damn Gabby!" I said as I turned the TV off and headed upstairs to my bedroom. I opened the drawer on the night stand and grabbed the bottle of sleeping pills from inside. "Oh well, here goes nothing." I said before I swallowed the pill dry. "Michael, please help me sleep tonight. I really need you." I closed my eyes and hoped that I wouldn't have any more nightmares tonight.

Gabrielle

On the other side of town, Gabrielle sat in a car outside of the place that she had followed Benjamin to.

There was no way I was going to be able to sleep tonight knowing that Benjamin was cheating on me with other women. When I first pulled up, I was shocked to see the filthy neighborhood that Benjamin had driven too. I watched as he greeted a much thinner woman with a scarf on her head at the door. He kissed her passionately before they finally went in and closed the door.

It felt as if my heart skipped a beat because he hadn't kissed me like that since our first year of dating. I watched the front bedroom light was turned off and then decided to get out of the car to see what I could see or hear.

I ran nervously across the street and dove in the small bush underneath the bedroom window. I couldn't see anything so I slowly stood up to get a closer view.

Inside, Benjamin was kneeling and the girl was still standing up against the wall. I pressed my face up against the dirty window a little more and looked around. The room was filthy. There were clothes everywhere and the bed was so close to the floor that it looked as if there was only a mattress.

"Cum all in my mouth baby. I want to taste it," said Benjamin. She moaned something unrecognizable and then yelled.

I immediately bent over and started to cough. I ran back across the street to my neighbor's car that I'd borrowed and sat inside. My thoughts were all over the place.

Should I confront him? Should I knock on the door and slap the bitch? Or should I flatten all the tires so that he can't leave?

I knew the last one was out of the question because it was my car that he was driving.I thought about calling Kyndal back to tell her to come get my car for me, but quickly changed my mind.

I didn't know what I was going to do about Benjamin just yet and I knew Kyndal would advise me to leave him alone after this. I finally decided to head home and wait for Benjamin to arrive. At least, that way, I would have some time to think about what my next move should be.

"Where the hell is he?" I screamed after throwing a glass across the room. I looked at the clock which read 2:33 a.m. and picked up the phone to dial his number.

Right as the voicemail picked up she heard a key turning in the door. She pulled the door open and slapped him.

"What the hell?" he screamed. She continued to punch him while he covered his face with both hands. "You lying piece of shit! How could you? " was all he heard. Once he became aware of the fact that he didn't really need to guard himself, he grabbed her by the arms and shook her.

"Gabby, what the hell is wrong with you?" he yelled.

"You, you, you? I should've left your ass alone long time ago," she screamed as tears ran from her eyes. "You should have told me you didn't want to be with me. What did I ever do to you Benjamin?"

He just stood and watched her in disbelief. "You're crazy. I haven't done anything to you. What the hell is wrong with you?"

"I saw you with that dirty bitch tonight Benny. I followed you all the way to 6969 Pinehurst. You parked my fucking car in the dirty bitch's driveway and stood there kissing her in the doorway as if you had no fucking worries. I can't believe this shit. I've wasted two years on your sorry, no good ass. If she wants your sorry ass she can have you."

"Oh so you followed me huh? Well that's what the fuck you get. And let me tell you one thing, that bitch don't mean shit to me. I love you," he said.

"Love!" cried Gabby. "Do you even know what the hell that means? I can't tell that you even like me half the time. You don't spend time with me. You don't kiss me. You don't even have sex with me anymore."

"That's because all you do is nag me all the time. It's hard to show you love when all you're doing is hollering at me all the time. Sometimes I just want to relax and chill with my woman. You don't even cook for me. That's why I visit my friends from time to time. They know how to treat me," he retorted angrily, as he relaxed on the couch.

"Oh they know how to treat you. I'm the one taking care of you and your kids. Isn't that my car that you drive all around the city every day of the week? If they know how to treat you so well, then go and be with them!" she shouted as she opened the door.

"Gabby, close the damn door. I'm not going anywhere. Come sit down next to me so that we can talk about this," he tried to calm her down.

She stood holding the door open for a few minutes, before finally adhering to his request. She sat on the end of the couch with her back towards him and said, "Benjamin, I've done all I can to make you happy. I can't understand why you continuously hurt me for no reason. I love you. But I need something more solid."

"Baby, I understand. That's why I want you to know that I'm ready to give you the baby that you want in a few months. But you're going to have to start working on being more supportive and domestic. Those are the qualities that I'm looking for in a wife and I know you can be that one day."

She slowly turned around and smiled at him. She knew that he would one day come to his senses. She just didn't know what it would take to get him there.

He walked over to her and gently touched her face, "Baby, I love you," he said before kissing her. He slowly removed her clothes and kissed every part of her body that he hadn't touched in months. He stopped once he reached her vagina and removed his clothes instead. She moved his hands back to her love area and whispered in his ear, "please kiss it baby." Instead of adhering to her request, he roughly shoved himself inside of her. After about two minutes she heard him say "Oh shit baby, here I come." She didn't want it to be over but before she could move he was done. He rested himself on top of her and closed his eyes. She wiped the sweat from his forehead before kissing it. "Baby, do you think that you can do something for me?" she asked. Receiving no response, she assumed that he fell asleep and slid from underneath him.

She headed towards the bathroom and showered. After getting out of the shower, she looked at her naked body in the mirror and frowned. "I just have to get myself together and he'll love me more, that's all," she said before turning off the lights.

She walked back into the living room area where he was still asleep on the couch. She looked at the clock on the wall, which now read 3:35 a.m. and decided not to wake him. She headed to the bedroom alone and cried herself to sleep.

Kent

"Hey Pops," I said as I sat next to him at the bar.

"What's up son?" he replied. "Did you have a chance to look at the game last night?"

"Oh no. I was at home chilling. But I did watch the replays on ESPN this morning."

"So how's everything going with the job?" he asked.

"Umm, not good," I replied. "They said that I couldn't get the job back so I'm just going to have to find something different."

"Aww son," he said. "You better find something soon, because the economy is on the verge of a collapse and many people are going to be losing their jobs. Soon, there won't be anything available, especially in your line of work."

I just sat there for a minute trying to decide if I should tell him about today's events with the girls. I knew that he would have something smart to say about my not using protection and go into the whole story of him teaching me how to use a condom at the age of 12.

I was 12 years old when my Pops caught me masturbating in my room with a stack of his erotic magazines. I was scared out of my mind because I had been doing this for the last year without being caught. I remember the very first time I saw one of those magazines. I was amazed at all the different types of beautiful women that were displaying all their goodies for my pleasure. I can remember getting so excited that my manhood would rise on its own. It wasn't until a month later that I decided that it was okay for me to touch myself as I had seen a man doing on one of the porn movies that I had also grabbed out of my dad's room and watched when he wasn't home. I didn't like the movies as much as I enjoyed looking at the women in the spreads.

Anyway, my dad caught me in my room on the same day that I had just had my first orgasm. It was great. I was lying down in my bed, smiling at the ceiling with the towel right next to me when he walked in. He said, "Son what the hell are you doing?" I immediately jumped up from my bed and fell over the stack of magazines on the floor. He laughed for a few minutes and then told me to go wash my hands before sitting next to him. After I was cleaned up, he asked me if I was having real sex yet and I answered that I wasn't. He explained that if I was going to start having real sex that I'd better know how to protect myself because he wasn't going to have girls' mothers coming to his house talking about their daughters being pregnant. He pulled out a condom and suggested that I go into the bathroom to put it on. When I got in the bathroom, I didn't know what to do so I just stuck the top half of my penis into the plastic and put my underwear on before going back out to show my dad. He laughed hysterically at me once he saw that the condom was still rolled up and too big for me. After a few moments he suggested that I go into the kitchen and grab a banana. He instructed me to put the condom over the banana and roll it all the way down until it wouldn't go anymore. Afterwards, he gave me a very long lecture about sex, protection and babies. He said that he was going to buy a case of condoms so that I wouldn't have any excuse for not using them when the time came.

His lecture worked well until I was 17 and had my first taste of sex without a condom. After that day I never went back to using rubbers because it felt so good without it. Right about now, I wish I had followed his rules throughout my adult life and maybe I wouldn't be in this situation now.

"Pops, I messed up man," I said.

"Messed up how son?"

"I got two new babies on the way, one with Sasha and the other with this chic named Angela that I'm not sure if that baby is even mine."

"Damn, son. Didn't I tell you to use protection man? Damn, do you ever listen to me?"

"I know," I said while shaking my head.

"So what are you going to do now son? Are they having the babies?"

"Yes both of them are," I replied. "But the messed up part about this is they all found out about it today?"

"What do you mean they all?"

I told him how everything happened and he didn't hold back telling me how irresponsible I had been. Once I was done telling him the story he said that I'd better try to find a job quickly because Friends of the Court wouldn't take any excuses. He also suggested that in the meantime, I needed to be as nice to them as possible and just maybe I could avoid the problems of going to court. I left the bar feeling worse than I had before I entered.

I headed home. Once I got in the parking lot, I noticed a red minivan with the lights on. I shrugged it off as being a visitor of one of the neighbors until I reached my door and heard Angela yelling at me.

"Kent you gon' act like you don't even see me?" she yelled. "I've been out here waiting for you for over an hour," she yelled.

"Well go home Angela," I said calmly. "I really don't have time for your games tonight. You've caused enough trouble.

She waved for the driver of the vehicle to leave. They pulled off and I turned around to face her, "Why the hell did you do that? You're not staying here!"

"Oh yes I am," she smiled. "I'm not going anywhere but in your bed tonight Kent."

I had to use every ounce of control I had to stop myself from slapping her so I opened the door and walked in. I tried to quickly close the door but she moved just as fast placing her belly in the way. I walked away from the door and flopped down on the couch with my head in my hands.

"Angela," I said. "Please call your ride and tell them to come back and get you before I get mad."

"You're already mad sweetie," she replied softly. "But I know just how to fix it." She quickly dropped down on her knees beside me. I stood up and looked down at her. "Get up Angela," I said.

"No, I like it even better when you're standing up," she said. "She reached towards my zipper but I removed her hands.

"Get the hell out of my house Angela!" I yelled. "You're fucking crazy."

"You're damn right I'm crazy Kent!" she yelled back. "But you made me this way, baby."

I stood looking at her with so much hatred in my eyes that she finally turned away.

"Kent I love you and I want us to be a family. Why are you acting like this all of a sudden? Is it that tramp you've been sleeping with? If so, I'm going to handle her so she won't be a problem anymore."

"What?" I asked looking at her in disbelief. "You've lost your damn mind for real." With that, I picked her up and carried her to the front door.

"Put me down Kent. I'm not going anywhere," she screamed. I grabbed my keys and closed the door. She yelled and screamed all the way to the parking lot. I opened the door to my truck and shoved her in, locking the door. She screamed and tried to get out but I was in the car by the time she found the unlock button. I put the keys in the ignition and pulled off. She continued to fight with me screaming the whole time.

"Kent can we please go back to your place? I just want to lay with you one more time!" she yelled.

I didn't answer. I continued to head towards the expressway to get to her home. Suddenly, the screaming stopped and she started mumbling about a pain in her belly. I ignored her and just kept driving. Once we arrived at her home, I could still see that she was actually in pain so I asked her if she wanted to go to the hospital and she agreed.

At the hospital, the nurse verified that she was, indeed, in labor. I decided that it was best that I stay with her because no one else had arrived on her behalf. Two hours later, baby Noelle was born. Angela was so happy and I couldn't help but share in her joy looking at the beautiful baby girl.

A few hours later, after Angela fell asleep, I decided that it was time for me to leave. I drove home but didn't have enough energy to get out of my car so I went to sleep inside.

While Kent, lay sleeping in his car, Sasha attempted call him three times.

"Pick up the damn phone Kent!" she yelled before hanging up the phone. "I hate you. I fucking hate him," she said before bursting out in tears. She cried continuously until she couldn't cry anymore. "You know what, I'm tired of crying over his sorry ass. He's going to pay for what he's done to me. I've wasted six years of my life trying to prove to him that I should be his wife. He owes me now," she said to herself looking at her plunging belly in the mirror. She rubbed her belly and smiled. "He's going to pay baby. He's going to pay."

Kyndal

"Hi Dr. Anderson, this is Kyndal, Marion's daughter," I said over the phone.

"Hi Kyndal, it's good to hear from you again. How's everything going for you?" she asked.

"Everything is fine except the fact that I've been having strange nightmares lately," I said.

"Hmmm nightmares huh?"

"Yes," I replied. "That's the reason I called you today. I would like to come in to talk to you about some of the dreams I've been having since Michael's death."

"Ok Kyndal," she replied. "What's a good day and time for you?"

"I would like to come in tomorrow early afternoon around 1 o'clock, if possible."

"1 o'clock will be fine Kyndal. I look forward to speaking with you then. Have a great day," she said before disconnecting the call.

The last two weeks have been horrible for me, since I haven't been able to sleep. The sleeping pills are working but, for some reason, the nightmares are getting stranger and stranger. Each night, I keep seeing people from my past coming after me. I keep dreaming about my father and I haven't spoken to him in years. I hope Dr. Anderson is able to help me in some way because I need to be able to sleep.

"Kyndal, you have a visitor in the lobby," the secretary said over the intercom. I picked up my phone to call the front desk. "Hi Kelly, this is Kyndal. Who is the visitor?" I asked.

"Ms. Melissa Graves," she responded.

"Oh," I replied, surprised that she was back. "Give me a few minutes."

"Ok I'll tell the young lady that you will be here shortly."

I couldn't understand why this girl continued to show up at the office unexpectedly. She said she didn't need help and honestly didn't act like it either. Why couldn't she just be like everyone else here and schedule an appointment for once? I cleared my desk and grabbed her file from the cabinet. I readjusted my skirt and headed towards the lobby.

"Hi Melissa," I said with a smile. "It is nice to see you again. Please follow me to my office."

She walked in to my office and headed straight for the window, as she did during her previous visit. Remembering her last outburst when I suggested taking a seat, this time I didn't ask her because I felt it would be a waste of time.

"How can I help you today?" I asked nicely.

"How many times do I have to tell you that you can't help me? How about asking why I'm here today? That sounds better," she said.

I just looked at her and noticed that she was wearing the same dirty men's jeans and camouflage pullover that she had on the last two times she was here. "Ok Melissa, what would you like to talk about today?" I asked cheerfully.

"Well I saw my holier than thou father this week. And you know what, he didn't even recognize me! He just walked right past me in the church parking lot. Hell, I can't blame him he hasn't seen me in months and he surely wouldn't recognize his precious daughter dressed liked this."

"Why do you say that Melissa?" I asked.

"You're funny Ms. Kyndal," she laughed. "Did you know that my dad was expecting me to be like you? You know, well dressed, proper and professional. That's what a preacher's daughter is supposed to be right?" she laughed. "Well, I chose to go out into the world on my own to find out what life was like outside of the cathedral walls of holiness. I sure found out alright! I found out what is like to be used by men because of my pretty face. I discovered what is it was like to get high and feel free from the worries of life. I learned what it was like to be the girl that everyone wants, but nobody really loves. And I damn sure experienced trying to live life after death. Cause that's how I feel. I feel dead inside. I'm all used up and nobody cares about me. My dad doesn't even notice me now," she said looking out the window.

"That baby didn't even feel that I was worthy of being a mother. It left me before I even had the chance to show it that I cared."

I got up from my chair and headed to the window. I placed my hand on her shoulder and she immediately turned into me and started sobbing. After a few minutes of crying, she jumped back and ran to the door. "I'm out," she said before slamming the door.

I couldn't help but feel for her. I closed my eyes and saw visions of all the things that she had just said to me and the nightmares that I'd been having since I first met with her three weeks ago. I immediately started crying because it was at that moment that I realized that her life story was the same as mine.

I was unable to sleep that night because I was scared of the dreams. I took two sleeping pills but that didn't work either. I finally got down on my knees and asked God to please forgive me for all the wrongdoings of my past. I prayed for him to release me from the crazy thoughts in my mind and to free me from the pain I was feeling inside.

I cried long and hard as I thought about how my life had changed over the years after the rape. My perfect view on life and attitude towards men had changed drastically. I tried to love them as much as they loved me, but I couldn't so I would leave. I just couldn't let anyone get close enough, out of fear that they would leave me as my daddy did.

I loved my father with all my heart. I was what many would call a daddy's girl. I loved being with him more than being with my mother. My father didn't have much but the little that he did have, he always found a way to provide. He was a worldly man that lived by the code of the streets. Every day was a struggle for him. He had to find ways to pay the rent because he only had a secondary level of education and could barely read and write. but he found ways to make money. I didn't notice the difference in the life that my family lived compared to anyone else in my neighborhood. My father was a provider and he promised me that he would always provide and look after me and my siblings.

He lived up to his promise until I reached the age of 16. At the time, my father's new hustle was selling drugs. One day, he decided to try heroin and from that day forward, he was no longer the father that I knew. My mother would cry every night as she waited for him to come home. He never did. He stopped paying the bills. He stopped coming around. For the first couple of months, I was in denial. I refused to accept that my strong father had allowed a drug to take over him in that way. Eventually, I started crying myself to sleep at night until one day I decided that I would go and find him.

I will never forget the day that I found my daddy. He was inside the apartment building, known as the drug house in the neighborhood. I walked in and asked if my daddy was there. A neighbor noticed me and told me that he would go and get him from the backroom. When he came out, he grabbed me and pulled me outside. Once we were outside, he started yelling at me. I pulled away from him and asked him why he hadn't been home and told him that we needed him. He slapped me and told me to go home. I started to cry and, through my tears, asked him if he even loved me. I could not understand why he wanted to be on drugs and away from his family. His response was, "Yes, I do love you, but I have nothing to live for. Drugs fill that void and make my pain go away." Shocked to hear that, I asked him, "Don't you see me daddy? You have me to live for." He looked at me bitterly and replied, "No, we are all alone in this world. You have you to live for," and walked away.

That night was the last night I cried for my daddy. I buried myself in my studies and decided that I would live for myself from that day forward.

I fell in love with one man after that but the emotional abuse that I suffered with him was just as bad as it had been with my dad. Shortly after, I was raped, so the little trust and comfort that was there for the few men that had been in my life in the past was now completely gone.

I finally understood that the men chasing me in my dreams were my victims. I hurt them with my cruel attitude, and now they were coming after me. Love was my drug of choice. They wanted what I had so I gave it to them and took it away when they least expected it. It was easy for me to walk away because I didn't have any expectations of men at the time. I told them simply that I expected them not to lie to me and, in return, I won't lie to you. I never make promises, and asked them not to make me any either. I told them, "I love you, but I'm not afraid to leave you." It was just that simple to me.

My destructive ways vanished when I met Michael. I loved him whole heartedly with many expectations for our future. I accepted his promises and never saw them being left unfulfilled.

Like Melissa, I had questioned God's reasoning behind why he would allow me to be happy and then take it away.

I realized that I was actually looking forward to my meeting with Dr. Anderson, hoping that, maybe, she would be able to give me some explanation for what I was experiencing in my life.

Sasha

"Who the hell does he think he is?" said Sasha as she picked up the phone to call her favorite Aunt Lolly. After three rings, she hung up the phone, because, suddenly, she wasn't sure if she wanted to go through with her plan. All she wanted was for Kent to realize his true love for her and come home. She had been his devoted friend and lover for too many years and now it was time that he gave her what she deserved. However, since he couldn't do it by himself, she was willing to go the extra mile to help him out.

She picked up the phone to call her Aunt Lolly from Louisiana again.

"Hello," answered a frustrated Aunt Lolly on the other end of the phone.

"Hi Aunt Lolly," she greeted her. "It's me, Sasha."

"Sasha wow, it's been years. How are ya ma love?"

"I'm fine," I replied.

"Hmph, I can feel the uneasiness in your voice ma' dear child. What's really going on with ya?"

"A lot," she replied. "I'm getting ready to have my second child and things aren't going too well with the baby's father."

"I see," Aunt Lolly acknowledged. "And that's the reason you called today my sweetie?"

"Yes, but I'm not sure what I want to do just yet," Sasha replied.

"Oh, sure you are, my dear. Ya' see, I feel that there is a strong love that you have for this fella. Still, ya' know things haven't been working out for you as you've planned. But ya' see, what you may feel you want, my love, is not always gonna be what ya' need," she continued. "Ya know, you young people have it all twisted when it comes to love, ya' know. Ya' think that having a man's baby will change him, when, in reality, the only person it changes is you. Do you think that you really love this fella my dear?"

"Yes, I love him, but I just don't know if he loves me the same way. I want us to be a family. We should be a family?"

"Ummm, you're already a family because the blood is connected, you are having a baby together. He will always be the father of your children and will be there for you. But I take it that you want more, aye?"

"Yes, I deserve more," said Sasha.

"And that's why you're really calling me today, my love," she asked.

"Yes in a way," Sasha agreed.

"Well, you know that I can do all things when it comes to matters of the heart. But remember, the soul works closely with the mind, and it is the mind that makes the ultimate decision."

"Yeah I know."

"If ya' think you're ready for love, my dear, I can definitely grant you that, but be prepared for the work that is coming your way," she warned.

"I'm ready Aunt Lolly. I'm ready."

"Okay, my dear. You just need to do two things to prepare yourself before I'm able to give you what your heart desires. Write down all the reasons why you love this man and find for me something with his DNA. Once you have these two things prepared, I will take care of the rest, my love. I will take care of the heart."

Once the conversation was over, Sasha lay across the bed, thinking about all the reasons she deserved to be happy with Kent. She took out her journal and started writing everything she loved about him. She pulled out a picture of them that they had taken two years ago at Layla's party and smiled. "I will have the family that I want, even if it takes something stronger than me to receive it. I deserve it." She closed the journal and headed downstairs to wait for Layla's arrival.

Kent

"Hi daddy!" Layla and Brittany yelled in unison.

"Hi my babies," I smiled.

I picked them both up and started kissing them on their cheeks going back and forth as they laughed.

"How was school today?" I asked.

"Good," said Brittany.

"Fine," added Layla. "But my teacher is crazy," she continued. "Do you know today, she asked us if we knew where babies came from?"

"Huh?" I said shocked.

"Well she was reading a story about a baby bird today and, in the story, there was a stork that brought the baby all wrapped up like a present. So I said, babies are not presents, they come from somewhere else. Then she asked us kids do we knew where babies came from?"

"Tell me what you said honey," I prompted, curious to see what she knew.

"I said they come from out of mommy's belly at the hospital. They are born naked. I know that because I saw a picture of me when I was born and I didn't have any clothes on."

I laughed, amazed by her clever response. "Well, you're right Layla. But babies are presents to their parents, baby. You girls were my best gifts ever," I said before tickling them.

I got in the car and dropped Brittany off at her place first. Taylor didn't even speak to me, so I figured that she was still mad about yesterday. I knew that I'd have to tell her eventually about the other baby, but I was too tired from yesterday's events to start another fight so soon.

I decided that I should go to the store to pick up the things that Sasha had asked for yesterday, because I knew that she too was still mad at me. I hadn't returned her calls either because I didn't want to hear her screaming at me.

Once we arrived at her place, I got out of the car and knocked on the front door. "It's open," she yelled. I walked inside and saw that she was sitting on the sofa, absentmindedly flicking through TV channels.

"Hey Sash, I got the stuff you wanted. I'll just put it in the kitchen for now."

"Hmph, thanks for doing something right," she replied nastily. I ignored the sarcasm and started walking away.

"Kent, can you come in here and get this magazine from underneath the table? I can't reach it."

"Sure," I said walking into the living area where she was seated. I knelt down in front of her to grab the magazine, when, all of a sudden, I felt her pulling my hair. "What the hell?" I yelled before getting up.

"Oh so you thought everything was good huh," she said before kicking me. "Get the hell out of my house Kent. I hate you!" she screamed.

I looked at her as if she was crazy and decided that it was best that I just walk away and not react. I turned to leave, but right before I got to the front door, a glass vase hit it. Layla came out of the kitchen with a glass of milk and screamed, "Mommy!" I walked right out the front door and got in my car.

"These women are fucking crazy," I said as I pulled off.

I couldn't help but feel for Sasha because she had been through this same situation with me before. KJ and Layla were only three months apart. It was hard for her to deal with the first time. This time was no different. But for some reason, she has never tried to force me into being in a relationship with her. She has always understood my situations with other women. She knows that I love to have sex with a variety of women. She has just been a great friend and I have never wanted anything more than our casual relationship. She knew that, even though I love her, I've never been in love with her to the point where I wanted to stop being with other women.

Ring. Ring. I looked down at my phone and saw that it was Angela.

"Hi Angela," I answered dryly.

"Where the hell have you been Kent?" she screamed.

I decided not to answer her question, "What do you want Angela?"

"What do you mean, what do I want? You're supposed to be here at the hospital with me and the baby," she said before bursting out in tears. "Kent we need to put all of our differences aside. We have a beautiful baby girl here now and we need you."

I held the phone in silence for a few moments trying to decide if I wanted to fight with her or just deal with the situation nicely. "Ok Angela, I'm on my way."

"Ok," she smiled. "Can you please bring me something to eat from McDonalds."

"Sure," I said. "I'll be there shortly."

"I love you Kent," she said. I hung up the phone.

I never understood how she would continuously say that she loved me even though I never responded. I may have told her that one night while I was drunk, but I am sure it had not happened since. I guess she was still holding on to that night.

I really needed to figure out how I was going to handle the whole paternity situation because I knew that it had to be done. There was no way that I was going to be taking care of a baby that wasn't mine.

Once I reached the hospital, I saw a few of Angela's girlfriends in the parking lot.

"There's that low life right there!" one of them yelled. "Look at him, looking all stupid! You better treat my girl right or we gon' whoop your ass."

I pressed the alarm on my car and headed for the entrance. Once I got up to her suite, I saw her mother holding the baby. She frowned at me, but forced a smile once she saw her daughter looking at her.

"Hello, how are you doing today?" I asked politely.

"We're fine," Angela replied, still staring at her mother. "Mommy, give Noelle to her daddy," she said.

I washed my hands first and walked over to her mother. She placed the baby gently into my arms before pinching my wrist.

I looked at her but decided to say nothing. Looking at Noelle's beautiful face and slender body, I instantly felt a connection. She looked just like the baby picture of me that my mom had displayed on her fireplace. I smiled at her and kissed her forehead.

"Hey baby girl," I said. "It's your daddy. Yes, it's daddy."

Angela's mother grabbed her coat and gave Angela and the baby a kiss before leaving the room.

"I'm glad that you came back, baby," Angela said. "The doctors said that she may have a little jaundice but she's fine otherwise. That is great news given that she's premature."

"That's good," I said playfully to Noelle. "Because daddy wants his girls to be good and healthy."

"Well I'm fine too Kent! Thanks for asking," she yelled.

"That's good Ang," I replied.

"What's the matter with you?" she asked. "Don't you love me anymore?"

"Ang, let's not go there. I will be here for the baby and nothing else."

"Bitch!" she yelled, "I hate you."

I placed Noelle back into her crib next to Angela's bed and kissed her. Angela grabbed my arm as I turned to leave, "I'm sorry Kent. I didn't mean that. Can you please stay with me, Kent? Please," she pleaded, as her eyes brimmed with tears.

"I think it's time for me to leave Angela. I just wanted to see the baby," I replied.

"You need to fill out that sheet for the birth certificate for the nurse before you leave," she said.

"Okay, I'll do it later," I said.

"No, do it now Kent. You know you're the father so I shouldn't have to go through this with you. Just do it!" she yelled.

"I picked up the sheet from the table and filled out the area as requested for father's information. I hesitated for a minute debating if I should write unknown but I wrote my full name 'Kent Travis' instead.

"Thank you," she said on my way out the door. "Thank you."

Angela turned the television down in her room and stared at her new baby for a few moments after Kent left. She picked her up from the crib and kissed her cheek. "Mommy's going to make sure that daddy does right by us. Trust me. That little piece of paper right there is proof that he agrees with ruining my life, so it's my turn to return the favor. Say 'sorry' to that poor little Karen girl, Noelle. She needs to make room for his new family. Because daddy's coming home. Trust me."

Gabrielle

"Hey girl," I said waving to Kyndal as she passed the waterfall. Since it was such a nice day, we decided to come down to Campus Martius Park for lunch. I'd grabbed a couple of subs from Subway on my way to the park, so that we could enjoy the local jazz group that was on stage today.

"Ooh girl, you know my feet hurt because I had to park so far away. These shoes were definitely not meant for walking, just flaunting," said Kyndal, laughing.

"Well you could have fooled me, because you sure came in here walking like a supermodel, strutting your stuff," I replied jokingly. I looked down at the red leather BCBG pumps that she was rocking and shook my head. "You know, I love me some pumps but I keep a pair of flats in the car just for days like this when I have to walk far," I said showing her my bedazzled gold flats.

"Those are cute," she noted. "And you look really nice today. Have you lost some weight?"

"Yes. Yes. A whole 25 lbs," I said, laughing. "But I haven't lost the things that matter," I said pumping up my breast.

"You can always give me some of those and some of that," she said pointing to my breast and butt. We laughed as we opened our sandwiches to eat.

"So what's been up with you lately, lovely?" I asked between bites.

"Nothing much, just working on some personal things to get my life back in order," she replied trying to shoo a fly away.

"Like what? You don't have much of a personal life these days. You're always at work or home."

"Yeah I know. But that's probably the best place for me. I'm way past the club days and I don't really have anyone to hang out with since you're always booed up with Benjamin," she laughed.

I wished that I could tell her the truth about how unstable my relationship with Benjamin really was, but I decided to do it another time. There was no need to ruin the beautiful day. On top of that, I didn't feel like being lectured. Plus, there were times that I was happy and I was willing to hold on to those moments for now. "Benjamin is my honey, but we're not doing much these days," I replied.

"Why not?" she asked. "It's not like he does much anyway," she commented sarcastically.

I decided not to respond and changed the subject instead. "Girl, you know, I'm getting ready to buy a new Benz. I'm thinking of getting a red one with four doors this time, so that I can have room for the baby."

"You still talking about a baby with that man. Girl, you crazy."

"I'm not crazy, girl. I just know what I want, and I want a baby."

"Ok," she replied. "Whatever happened that night after I told you about that lady in your car?"

"Oh nothing. He said that it was his sister's friend, remember? I told you that." I said flatly.

"Oh yeah," she replied. "Well I probably would have gone snooping around after that if it was me back in my detective days with Roderick. Girl, you know, he almost drove me crazy with all that cheating mess. I am surely glad that that chapter of my life is over."

"Ummm hmmm, I remember," I laughed. "Out in the middle of the night, doing drive-bys with me on the phone. Remember the time you knocked on the girl's window, screaming for him to come out." I laughed just thinking of some of the things Kyndal used to do when she was with her college love Roderick.

"Yes girl, but please believe, I will never allow another man to drive me as crazy as Roderick did. Those lying cheaters are the worst kind. They will drive you insane, and you will lose all the energy trying to uncover their stupid lies they have you believing are true," she responded.

"Yes, yes," I laughed. I hadn't told Kyndal about what really happened the night she saw Benjamin with another woman yet, as I hadn't figured out what I was going to do about him just yet. I still loved him and still wanted to start a family with him. So I decided that it was best that I kept that night to myself.

"That's why I think that you should really think about the whole baby and marriage thing with Benjamin," she said interrupting my thoughts. "I love you Gabby and I know that you deserve better than him. He may say that he loves you, but I can certainly tell that you aren't happily in love with him. Not to mention that he has eight kids already that he may or may not be taking care of. I want the best for you and he ain't it!"

"Whatever Kyndal, I love him and we'll be fine," I replied looking away from her.

"No he'll be fine. You'll be crazy by the time you're done with him. I know what it feels like for a man to really love you and care for you. He will be willing to do whatever it takes to see that you smile every morning and night. He will express to you how he feels with no worries. He will accept you for who you are and not try to criticize you for every little thing. I hope that Benjamin will wake up and be the man you love and not just the man you want Gabby. But I'm having a hard time believing that this will happen anytime soon. I know his type."

"Kyndal, I hear you, but you don't even know him," I objected.

"My point exactly," she replied sarcastically. "I'm your best friend and I have yet to meet him."

We sat in silence for the next 15 minutes before we packed our things to leave.

"Thanks for coming Kyn," I said as we parted ways.

"No problem. But please remember that I love you no matter what and I'm sorry if I hurt your feelings in anyway," she said before kissing me on the cheek.

"I love you too," I replied.

As I walked back to my car, I couldn't help but think about some of the things that Kyndal had said. I knew that Benjamin loved me. He just wasn't the type to express how he felt openly. However, I was missing those passionate kisses that we used to share in the beginning of our relationship. Now, he's sharing them with another woman, which is driving me absolutely crazy.

After the incident, I spent the next few days checking his phone while he slept and one night I even followed him again. I was lucky that night because he went straight to his friend's house and didn't leave until 2 a.m.

I never would have thought that this would happen to me. I mean, I've had my share of married men and cheating men in the past, but I never would have thought that the man I chose to love would do this to me.

I couldn't believe that he expected me to accept what he was doing and move on. I wish it was that easy. I spent the next few weeks trying to accept the fact that men cheat and that he would love me anyway. I continued to play step mommy with the kids and even spend some of my evenings riding around with him to visit his friends in the hood. My life was slowly becoming his because I never had time to do anything for myself. I'd stopped going to church months ago and a girls night out was unheard of because I had no car to get there. However, I couldn't tell my friends that because I was too embarrassed by my own situation.

The only thing that I was happy about was the fact that Benjamin was now making an effort to come home before 11 at night. I no longer had to sleep alone and we were starting to have sex again. This was definitely the happiest I'd been in months.

I activated my Bluetooth inside the car to call Benjamin.

"Hey honey," I said.

"Hey," he replied dryly.

"What are you doing?" I asked.

"Chilling. What's up?"

"Nothing, I was just thinking about you and wanted to call to let you know."

"Oh, cool," he replied off-handedly. My heart dropped for a moment because I was hoping that this would be the one time that he would have a better response.

"Anyway, I was hoping that we would be able to go to dinner tonight at Oslo's so that we can talk about our future."

"Future huh?" he asked nonchalantly. "We can talk about it now, if you want to."

"Ok," I said. "Well, I was thinking that, since we have been together for the last two years, I think it's time that we get more serious. You know, like move in together and make plans for our engagement."

He laughed, "Engagement? You don't plan an engagement. You just do it!" He continued to laugh.

"I know that but I can't understand what you're waiting on," I objected, not finding his laughter humorous at all.

"I'm not waiting on anything. I just want you to get your stuff together and then I'll propose to you after I see that you can give me what I need."

"What you need?" I said.

"Yes, I told you that you need to lose some weight. I told you that you need to learn how to cook. I expect you to be down for me no matter what. And until you've shown me that you can do these things, I'm not proposing to you."

It took everything in me not to let him have it. But I didn't want to start an argument with him because he would only get mad and that would make things worse. "Okay honey," I replied instead. "I'll get on it."

He hung up the phone without even saying goodbye. I parked my car in my assigned space in the parking lot and just sat there, looking at my reflection in the mirror. "I'm pretty," I tried to convince myself, but for some reason, I couldn't make myself believe it. I picked up my phone and scrolled through my phonebook to find the number to Dr. Ellis that I had saw on a liposuction commercial earlier that week. I quickly pressed send to dial the number before I changed my mind. "Hello, Dr. Ellis House of Beauty," the receptionist answered. "Ummm hello," I stuttered. "My name is Gabrielle Williams and I would like to schedule an appointment for a consultation."

"Sure," she replied. "We have Monday morning at 9 available. Will that work for you?"

"Yes, that will be great," I replied.

"Just remember to download our questionnaire from the website and fill it out before coming in. Thank you for calling Dr. Ellis's House of Beauty where beauty is only one appointment away."

I hung up the phone, got out of the car and went back to the office. Just as I reached my desk, I saw Bill leaving John's office, smiling. He stopped by my desk and said, "I hope you had a great lunch today Ms. Williams," and walked away.

I didn't know what had just happened in the office but I was sure that it was something that I wasn't going to like. "Oh well," I said to myself. "I have bigger problems to deal with."

Kyndal

"Hi Kyndal, it's good to see you," said Dr. Anderson.

I closed the door to her office and sat down in the chair directly across from Dr. Anderson. I couldn't believe that I was back again after last week's session either. I thought that telling Dr. Anderson all about my past would stop the dreams and the pain but for some reason I'm still not feeling fully satisfied yet.

"Yes, I'm back," I said. "I can't understand why, but I guess, that's why I'm here," I said, smiling uneasily.

"Well, last week, you really put everything out on the table, which is very good. But, if you're still feeling uneasy about anything, please feel free to share it with me," she offered.

"I'm not quite sure that I know exactly what it is, but for some reason, I'm feeling very angry whenever I think of Michael. I feel as if he left me for no reason. He made all these promises that he knew he couldn't live up to but I was stupid enough to believe that he would be the one to set me free of all my problems and past hurts. Maybe I'm just mad at myself for allowing someone to get that close to me again. Maybe I mad because I knew that I shouldn't have trusted him because he's a man and all they do is hurt you. I don't know Dr. Anderson. I just don't know."

"Kyndal, you have every right to be angry. But it sounds like you've been angry for many years prior to Michael, based on what you told me about your past relationships along with the abandonment you experienced when your father left. Have you ever forgiven your father for leaving you?" she asked.

"I, ummm, I don't really know. I mean I guess, I never really think about it," I answered.

"In order to move forward, you really do need to think about forgiving those who caused you so much pain in your past—not just your father, but anyone who has done wrong by you. Do you understand?"

"Yes, I guess. I mean, I haven't allowed anything from my past to affect my life at this point. I put all those things behind me years ago."

"You may think that you have, but its' still evident to me here today. Think about some of the ways Michael's death caused you to feel abandoned, hurt and cheated out of your dreams for the perfect future. Think about all the things that happened to you in your past and compare your current feelings to those from the past. Once you recognize that these feelings are still present, you'll be able to acknowledge them and work on forgiving those that caused that pain. "

I sat in silence for a few minutes, thinking about what Dr. Anderson had said. I could definitely understand how Michael's death might have triggered old feelings, but I had already accepted them and moved forward with my life. The one thing that I had not done was forgiven my father. But how could I? I mean, he left my family with almost nothing and he hadn't looked back, so why should I?

"I fully understand what you're saying Dr. Anderson. But it's so hard to forgive someone that you can't see. I mean, I love my dad and all, but I haven't seen him in years, and the pain is still there."

"I know it's not something that will come to you easily. But you'll figure out a way to handle it. Forgiveness is the most important step in moving forward," she said.

"Thank you Dr. Anderson, I really appreciate your time," I said before standing to my feet to leave.

"Don't hesitate to come back, Kyndal. I'll be here if you need me," she replied kindly.

When I left Dr. Anderson's office, I decided to drive through my old neighborhood. It saddened me to see that the block that I grew up on was filled with vacant lots and trash. There were only a few homes left on the 13000 block of Kilbourne St. and those that were still standing looked abandoned. I circled the neighborhood until I reached the Fred's Market, where four men were standing outside asking for change. I noticed one of them as my old next door neighbor so I slowly rolled down my window and called his name.

"Jimmy!" I yelled. He smiled and walked over to the car. "Hey Jimmy. Do you remember me?"

"Hmph. You're so beautiful that I wish I did. What's your name sweet thing?" he asked.

"Kyndal," I said. "You know my father LJ, Leon."

"Oh LJ," he said. "He locked up ain't he?"

"Umm, I'm not sure. I haven't seen him in a while."

"Oh, he got caught trying to rob a liquor store with a knife a few months ago. He was dumb. Didn't even wear a face mask," he said, shaking his head, as if in disbelief.

"Oh," I replied, not knowing how else to react.

"Well it sho' is good to see his daughter is doing good," he said smiling showing a few missing front teeth. "Do you think you can give me a little change to get something to eat?" he asked.

I reached for the cup holder where I placed most of my spare change and handed it all over to him.

"Thanks," he said. "I'll tell your uncle Kevin that I saw you. I am sure that he will tell your daddy."

"Thank you," I replied before pulling off. I headed towards the I-94 expressway to go home. I picked up Noah on the way and decided to stop by my mother's.

"Hey mom," I said as I entered her living room.

"I see that you still have my key," she said. "So there's no reason for you to stay away for long periods of time. Come here, grandma's baby," she said to Noah. He ran over to her to give her a hug and a kiss. I walked over to the dining room where the picture stand was. I looked at the pictures of my sister, Calle, my brother Derrick and me in our younger years. Boy, had we come a long way! I moved those pictures to the side and pulled the distorted one of the whole family together, including my father. I can't say that we looked happy in the photo because it was really old but we were all together and that's what I loved about it.

"Kyndal," my mom called. "What are you doing in there?"

"I'm just looking at pictures mom," I replied.

"Don't get sticky fingers like you always do," she yelled. "I need my pictures."

I laughed because whenever I came to my mother's house I would take something from her. It didn't matter if it was jewelry or food, if she complained about it, I took it just to drive her crazy. "Mom, I'm not going to take anything," I said.

"Well come back in here where I can see you," she said. I placed the picture back where I got it from and headed to the living room where my mother was seated. Noah had already convinced her to turn to cartoons so he was seated right in front of the television watching Power Rangers.

"Mom, I don't like for him to watch violent cartoons," I said.

"Girl hush, he's a boy and all the cartoons these days are filled with action. You can't shelter that boy from the real world," she said.

I looked at her sternly, but decided not to go there with her because I didn't want her to yell at me about how he needed to be raised around real men in order to be tough in the streets. I always found that funny because none of the men that she considered real had ever held a job for half of their lives, including my little brother. I was never going to allow my son to live the "street life" if that's what it took for him to be considered a real man.

"Okay mom, you're right," I said, hoping to end the conversation.

"Something must be wrong with you if you're telling me I'm right," she said. "Do you have a fever or something?" she laughed.

"No mom, I don't have a fever. But I do have a question. When was the last time you spoke to daddy?" I asked.

She paused for a few moments before turning her head to look at the television, "It's been a while," she replied.

"A year or two?" I asked.

"Not that long," she said. "He stopped by about six months ago before he stuck up that liquor store."

"Oh, you knew about that?" I asked surprised.

"Yes I knew," she looked at me dumbfounded. "I know everything about your daddy. He is still my husband, you know."

"Hmph," I sighed. "I don't know why you never divorced him. He's been gone for over ten years."

"Sometimes you just need to leave well enough alone," she replied. "It's not like I'm getting married to anyone anytime soon," she said.

"Mom, why haven't you dated anyone since daddy left," I asked.

"Because, sometimes, you never get over your first love," she said sadly. "Not to mention the fact that it's hard to date when you have three bad kids running around."

"Don't blame it on us," I laughed. "We all moved out at 18 so you've been free for over seven years now."

"Don't get me wrong," she continued. "I've dated a few men, but I didn't want to marry any of them. I couldn't even kiss any of them."

"I see that daddy scared you straight after all," I laughed.

"Your dad was a really good man before the drugs," she said. "He just couldn't deal with the pressures of the world. I don't think that that's his fault."

"It is his fault, mom. He's a man and he always told me that a man makes his own choices. He chose to stick that poison in his veins. He chose not to come home and take care of us. He chose to be a bum. Those were all his choices. His choices," I said with tears forming in my eyes.

She walked over to me and grabbed my face, "I understand exactly what you're saying, Kyndal. But drugs can be very powerful and lead you to do things that you wouldn't ordinarily do. I accepted the fact that your father is out of control because of the drugs, but you're going to have to choose to let that go, Kyndal."

I moved her hand and walked away. "I already have mom," I replied, taken aback by her reaction.

"Well, please try a little harder, because you're still very emotional whenever we talk about your father, honey."

"I'm fine," I said. "Just fine."

We stayed for dinner and headed back home around 8:30. I carried Noah upstairs to his room and headed back outside to retrieve the mail from the mailbox. It was still light outside because summer was approaching. Right before I reached the corner, a car drove up beside me and stopped.

"Hey lady," a man spoke through the rolled down window with a deep voice. "How are you today?"

I said 'fine' and began to walk faster.

"So I take it that you don't remember me from college," he said.

I turned my head to see who it was. His face looked familiar, but I couldn't remember his name.

"Gerald," he said. "I don't think we ever introduced ourselves in school."

"Oh," I replied, still walking towards the mailbox.

"I noticed you a few weeks ago walking to get your mail, but I didn't want to scare you because it was so late," he said. "Why don't you ever check your mail during the daytime?" he asked.

For a moment, I didn't know how to respond because I didn't know if he was stalking me or just very observant. "I don't know," I replied.

He laughed and continued to tell me that he usually worked out in the evenings, which is why he got home at different times. He said that he was hosting a poetry event later that week and wanted to invite me to come out, if I could. He gave me a flyer and we said our goodbyes before I headed back to my place.

I looked down at the flyer, which read, *"God's Trying To Tell You Something"—poetic verses session at Jubilee Lounge on Friday night.*

I picked up the phone to call Gabrielle.

"Hey girl," she answered.

"Hey girl, how are you?" I replied.

"I'm good. Trying to cook this Mediterranean chicken for Benjamin," she said.

"You cooking?" I laughed. If there was one thing I knew about Gabrielle it was that she definitely could not cook. In all the years I'd known her, everything that she attempted to cook was either burnt or so nasty that a dog would give it back if he tasted it.

"Why are you laughing?" she asked. "I got Patti's *Labelle Cuisine's Cookbook: Recipe's you can sing about."*

I laughed. "Well, let's just hope he's singing lovely tunes and not an 'Oh my god' tune on the toilet once you're done." I said.

"I see you got jokes," she replied. "I think I'm doing good."

"Let us pray," I said jokingly. "Speaking of prayer, girl, I just ran into this guy that used to go to WSU with us."

"What was his name?" she asked.

"He said that his name was Gerald. But I don't think we ever said anything to each other in class back then."

"Oh," she replied. "Well, was he cute?" she asked.

"I guess," I replied shyly. "He's very attractive."

"Ooh I think I remember exactly who that is. He was one of those Glory Phi God guys that we used to walk pass in the student center."

"Oh well, that makes sense. You know that I wasn't into praising God back then, so I surely would have passed him up," we laughed. "But he invited me to this poetry session tomorrow and I wanted to know if you would be able to go."

"Hmmm, look at you, miss 'back in action'," she joked. "You must like him. Did he look as if he had some money girl?" she asked.

"Umm, I don't know. He was driving a nice car; not a Benz, but still nice, and he looked clean and well groomed."

"Ummm huh. Look at you paying attention to details. Looks like you're going to be back in action in no time. But just watch out for his kind because you know he don't believe in sex before marriage and I know you can't hold out." We both started laughing until I heard Benjamin yell "Who are you talking to?" Next thing I knew, Gabrielle said good-bye quickly and hung up the phone. I started to call her back but then decided against it because she never answered the phone when he was around and I knew tonight wouldn't be any different.

I went upstairs and slipped out of my work clothes and into a one-piece negligee. These past few nights had been difficult for me because I was starting to feel the need to be comforted during my late nights. I closed my eyes and tried to think about something besides the burning desire between my legs. But I couldn't so I got up and turned on the television instead. I laughed at what Gabrielle had said about me not holding out. It had been a year since I had been touched by anyone and I didn't see the situation changing anytime soon.

Kent

"Baby, I miss you," I said to Karen after she finally answered the phone.

"Kent, I don't want to talk to you, so please stop calling me," she replied.

"I just wanted you to know that I miss you and I'm sorry for any pain that I caused you in the past. I really want to see you. Can I stop by later?"

"No!" she yelled. "I don't want anything to do with you. Why don't you call one of your baby mamas, like you were doing while you were with me."

"Here we go," I replied. "I know that you're still angry with me, but I really want to see you tonight. I'll be there at eight, so be ready for me."

"Don't come to my house, Kent," she yelled before hanging up the phone. I smiled because I could sense in her voice that she really missed me too. I knew just what I would have to do to get her pass this.

I headed to the flower shop on Jefferson and told the florist to give me something extra special. She went to the back and brought out a beautiful dozen of multi-colored roses. I hadn't seen anything like it before so I knew that Karen would love them. She loved flowers and I had yet to bring her any since we'd started dating, even though she often gave me hints. I felt like roses are for special occasions only and this was definitely a special occasion. I hadn't had sex in over two weeks and I needed some bad. I could have called someone else, but I really wanted Karen.

My life has been full of baby mama drama these last two weeks, with Angela needing this or that for the baby all day long. Not to mention Sasha, who had increased her phone calls as well. She didn't use to call me for much but now she wants me to do everything for her. She claims that she can't do anything because the baby is making her sick. They are both driving me nuts. Hell, it feels like I'm working a full time job even though I have yet to find one.

But tonight, I didn't want to worry about any of that mess, I just wanted to chill with my baby. I pulled into Karen's parking lot at 7:55 exactly. I knew that she would put up a fight at first, but would eventually give in, once I put one of my special kisses on both sets of her lips. She loved when I played with the tip of her clit while I kissed her passionately on the lips. I was starting to get excited just thinking about her. I grabbed the bouquet of roses and got out of the car. Once I reached her place, I saw a green Ford Taurus speed by the complex, almost hitting a man crossing the street. I shook my head and knocked on the door.

After three knocks with no answer, I picked up my phone to call Karen. She let the phone ring several times before it went to her voicemail. I decided to knock again before leaving a message. She still didn't answer. I looked in front of the building and saw that her car was parked in her usual spot.

"Karen," I said. "I know that you're in there. Open the door, baby."

Still no response. "I guess you're really mad at me this time huh," I continued. "Well, I guess I'll just leave these here for you." I placed the roses inside her doorway and walked down to her car to leave the card that I had for her. I knew that she would have to read it when she saw it on the windshield wiper in the morning.

I walked around the building to the visitors' parking lot where my car was parked. I tried to call her one last time but she still didn't answer. I sat there for a few moments longer, hoping that she would open the door to get the flowers and come looking for me, but once that didn't happen I eventually drove off.

****

"Look at his silly ass," Angela said to her friend. "He didn't even notice us following him the whole time. But I'm going to teach his ass to not call me back because he's trying to get back with this tramp." She got out of the car and walked up the stairs that led to Karen's apartment. She quickly grabbed the bouquet of roses and started to walk off.

"Hey, put those back," yelled the neighbor. Angela turned around to see who was yelling at her, and hesitated to respond when she noticed the little old lady dressed in a robe with huge rollers in her hair.

"Yeah you," she said to Angela. "I'm sorry ma'm, but these roses don't belong to her. They belong to me," she replied before walking off. The lady continued to scream at her but she walked back down to her car as if nothing had happened, the roses fixed in her hand.

"Those are cute," her friend said when she got back in the car.

"Hmph," sighed Angela. "Girl, be quiet. He ain't never bought me anything like this before. But he'll learn to always return my calls after this," she laughed before driving off. When she reached her home, she walked inside and went straight for Noelle.

"Hey baby," she said. "Did you miss mommy? That's okay, because both daddy and mommy will be here for you tonight. I promise."

She picked up the phone to call Kent. When he didn't answer she picked up the roses to smell them.

"Oh, these roses are pretty as can be, but too bad they weren't for me. But that's okay, I don't want them anyway. I'll get something better and daddy's gonna pay. Yeah, daddy's gonna pay," she sang while looking at herself in the mirror.

****

By the time I got home, I was so sleepy that I jumped in bed fully clothed. After lying there, trying to fall asleep to no avail, I grabbed the remote and turned to ESPN to watch the highlights from past games. However, my mind was somewhere else. I needed to get some quick. I was horny as hell. I couldn't remember the last time I'd waited more than two days to have sex, so these two weeks were driving me crazy. I picked up my phone but I didn't know who to call and didn't really want to call anyone in particular. All of my fun ladies were probably already out with other men, since I haven't spoken to any of them in months, and Angela and Sasha were definitely out of the question.

I grabbed my keys and ran out the door. I knew just where to go for a variety of beautiful naked women and a little rubbing action. I headed straight for *Déjà Vu*. I hadn't been in a while so I was hoping to see some fresh faces.

It took me all of five minutes after my first lap dance to figure out that I was in the wrong place because I desperately needed to have real sex bad and this grinding on me wasn't gone cut it. I walked out of the club and picked up my phone to call Sasha.

"Hey," I said when she answered the phone sleepily.

"What do you want Kent? Its' almost midnight," she said.

"I wanted to come over," I replied, changing my mind as quickly as I said it.

"No, Kent don't come over here. I'm not having sex with you, so you might as well go home."

"Alright then," I said quickly, hanging up the phone. Two seconds later, Angela called.

I answered, "Yes, Angela?"

"Hey Kent," she said seductively. "Why don't you come sleep with me tonight?"

"For what?" I snapped. "You can't give me what I need."

"But I can give you something better," she smiled. "My lips are fine. Come let me taste you."

As soon as she said the words 'taste you', my manhood answered for me. "I'll be there in ten," I said.

"Alright baby, I love you," she said. I hung up the phone. I knew that going over there was a bad idea, but I needed to do something quick.

When I arrived at Angela's place, she opened the door dressed in an all black lace baby doll dress and a pair of patent leather stripper stilettos. She pulled my hand and led me to her bedroom. I glanced over at Noelle's crib to see if she was sleeping. She was, so I moved quickly over to the bed.

"Baby, I really miss having you here with me at night," she said.

"Uh huh," I replied. She started kissing me while unbuttoning my shirt. She grabbed my nipples before heading down to unzip my pants with her teeth. I closed my eyes so that I could feel the moment versus seeing her in action. I opened them when I noticed that she had stopped. She was standing over me smiling.

"What's wrong Ang, why you stop?" I asked.

"Because I just wanted to look at your face before I went to work," she grabbed my manhood and went to work. She was licking the shaft just how I liked it and didn't hesitate to take me deep into her throat until it was time for me to cum. I exploded and she swallowed every bit of me. I lay down on the bed, as she tried to climb on top of me.

"No Ang," I said. "We can't do that it's only been two weeks since you had the baby."

"I know but I really want you bad right now. Come on, Kent, please let me satisfy you all the way," she whined.

I looked her as if she was crazy. There was no way I was going into all that mess even if I was hornier than two dogs. "Hell naw, Ang, I can't do it," I said, getting up from the bed. She pushed me back down on the bed and reached for my penis again. I moved and quickly grabbed at my pants.

"Come on, Kent. I thought that you knew how to please a woman. Let me see how nasty you really are."

"I'm not that nasty Ang," I replied, pulling my pants up. "I'll see you tomorrow. "

"Kent baby, please don't leave," she said when I reached the door. "Can you just stay the night with us? I promise, I won't bother you," she pleaded.

I looked at her. She looked so cute and innocent lying there. I decided that I would stay the night, since I was already too sleepy to drive home. "Okay Ang, I'll stay," I said.

"Thanks baby, I love you," she replied.

Sasha

"He had some nerve calling me at midnight," Sasha said to herself. "Who the hell does he think I am?"

She picked up her phone to call her Aunt Lolly.

"Hello, Lolly speaking," she answered after a few rings.

"Hi Aunt Lolly, it's me, Sasha."

"Oh how are you ma' dear?" she seemed pleased to hear from me again.

"Well I'm fine, I was just calling to see if you received the package yesterday?"

"Oh, yes I did, honey. But let me ask you this Sasha. Are you really sure that you want this man?"

"To be honest Aunt Lolly, I'm not sure about anything when it comes to Kent. I know I love him but I'm not in love with him. But I do want us to be a family because that is what we should be right. I mean, we have two kids and we're good friends. I just want the respect that I deserve, but he won't stop cheating. I'm not sure if I want him like that. I'm confused."

"Yes you are, ma' dear. I think that you should take some time to think about this before I mix up the potions for ya," Lolly advised.

"No! I know what I want so you can make them and I will handle it after that."

"Ok ma dear," she hesitated. "Well, you know, there are two spells under Tata Remi that I can do for ya. One will bring your lover back and Palo Mayombe is the spell to stop all the cheating and infidelity. Which one would you like?"

"Well, it seems that I need them both," Sasha laughed. "I can't have one without the other. I want him to love me but I also want him to stop sleeping with other women."

"Oh," laughed Lolly. "This is going to be some strong potion here. Just hope that they will work well together because it can either lead to strong love or a terrible disaster. In most cases, it works more towards strong love," she laughed again. "But you will have your work cut out for ya, my love. Because it sounds to me that you want love, but are unwilling to give love back."

"Uh huh," Sasha replied.

"Ok ma love, I will mix this potion for ya, and you will surely have that man back within days. But ya have to wait until after your pregnancy because I don't want to curse the little baby."

"Ok Aunt Lolly, I'll wait," Sasha replied.

After disconnecting the call, Sasha sat at the edge of her bed, thinking about the way she wanted her life to be. She believed in family and wanted her home to reflect those beliefs. She stood to her feet and looked in the mirror.

"Only four more weeks and you'll be here. We will be a family baby. We will be," she said.

Gabrielle

"Where the hell are you Benjamin?" I yelled as I looked out the window. I told him I needed him to bring my car back two hours ago. But he's still not here. Kyndal is going to be so mad at me if I don't show up to this little poetry session thing. It's been a while since she even wanted to go anywhere, so I know she's going to pitch a fit if I don't come, especially if I tell her the reason why.

I picked up my phone again and dialed Benjamin's number.

"Hey babe," he said loudly over the music in the background. "I'm about to pull up in five minutes so come on down," he said quickly before hanging up.

"Five minutes!" I said before noticing that he'd disconnected the call. "This is gonna be the last time I let him drive my car and that's my word."

I grabbed my purse and headed down the stairs to wait for him in the lobby. Ten minutes later, he pulled up with the music still blasting. I couldn't believe that he had the audacity to bring his dirty, low life friends to my place to pick me up. I decided it was best if I just kept my mouth shut until I remembered that he was supposed to be getting dropped off at home.

"Benjamin," I said softly. "Are your friends going to your place with you because I'm late?"

"Oh nawl," he replied. "I was just going to drop you off."

"Drop me off?" I asked sarcastically. "Oh no, you're not! I'm going to drop you off and take my car with me."

"Baby look, don't trip," he said. "I'll come pick you up on time, I promise."

"You don't have to promise, because that's not going to happen," I said before answering my phone.

"Hey Kyndal, I'm on my way," I said softly.

"Hurry up," she said. "I'm going in without you."

"Okay," I replied and turned to look at Benjamin. "Take me to Jubilee lounge down in the new center area. I'll ask Kyndal to bring me back."

"Cool," he said, heading towards I-75. I turned my head and focused on the road in front of me.

I couldn't understand how my life had changed over the last three years. I was so happy that I had finally found someone that adored me as much as I adored him. I was happy to spend my days and nights with him and we shared so many common interests. I just knew that I had found the one, regardless of his history with women. I knew that I was different and that he would recognize my efforts and reward me with marriage and a child.

But these last two years have been very trying. He no longer adores me hell, he doesn't even say 'I love you' anymore. He puts me down constantly and never thanks me for my efforts.

"Babe, which way do I go from here?" he asked, interrupting my thoughts.

"I wish I knew the answer," I replied. "But make a right on Grand Blvd and a left on Second Ave."

"Okay," he replied.

When we reached the lounge, I was surprised to see how many parked cars were in the lots and on the streets. I knew people loved poetry, but I didn't know the Christian community would support the event to this capacity. I got out of the car without saying goodbye to Benjamin. He drove off with no hesitation.

I stood in line for almost 15 minutes before I was finally in. I picked up my phone to call Kyndal, but right as I was pressing 'call' button, someone grabbed my arm from behind.

"Hey Gabby," someone spoke, and I turned to see my old college buddy Marcus.

"Marcus," I said hugging him. "How are you?"

"I'm fine, praise God," he said. "What brings you out tonight? I've never saw you here before."

"My friend Kyndal is in here somewhere," I said, looking around.

"Oh Kyndal, I saw her over there talking to Gerald earlier," he replied, pointing towards the front of the stage. "C'mon I'll walk you over there," he said grabbing my hand. I felt a little indifferent about him holding my hand, but I allowed him to take me to Kyndal anyway.

"Hey girl," Kyndal greeted me, turning to look at Marcus, who was still holding my hand. I quickly snatched my hand away and thanked him for showing me the way.

"Well, I hope to talk to you some more before the night is over," he smiled.

"Ok," I replied nervously. I wasn't sure how to take him because I definitely wasn't interested in him. I guess, I would just tell him that later, if he tried anything. I smiled and turned my back to him to greet Kyndal.

"Hey friend," I said before taking my seat next to her.

"Don't 'hey friend' me," she teased. "What's up with you and Marcus?"

"Nothing!" I quickly replied. "I just bumped into him on the way in and he showed me where you were. That's all."

"Uh huh. Well it looks like he was all into you, judging by the way he was holding your hand and smiling at you."

"Girl please, you know that he is not my type," I replied.

"He should be," she replied. "He is certainly better than that Benjamin boy that I have yet to meet. Why didn't you bring him tonight?"

"Girl please, you know that he wouldn't come to a place like this. This is definitely not his type of spot."
I laughed at the thought of him being in a place filled with Christians talking and rapping about God.

"Hmph," she replied. "I thought that was the type of man you wanted years ago. You know, back in your Christian days. 'I want a man that can stand before God with me with no hesitation' were your exact words. But I'm not one to preach because I have yet to lay all my burdens on the altar. "

"Yeah, let's not start the preaching tonight Kyndal. I want to have some fun," I replied.

"Me too," she replied. "But we can only drink sparkling grape juice in this place."

We both laughed.

"Is everything alright?" Gerald asked, as he approached us from behind.

"Yes," I replied, looking up at him admiring how handsome he was. I smiled at Kyndal and she smiled back. She introduced us as we exchanged handshakes.

"Good," he replied. "The show is about to start. Enjoy."

"Enjoy Kyndal," I whispered. "Cause that right there is one fine man of God that you need to get close to."

"Girl, whatever. I just want to see the show," she replied. "But he is kind of cute, huh?"

"That's way beyond 'kind of'," I teased. "But I know that you'll get him with no questions asked."

"I'm not thinking of getting anybody Gabby," she replied. "I have too much mess to clean up before I let anybody new enter the picture."

"Nobody said anything about him staying in the picture, just get what you need, girl. Get what you NEED!"

She laughed, "We shouldn't be talking like this in the house of God," she giggled, raising her hand, mocking churchgoers saying 'Hallelujah'."

"Whatever," I replied. "We'll see."

The place was packed and I was surprised at how good the poets and singers were during the first half. It really felt as if we were at a church service with all the praising we were doing. During intermission, Gerald came back to the table to see how we were doing. Marcus came shortly after, asking me questions about my work and love life. I told him where I worked and how I was in a committed relationship. He said that was good, but I shied away from him when he asked if I was happy. I didn't feel the need to answer that question because it wasn't any of his business. He got the hint and excused himself from the table. Once we were alone again, I teased Kyndal about Gerald some more and she joked about Marcus.

When the second half started, everyone turned to the stage to hear a young man with a beautiful strong voice singing, Marvin Sapp's *God*

Favors Me. I watched as Kyndal shook her head from side to side and I began to praise God more than I had all night. I closed my eyes once he began to sing the second verse:

*"I don't know what you're going through
but I want you to know tonight you got favor
In your trial, in your test, in your hard time
Don't worry (God favor's me)
Attack your character, attack you integrity
Don't' worry NO NO (GOD favors Me)
Touch your neighbor,
Encourage the person next to you
Tell him I got it. I Got it.
I can say yes, to your will, During hard times…….*

When I finally opened my eyes, I turned to see Kyndal crying, which took me by surprise. I placed my hands on her shoulders and began praying for her. I almost never saw her cry, so I grabbed some napkins and handed them to her. I got teary-eyed watching her, but I thought it was best to be strong for her, so that she would be able to let go of all the grief she was dealing with. Once the young man finished singing, everyone stood to their feet and clapped for him.

Gerald walked onto the stage and said," "The presence of God is surely in this room tonight. And I don't know if you know Him like I know him, but I would advise you to get to know Him because His favor is amazing. I know that we have a room full of Christians, but I do believe that there are some souls that need some healing as well. Don't worry, God's favor is upon you, but you have to be willing to put your life in His hands in order to receive His favor."

He said a few more words before handing the mic to the next performer. As I turned towards Kyndal, I could see that she was still crying with her head on the table. I whispered in her ear to ask her if she was ready to go. She nodded in agreement. I grabbed a few more napkins for her. Once she was finished drying her face, she opened her purse to retrieve her lip-gloss. I smiled.

"Girl, you're silly," I tried to cheer he up. She laughed when she finally realized what she was doing.

As we headed towards the door, Gerald approached us. "Hey, I just wanted to thank you for coming and I hope to see you two again."

111

We said our goodbyes and headed to the parking lot to Kyndal's car. She turned to me before pulling off and said, "Gabby, I'm so glad that we came here tonight. I really needed that."

"Me too," I replied.

"I know it's been a long time since I've been to church, but I think it's time that I get back on that path because I've been going through a lot lately. I haven't told you much about it, but I promise that I will soon. I just think that it's time that I try God again."

"I hear ya," I replied softly. "I need to get back too, trust me."

We drove to my place silently. I think we were both thinking about how our lives had changed for the worse since we started living for ourselves. We had both been through so much during the last two years that we needed another source to seek outside of ourselves.

I walked into my apartment and dropped my keys on the counter. I decided not to call Benjamin because I didn't want to ruin my night. However, when I reached my bed, instead of getting right in, I did something I hadn't done in two years—I got down on both knees, clasped my hands together, closed my eyes and began to speak to the Lord.

Kyndal

As soon as Gabby got out of the car I cried relentlessly for the entire drive home. When I pulled into the garage, I sat in my car for a while, thinking about all the pain I was dealing with—all of the burdens that I needed to let go of in order to move forward. I thought about Dr. Anderson's speech on forgiveness and I started reciting a verse from a song that I recalled the choir singing on one of my church visits:

"I want a heart that forgives, a heart full of love
One with compassion, just like yours above
One that overcomes evil with goodness and love.
Like it never happened,
Never holding a grudge.
One that lives and let's live
One that keeps loving over and over again,
One that MEN can't offend,
Because your word is within,
One that loves without price, Like you lord Jesus Christ......(Kevin Levar)

I cried until I couldn't cry anymore. An hour later, I got out of the car and went inside. I picked up the phone to call Mom, but she didn't answer so I undressed and went to bed.

When I arrived at work on Monday, I was surprised to see that Melissa was in the lobby waiting for me. I smiled at her and motioned for her to come into my office. I sat my things down on my desk and pulled my chair out to be seated.

"Ms. Kyndal," she started, while staring out of the window, as usual.

"Have you ever wondered why streetwalkers walk the streets?" she asked.

"Sometimes," I replied. "But then I realize that everyone isn't as fortunate as others in life."

"Fortunate?" she questioned. "I don't think being fortunate has anything to do with it. Look at me. My father's a very wealthy pastor at a renowned church. My parents live in a big mansion with acres of land surrounding it, right here in Palmer Woods. So, in my view, being fortunate has nothing to do with it. But, I guess, if you come from money then you have a right to think that way."

I sat silently waiting for her to continue as she continued to stare out of the window.

"I believe that the lives of people that walk the streets are no different than yours and mine. They got hurt and lost somewhere along the way and just couldn't find their way back. I tried to go back to my father's house, but he wouldn't allow me. He told me that due to the fact that I wanted to be a part of the world, I should find out what it's really like to live life on my own. I cried because I couldn't believe that my father, the pastor, would turn his back on his own child after seeing me in this condition. Look at me. I'm a bum. I'm a streetwalker, even though I come from a 'fortunate place', one that praises the Almighty God for everything. I'm a bum, nonetheless."

"But you know what Ms. Kyndal?" she asked.

"Yes, Melissa," I said.

"I'm not blaming this on God because it's the choices I've made along the way that have gotten me to this unsettling place. I've been walking around with all this self-inflicted pain that I've forgotten that I still have a life to live. And I deserve to live a good one," she said smiling at me.

I smiled back at her because I knew that she had finally reached that place of hope and forgiveness. The place that I knew would allow her to move forward.

"It's great to hear that you're ready to live Melissa. That's exactly where you need to be in order to move forward."

"Ms. Kyndal, I wish that life was that easy but I'm willing to take it one step at a time. My first step will be going back to my father's church on Sunday morning and giving my life back to the Lord."

"That's great Melissa. That's Great!" I replied sincerely, truly happy for her. I rose from my chair to hug her. This time her embrace seemed warm and genuine. I could feel the happiness that she was trying to hold back inside. When she started crying, I rubbed her hair and began singing,

"Lord we wanna let it go
God we need to let it go
Lord it's been holding us back
And we don't want it, we don't want it, we don't
we don't want it no more
We don't know how to get rid of it, but
Here I am Lord Jesus, here I am ohhh, Here I am Lord Jesus,
Lord I need you, I need you, I know this is me you're talking to
This is me, this is me, this is me Lord, this is me..........(Kevin Levar)

Just as I was ending, Melissa pulled away from me and went back to the window. To my surprise, she began to sing,

"Lord I let it go, every person that's ever hurt me
God I let it go,
every single hurt
God I let it go,
Every single pain
God I let it go, I let it go, I let it go
Lord you can have it, Lord you can have it
Take it now, Take it now Lord
Cause I don't want it no more." (Kevin Levar)

We hugged again and then Melissa turned to the door to leave. "Thank you Ms. Kyndal. I thank you for everything."

I watched her as she walked out the front door of the crisis center and across the street to the gas station, but this time she didn't go inside. She walked straight to the bus stop and stood smiling.

"No, thank you Melissa! Thank you," I said softly to myself.

I went to Dr. Gordon's office to inform her that I would be leaving early. A few minutes later, I grabbed my things and headed to the parking lot to my car. I could feel my phone vibrating inside my purse but decided to ignore it because I needed to get home so that I could take care of a few things.

I pulled into the garage and headed straight to the mailbox since I hadn't checked the mail in two days. The street was quiet but that was probably because it was midday and all the kids were at school. I retrieved the mail from the box and headed back to my place.

"Hey Kyndal," I heard someone yell right as I reached the front porch. I turned to see who it was and recognized Gerald jogging down the block. I admired his physique and kept watching him as he got closer to where I was standing. "Hey Gerald," I replied.

"I know I'm all sweaty and out of breath but I wanted to say hello anyway. How are you today?" he asked.

"I'm fine," I replied, smiling.

"That's good. So did you enjoy the poetry session?"

"Yes I did, it was wonderful and I look forward to going back very soon."

"Well, you should. I host this session every other Friday night and we are always looking for new faces and fresh voices."

"Oh no," I said shaking my head. "I'm not good with speaking or singing in front of other people. I'll just enjoy the word," I said jokingly.

"Enjoying the word is always good. But remember that if you really need to seek the source, you will need to speak the word directly," he said seriously. He must have sensed my uneasiness, so he laughed and said that he was just joking.

"What church do you belong to?" he asked.

"Ummm, my family belongs to Deliverance Temple," I replied.

"Ok," he said. "Well if you're ever in need of the word or looking for a great service, feel free to stop by my church, World Outreach, anytime. I hope to see you soon."

"We shall see," I replied.

He jogged away and I went inside. I picked up the phone to call Dr. Anderson.

Kent

"Kent, please come now. I think the baby is coming," Sasha yelled into the phone.

"Okay, I'm on the way," I said making a U-turn in the middle of Warren Ave. I headed towards the freeway but all I could think about was Karen and how I was finally able to get her to meet me for lunch. I picked up my phone to call her.

"Hey baby," I said when she picked up.

"Hey Kent," she replied.

"Are you ready for lunch?" I asked.

"I was just getting ready to leave the house," she replied.

"Well, something came up. Do you think we can do dinner later?"

She was silent for a moment before she responded. "Maybe, it depends on what came up. What's going on Kent?"

"Um, Sasha is ready to have the baby and I…."

"You have to be there, right," she responded. "Look Kent, I really don't think that this is going to work out for us because I'm never going to be able to accept the fact that you will always have these other women in your life and they will come before me, no matter what you say. I refuse to put myself through unnecessary pain because of you. I've been through too much already. So I think it's best that we just go our separate ways."

"I'm sorry that you feel that way. I'm sorry that any of this happened and I wish I could take it back, but I can't."

"That's right Kent, you can't. And I don't want to be a part of it. Good bye," she said before disconnecting the call.

"Damn!" I yelled, throwing the phone into the passenger seat. When I arrived at Sasha's, I walked right into the front door and headed upstairs to her bedroom where I found her lying down, moaning in pain.

"You ready?" I asked nonchalantly.

"Yes, I'm hurting Kent. I think the contractions are five minutes apart now," she said. I grabbed her slippers and the bag that was next to the door. She sat up on the bed and gestured for me to come and get her. I helped her downstairs and into the car.

When we got to the hospital, the nurse checked her and told us that Sasha was fully dilated and was ready to start pushing. An hour later, my son Korey was born. I stayed at the hospital with Sasha and the baby all night.

The next day, I went out to run some errands. While I was at the grocery store, I ran into a friend of Karen's. She asked if I knew how Karen was doing and I told her I thought that she was fine. She asked if we would be attending their mutual friends Henry's gathering this weekend and I said that I was unsure. She told me to tell Karen and the baby hi and walked away. I didn't understand what she meant by this and wondered if she thought that Karen was pregnant.

I pulled out my phone to call Karen but she didn't answer. I decided that I would just stop by on the way back to the hospital because she lived pretty close by.

I pulled into the visitors' parking lot and walked up the stairs to her apartment. She answered the door told me to wait a moment, and closed it again. Confused, I waited for a few minutes before I knocked on the door again. She finally came out dressed in sweats and gym shoes and told me that, since she was getting ready to go running, if I wanted to talk to her, I would have to join her.

I asked how she was doing and we made small talk about things that had recently happened to us over the past four weeks that we hadn't spoken to each other. I tried to refrain from saying anything about the babies because I knew that would upset her. So I told her about the encounter with her friend and she looked shocked.

"Are you pregnant?" I asked.

"Um no," she replied.

"Good," I said.

"Yes, very good. Because I wouldn't want to be added to your long list of baby mothers," she snapped.

"Ok, I see where this is going and I don't want to argue with you. We were having a good time and I hope to continue that," I replied. "Let's change the subject."

"Let's," she snapped. "You know, I will never understand men. I will never understand how you can just lay with so many women and not care about how it makes them feel to be taken advantage of. Used. And be made to feel worthless after having a child."

I was shocked at her change of tone because I had never heard her speak this way. "I'm so glad that I found out who you were early in our relationship, as it allowed me to walk away before I became one of your victims, Kent. You're a piece of shit just like the rest of the men I know."

"Okay Karen," I said grabbing her by the shoulders. She yanked away from me and slapped me.

"That's for all the women you used. Now, stay the hell away from me!" she yelled, running off.

I decided that it would be best not to run after her because she seemed really upset. I didn't even know what caused this whole argument because we were doing just fine until I brought the whole friend and baby thing up. Well, at least I knew that she wasn't pregnant.

I walked back to my car and got in. I pulled my cell phone out of my pocket and turned the ringer back on. I noticed that I had two missed calls from Sasha and three from Angela.

"Hey Sasha," I said into the receiver after dialing her number first.

"Hey Kent," she said softly. "Are you coming back today? I'm hungry."

"Okay," I replied. "What do you want to eat?"

"Can you stop by Motown's and grab me some chicken, mac'n'cheese and yams."

"Yeah," I replied. "I'll be there shortly."

"I knew he was with her," said Angela to her girlfriend as they sat outside of Angela's Apartment.

"Look, is that her jogging back up the street," Angela's friend asked, pointing to Karen.

"Yeah, that's her. Long hair and all. But where's Kent? I know I saw his car earlier."

She looked over towards the parking lot where his car was parked and saw that it was gone. She continued to watch Karen as she got closer to the area where they were parked. Angela quickly opened the door as Karen jogged past the door. She quickly grabbed her hair from behind and yanked at her hair continuously, screaming, "Now what bitch? Look at you now! I told you to leave my man alone!"

Karen was shocked as she turned to look up and saw Angela's face. She recognized her even though they met only once before. She instantly grabbed Angela by the neck and screamed. "What the hell is wrong with you? Let my hair go."

They squabbled for a few minutes longer until Angela screamed, "Leave my fucking man alone, bitch!" Karen struggled to keep her grip around Angela's neck, so she bit her instead.

Angela screamed out in pain, "Kim, come get this bitch off me! She's biting me."

Karen bit harder, refusing to let go until she felt the grip on her hair loosen.

Angela's friend quickly got out of the car and came to her rescue. Right as she approached the two, Karen's nosey neighbor came out with a bucket full of water and threw it on all of them.

"What the hell?" yelled Angela.

Karen took a step back to catch her breath, while looking at her neighbor.

"Look at you! You stupid little young girls, fighting over a man that isn't here for either one of you," she said. "You ought to be ashamed of yourself," she pointed to Angela and Karen.

They looked at each other.

"I don't know what you think is going on between me and Kent but we're not together anymore, stupid!" Karen yelled at Angela, trying to catch her breath. "I broke it off with him a month ago."

Angela looked at her friend who turned her head to the side. "Well you deserved it anyway for trying to break up our family," said Angela holding her neck.

"What family?" said Karen walking away shaking her head. "I don't want Kent and never will."

Angela and her friend got back into the car and drove off.

"Do you think she was telling the truth?" said Kim.

"I don't know, but I really feel like a fool if she was," said Angela. "Look at me! I am 29 with two kids at home, fighting over a man that belongs to no one. I think it's time that I move on, seriously."

"Yeah," Kim replied. "You need to move on."

****

The following day after Sasha was released from the hospital, she asked me if I wouldn't mind staying at her house few days to help her with the baby and Layla. I agreed.

The first few days were a breeze. I woke up to feed the baby in the middle of the night and took Layla to school in the mornings. I prepared dinner for all of us and I'd even gotten used to sleeping in the bed with Sasha again. I didn't realize that I had missed out on so much in the past not being there to care for the kids when they first arrived home. It felt good and I was even considering working things out with Sasha to try the whole family thing out. I knew that's what she wanted and I just hoped that I would grow to love her over time.

After dinner, I decided to talk to Sasha about us being together, so I put the kids to bed a little early and asked her to wait for me downstairs.

When I got back downstairs I was surprised to see that she had two glasses of red wine waiting at the table. I walked over to her, kissed her on the cheek and sat down in the chair next to her.

"You aren't tired, are you?" she asked.

"A little," I said before picking up the glass.

"Let me first say thank you for helping me out these last few days. I really appreciate you," she said getting up from her seat. She walked over to me and started massaging my neck and shoulders. I relaxed and drank more of the wine.

"No problem Sasha, I really enjoy being here with you and the kids. As a matter of fact, I was thinking that maybe we can try to work things out between us."

She stopped massaging and sat back down in her seat. She picked up her glass and took several gulps before responding. "Umm, I was thinking the same thing Kent. I don't see why we shouldn't work towards being a family."

"Well, I'm willing to try and I know this won't be easy at first, but we both have to be willing to make it work."

"Okay Kent," she said nervously. I walked over to her and kissed her. She seemed a bit nervous, but I continued.

"Kent, please stop. You know we can't do anything yet," she said nervously.

"Alright," I said. "I'll just go to bed. Are you ready?"

"Give me a minute and I'll be up in a few."

"Okay," I said heading up the stairs.

Sasha went into the bathroom and closed the door. "Damn, that worked fast," she said laughing at herself in the mirror. "Looks like it's not going to be so bad after all." She cut off the lights and went upstairs to lie in the bed beside Kent.

"Kent," she said.

"Yes," I replied.

"Do you think we can fall in love again?" she said moving closer to my chest.

"I hope so," I replied. "I hope so."

Gabrielle

"How in the hell could this have happened to me?" I screamed once I was inside the car. I threw the ultrasound photo down and started crying. I turned on my Bluetooth and started dialing Benjamin's number. I hung up after the third ring and dialed Kyndal instead.

"Gabby, what's wrong?" Kyndal asked.

I couldn't speak, so I just held the phone. "Where are you she asked?"

I still didn't respond. After a few minutes of not answering her questions, she threatened to call the police and send them to my home if I didn't answer her.

"I....I. I don't know how this could've happened," I said. "Why me?"

"Why you what, Gabby? You're scaring me? Where are you?"

"I'm sitting outside the doctor's office," I replied.

"What's the address?" she asked.

"10777 W. Ten Mile Rd," I replied. "I don't think I can make it home Kyndal. Please come now."

"Okay, I'm on the way, Gabby. Please don't go anywhere," she said.

I hung up the phone and laid my head in the passenger seat until she arrived.

"Gabby," yelled Kyndal as she knocked on my car window. "Are you alright?"

I pressed the 'unlock' button for her to come inside. "My life is over Kyndal," I cried, throwing the ultrasound photo at her.

She grabbed it and looked at the cloudy white images on the paper. "Are you pregnant?" she asked.

"No," I answered. "I'm never gonna be able to get pregnant Kyndal."

"What do you mean Gabby?"

"This stupid doctor just told me that I can never have kids because I'm going to have to have a hysterectomy."

"What?" asked Kyndal. "How is that possible you're only twenty…"

"Twenty-seven," I began to cry.

She sat silently for ten minutes before saying anything. Finally, she composed herself and spoke, "Okay Gabby, we need to get you home." She got out the car and motioned for me to move over to the passenger's side. We drove to my place in complete silence. Once we arrived, we went straight upstairs to my apartment, where I fell unto the couch. Kyndal went to the kitchen and made some herbal tea for both of us.

She walked back into the dining area and asked me to join her.

"Tell me exactly what happened, Gabby," she said. "What did the doctor tell you?"

I started not to tell her about my visit to Dr. Ellis for the liposuction consultation, even though that's where it all started. Finally, I told her everything anyway.

"Well, you know that I've been trying to lose weight these last few months. I've also been taking diet pills because I got lazy with the workouts and stuff. Last week, I called the plastic surgeon to have liposuction done."

"You what?" she yelled.

"Let me finish, Kyndal, please," I said before continuing. "I was asked to answer a questionnaire concerning my health, which I answered honestly. After speaking with the doctor about my irregular menstrual cycles, she advised me to go to see my doctor before coming back for the operation. I called my doctor immediately and, once I informed them about my irregular cycles, he suggested that I come in to have a pap smear done. A couple days later I received a call from them saying that my pap was irregular and that I would need to come in for a pelvic ultrasound. So today, I went in to have the exam done, and the doctor couldn't believe how large the fibroids were in my uterus. He said that they are dangerous at this size and suggested that I have these removed immediately. However, in order for them to do this I would have to have a hysterectomy performed." I broke down again.

Kyndal tried her best to console me, but after an hour had passed, I politely asked her to leave. She said that she didn't want to leave, but she had to because she hadn't asked anyone to pick Noah up from school. She left and said that she would take him to his dad's and come back later. Although I didn't want to be alone, I knew this was something that I would have to deal with on my own.

An hour later, my phone rang. I looked down at the caller ID and saw that it was Benjamin.

I hesitated before answering, "Hello honey," I said.

"Hey babe. What are you doing?" he asked.

"I'm home, resting," I replied.

"Good, I'm getting ready to swing by and grab the car," he said.

"Okay," I replied dryly and disconnected the call.

I went into the bathroom to clean myself up a little before he arrived. I didn't want him to see me like this. I cleaned the dining area and removed the glasses from the table. I opened the windows and door to the patio and sprayed some air freshener inside. Shortly after, the buzzer was ringing.

I opened the door for him and before I could sit down, he asked why the car wasn't outside. Then I remembered that Kyndal had driven my car to pick up Noah.

"Oh honey, I'm sorry I forgot that Kyndal took the car," I replied.

"What do you mean, she took the car? She has her own car, right?" he asked, sounding irritated.

"She picked me up from the doctor's office earlier and left her car there. I'll call her to see when she's coming back." I picked up the phone but before I could dial her number he smacked the phone out of my hand.

"You know what, you're stupid!" he yelled. "Why the fuck didn't you tell me that before I got dropped off over here? Now I'm stuck here with yo' dumb ass," he shouted, pacing back and forth.

I sat frozen on the couch in disbelief. "Benjamin—" I started to explain.

"Don't say my fucking name, Gabrielle! You do the dumbest shit and still expect for me to marry you, please! You can't remember shit. You can't cook and you can't fucking clean. Look at this place! You think because you sprayed a little air freshener that it makes it alright. Get the fuck up off your ass Gabrielle," he said, yanking me from the couch.

"Go ahead and call your little girlfriend and tell her to bring the car back right now!" He threw the phone at me.

I stood there shaking, until he started approaching me again, "Dial the fucking number, Gabrielle!" He ordered menacingly.

"Hey Kyndal," I said, trying to sound calm. "Where are you?"

"I'm just grabbing Noah some food before I take him to his dad's. Is everything alright?"

"Um yes," I replied.

"Are you sure? You sound different."

I looked up at Benjamin to see him mouthing "Tell her to bring the car back right now."

"Kyndal, can you just do me a favor and bring the car back right now? I promised Benjamin that he could use it tonight and he needs to leave right away," I said.

"Okay," she replied. "I'll just see if Noah's dad can meet me at my car and drop me off."

"Please do it as quickly as you can," I said before hanging up the phone.

"She'd better get here soon or else," he warned me. "Now get in the kitchen and fix me something to eat."

I got up from where I was sitting and walked into the kitchen. I opened the refrigerator, pulled out a package of turkey and grabbed some cheese. I took the skillet from underneath the cabinet and thought about all the things that had happened to me today.

128

First, I find out that I have tumors growing inside of me, which means that I can't have kids after the surgery and then I come home to be verbally abused by the man I love. I dropped the skillet and headed towards the living area where Benjamin was seated. I picked up the lamp that was sitting on the table, but quickly sat it down. I went back into the kitchen and grabbed the wooden broom. I walked back into the living room and hit him right upside the head with it and continued hitting him.

"I'm tired of you. Get the fuck out of my house!" I yelled while still hitting him with the broom. He was trying his best to grab the end of it but I moved with such force and agility that he couldn't stop me.

"I'm gonna kick your ass as soon as you stop," he yelled.

I grabbed the lamp and threw it at him, but I missed. He ran to the dining room table and tried to catch me. I ran around the table grabbing everything in sight and started throwing it at him.

"Get out!" I yelled at him

"I'm not going anywhere!" he yelled.

"She said, get out!" Kyndal yelled as she entered the apartment.

He looked at her and smiled but didn't move. "I'll kick both of yall asses if that's what it takes."

Kyndal reached in her purse to grab her phone and dialed 911. He frowned at her and walked towards the door. "I'll be back, Gabrielle. This ain't over."

Kyndal ran to lock the door as soon as he left out. "Are you okay Gabby?" she asked running to my side.

"I don't know what just happened," I cried. "I just got so mad that I couldn't take it anymore."

"That's okay," she said calmly. "Everything is going to be alright."

When the police arrived, I told them what had happened and decided that it was best that I not pursue charges against Benjamin because I was the one that started the whole mess. After the officers left, Kyndal wanted to talk about everything that was going on in my life. I told her that we would have to talk about it another day because I couldn't even begin to explain my situation at the moment.

Kyndal stayed the night and said that she would call into work tomorrow to stay with me but I told her that it wasn't necessary.

I tried to go to sleep, but I couldn't keep my eyes closed long enough without hearing the words of the doctor saying, "You'll have to have a hysterectomy to remove the tumors; therefore, you won't be able to have kids in the future."

I had spent the last three years thinking about my future. Now it was hard to deal with the fact that what I dreamed of would never be a reality.

Kyndal

"During your last session, we talked about you overcoming the pain your father caused you and the negative experiences with the men that you have dated in the past. We spoke more about how these challenges made you feel and why you may have responded the way you did after Michael's death. We also talked about how you would have to truly forgive each one of these men on a different level in order to move forward. Have you given any thought to how you are going to do this Kyndal?" asked Dr. Anderson.

"I have," I replied. "I had to think long and hard to come up with something that would be beneficial both to me and to others. I know that, in the past, I may have voiced my willingness to forgive alone. But, this time, I know that I'm going to need some help. I need something much stronger than anything that I can do for myself. I've decided that I'm going to give my life back to the Lord." As I said that, I smiled and walked towards the window. I looked out at the sun that was shining brightly and said, "You see, my life needs something more powerful than I am. And I realize that this is exactly what I've been missing."

"That's great to hear, Kyndal," said Dr. Anderson. "Absolutely great. But I want you to know that this will also require hard work and dedication and it will not be easy. However, as long as you make the first step, the rest shall follow."

I left Dr. Anderson's office feeling relieved. I pulled out my phone to call Gabrielle to ask her if she wanted to attend service with me on Sunday. She didn't answer, so I got in my car and drove home.

I noticed Gerald jogging up the street as I pulled into my driveway. I got out of my car and walked to the front yard to see if he was still there. I waved my hand for him to come over, as he continued to jog my way.

"Hey Gerald," I greeted him with a smile.

"Hey Kyndal," he replied. "How are you today?"

"I'm great actually," I smiled. "I just wanted to tell you that I'm going to take you up on your offer to come to your church's service this Sunday."

"Well that's great news," he said smiling. "We'll be glad to have you."

"It's been awhile, so I hope your pastor is good," I joked.

"He's far better than good. He's phenomenal. But I'll let you see for yourself," he said. "Is anyone joining you?" he asked.

"I'm trying to get Gabrielle to come with me. But I may just come by myself," I replied.

"We'll be glad to have you, either way," he said. "See you on Sunday, Kyndal," he said before jogging off.

I watched him as he jogged away. He was an extremely handsome man and his body was definitely something to remember. I smiled as I bit my bottom lip thinking of him. "Hmm, I just may have found what Gabby wanted in her man—an awesome man of God."

I went into the house and went upstairs to my bedroom. I pulled the comforter off the bed and fell face first into one of my huge pillows. I slowly turned my head up to the ceiling and smiled.

"Hey Michael, it looks like I'm finally going to be alright without you," I said aloud.

When Sunday arrived, I was extremely nervous. It took me almost two hours to get dressed. I chose the perfect blue aqua green two piece suit with a white ruffle blouse. I couldn't make up my mind rather to wear a 3-inch or 5-inch heel, so I called Gabby and she suggested the lower ones, so that I wouldn't look as if I was going to the club, as some of the other members did. I didn't want to make a bad impression on Gerald either because from what I could tell, he took the word seriously.

As I thought about Gerald, I couldn't help but smile. But, for some reason, I found it strange that he hadn't made a pass at me yet. I had yet to see him with a woman and I didn't see a ring on his finger, so I knew that he couldn't have been married. I made a mental note to pay attention to him at service to see if he was taken or not. I was not ready to enter a relationship just yet, but I knew that I wouldn't turn him down if he asked me out.

I was so glad that I had left Noah with his dad the day before, or I would have really been later than the 30 minutes I was running behind already. When I pulled into the church parking lot, I couldn't believe how large the building really was. I parked and hurried towards the building. Once at the door, I was greeted by several members before entering the sanctuary. The place was packed. There had to be at least 3000 people inside. I looked around and saw that there were people on both levels of the balcony and on the ground level. I scanned the room for a seat until one of the ushers waved for me to come forward. I found it odd that this church had chairs instead of pews.

As the choir finished their last song, the pastor rose to his feet. The congregation cheered as he gave his praise greeting before asking everyone to be seated. I tried looking around to see if I saw Gerald but I knew that it would be hard to find him amongst 3000 people. Towards the end of his sermon, the pastor asked everyone to look at their neighbors and tell them "I love you because Jesus loves you." We did as told. A few moments after, the pastor spoke of his daughter that had decided that she wanted to venture off into the world to see what it was like outside the sanctuary. He talked about all the things that she had learned and the bad choices that she had made during the year that she was gone. He said that he was happy to say that she learned that she needed Christ in her life in order to survive, which brought her home once more. He asked his wife and daughter to stand up. I broke down in tears when I saw Melissa rise from her seat. Pastor Graves motioned for her to come to the podium and the congregation applauded and rose from their seats. The entire church was praising God and screaming 'Hallelujah'. I was still seated, crying and thanking God for this wonderful experience. The pastor came back to the podium and asked the congregation to calm down because his daughter wanted to say a few words.

I watched as she adjusted the microphone and spoke:

"I just want to say 'Thank you Jesus'. Thank you Jesus, for your mercy, your grace and your favor on my life. Lord, I thank you for my life. I thank you. Let me tell you something," she said turning to the seated people, "You know, I left my father's house, thinking that there was something far better in the world then I could find here. There were times when I felt that I was truly missing out on life because my father wanted to keep me so close to him. I fought him all the time because I felt that I wasn't living the life I wanted to live. So I ventured out into the world to get a taste of what I thought was the good life. The devil is a liar.

However, I didn't recognize that all good things soon come to an end when you're faced with reality. My father had taught me a lot, but because I wanted to be a rebellious child, I refused to use those teachings. In fact, I ignored everything that he had ever taught me and did the exact opposite. Now, I won't tell you my entire story, but just know that I learned a lot more outside these walls of what not to do firsthand, than what my father had instructed me not to do in his house.

I would actually call this a storm, but I feel like the past year has been more of a tornado or hurricane. I've had to fight to keep my head above waters while holding on to what meant the most to me and that was my faith in GOD. Thank you Jesus. But I'm here to tell you today that you must recognize that God's will for your life is the truth and you must rely on the word of God to see you through. I almost gave up, but there was a voice in my head that kept saying 'It ain't over until God says it's over'. It ain't over until God says it's done.' I'm so glad that it ain't over. I'm so glad that my father is an awesome man of God. I'm so glad that he taught me the word of Jesus. I'm grateful that the God I serve gives second chances. I'm blessed to be standing here today to ask God to forgive me and to give me a second chance."

She bowed her head and said, "Father, I know that I have broken your laws and my sins have separated me from you. I am truly sorry, and now I want to turn away from my past sinful life and towards you, Lord. Please forgive me, and help me turn away from sin. I believe that Your Son, Jesus Christ died for my sins, was resurrected from the dead, is alive, and can hear my prayer. I invite Jesus to become the Lord of my life, to rule and reign in my heart from this day forward. Thank You for sending your Holy Spirit to help me obey you, and to do your will for the rest of my life. In Jesus' name I pray. Amen."

As she said her last words, she began to cry and praise God for his will. Pastor Graves and his wife hugged her and took her back to her seat.

"Thank you Lord for bringing my daughter back to me," he said. "Thank you for giving a second chance to those that need it. It is at this time that I would like to call all those that need a second chance to come forth and declare your need for salvation."

Before I knew it, I was at the front of the church with my hands raised high asking for God's love and salvation. I got down on both knees and asked for forgiveness and salvation.

The choir began to sing, Hezekiah's Walkers *"Moving Forward"*

"Not going back, I'm moving ahead
I'm here to declare to you, my past is over in you
All things are made new,
Surrendered my life to Christ, I'm moving, moving forward
You have risen with all power in your hands,
You have given me a second chance
Hallelujah, Hallelujah
Yeah, yeah, yeah
Moving, moving forward"

"Congratulations," said Pastor Graves, "Welcome to the family of God!"

Kent

"I'm glad to see that you and Sasha have decided to work things out Kent," said my mom.

"Yeah," I said softly. "We're doing pretty good so far."

The last two months had been pretty good between Sasha and me. We spent most of our days and nights together and I hadn't had the urge to call anyone else. We were in a good place. I couldn't stop making love to her either, which she seemed to enjoy immensely. I was really falling in love with her, seeing as though I hadn't expected any of this to happen so soon.

"She seems to be pretty happy now, Kent, even with the kids," she said. "Now I hope you're going to do right by her son."

"I'm doing right by her now, Mom," I replied.

"You know what I mean son," she said pulling my face towards her. "Although you two have had your issues in the past son, it seems as if you've both decided to move past those things. Am I right?"

"Yes, you're right, Mom. Sasha has been great with accepting all the kids as her own which Is one of the biggest reasons I love her."

"Well I hope that's not the only reason because it takes a strong woman to do something like that, son. She must really love you."

"Yeah, she says that she does, Mom. She does."

"I'm not telling you to rush anything but you may want to start thinking about the future with her, son," she said patting me on the back.

"We'll see mom. We'll see."

I watched Sasha as she pushed Layla and Brittney on the swings and smiled. She was a good mother to my children even though she sometimes complained about having all of them at the house every weekend.

We'd decided to come over to my mom's to visit since she hadn't seen the kids in a while. When we arrived, she had already fired up the grill in the yard and had the music playing.

"Kent, go check the chicken again because you know I don't like it too dark," she said.

I got up from my chair and headed to the grill. "Daddy, can we have a hot dog?" said Brittney.

"Sure baby," I said. "Just let me grab the buns from the kitchen."

She ran back over to the swings where Sasha continued to push them. I watched KJ jump from the top of the slide to the ground. My mother was now singing to the babies, who were lying on a blanket on the grass.

I smiled as I thought of how good everything had turned out so far. I was glad that I had decided to make everything work with Sasha. Angela had stopped calling as often as she used to and I heard that she was even seeing someone else. She made sure to drop Noelle off every Wednesday and Friday, so that she could have her "night off", as she called it. I had tried calling Karen again, but she never answered my calls. In truth, I hadn't had the desire to keep trying with her either.

I was happy with my life, despite the fact that I hadn't found a job yet. Everything seemed to be working just fine.

I grabbed the buns and yelled for Layla, KJ and Brittney to come over to the grill to get a hot dog. "Daddy KJ hit me," cried Layla.

"KJ, you know better than to hit your sister!" I scorned.

"Yes, daddy. But she keeps calling me bad names and telling me to go home to my own mom."

I looked at Layla and told her to go inside the house to wait for me.

I fixed hotdogs for Brittney and KJ and went inside to talk to Layla. This wasn't the first time I'd had this talk with her, as she would sometimes tease Brittney, saying that Daddy loved her more because he lived with her and her mommy and not your mommy. I scolded her each time, but I knew that, this time, I would have to use a little more than tough love because she was getting out of hand.

"Layla," I yelled because she wasn't sitting on the couch where I told her to be seated.

"Here I come, daddy," she said as she came down the stairs.

"Layla, haven't I told you about teasing your brother and sisters about going home when they come over."

"Yes daddy. I'm sorry," she said nonchalantly.

"Sorry is not enough this time Layla," I said removing my belt. "I want you to know that I love them just as much as I love you and Korey. It doesn't matter where I live, I love you all the same. Those are your sisters and brothers and you will not treat them any differently. Do you understand me?" I said.

"Yes daddy," she replied looking sadly at Sasha as she came through the door.

"Kent" Sasha yelled, seeing the belt in my hand. "What the hell do you think you're doing?"

I quickly turned around and said "Layla go outside."

I waited for Layla to leave the room before I said anything. "She needs to learn to respect her sisters and brothers, all of them," I said.

"Hmph, well if you didn't have so many damn kids, she wouldn't say half the things she says."

"Don't tell me that you condone this type of behavior? Is that the way you want her to talk to the rest of the kids?" I asked, now getting angry with her too.

"Well, if the shoe fits—" she started to respond, but stopped herself before adding, "She just says what she feels and I would probably feel the same way if I had three extra kids sharing my living space every weekend. Damn Kent, can't you tell their moms to keep them at home sometimes. We need our space. To be honest, I'm getting tired of them too running through my house tearing things up and that baby stays up all night crying. I'm just getting tired of it all, Kent. I need a break."

"Oh so you need a break now huh?" I yelled, getting angrier.

"Yes, a break, Kent. Do you know what that is?"

"You should have thought about all this before you agreed to make things work between us. But it's good to know that this is how you really feel, Sasha."

"No, I really feel like I'm tired of all of this, Kent. I'm tired of taking care of you and your little heathens while you sit at home all day doing nothing. Why haven't you found another job yet? What kind of man let's his woman go to work while he stays at home. That's not a man, Kent. You disgust me and I really want you gone!"

She walked out the back door and went back to the swings, where the kids were still playing. I sat down at the kitchen table in total shock because I couldn't believe what she had just said to me. Here I was, thinking of marrying her, and she told me that she was disgusted by me. I'd tried my best to please her every day and this was the way she felt.

I spent the rest of the evening in silence, watching her as she appeared to be having so much fun with the kids and my mother. How could she put on such an act if she felt this way?

Right before we left, my mother pulled me to the side and said, "Kent, promise me you'll try to make this work. Sasha is definitely a sweet girl and the kids love her. Promise me son."

"Yeah Mom," I replied. "I'll try."

We drove home in complete silence. When we arrived at Sasha's place, she told me to bring all the kids in for bed because it was too late for me to be driving them around. After putting them to bed, I asked her if she wanted me to leave.

"Come here," she yelled at me while undressing. "All I want you to do is please me," she said while pushing my head down between her legs.

Before I could say anything she pushed the back of my neck and demanded for me to continue. "No talking tonight, Kent. Just do what I tell you."

I was a little bit turned on by this, so I continued without saying anything. Right as she was about to climax, she dug her nails into the back of my neck and screamed.

"I fucking hate you Kent. I hate you." I tried to stop but she pressed my mouth right back into her flesh. When she finally reached her peak, I undressed and tried to climb on top of her. She slapped me and turned her back towards the door.

"What the fuck is wrong with you Sasha?" I asked, grabbing her by her shoulder.

She laughed and looked me dead in the eyes and said, "Nothing's wrong with me, dummy. I only wanted you to please me. Now get the fuck out of my bed and go downstairs to sleep on the couch."

"You're crazy," I said, laughing trying to turn her over.

This time she kicked me, "I'm not playing with you, Kent. I don't want you in my bed tonight, so go downstairs."

"I don't know what the hell is wrong with you, but you're crazy as hell if you think that I'm sleeping on the couch. I'll leave." I grabbed my clothes and headed towards the bedroom door.

"You're not going anywhere, Kent, unless you take all the kids with you," she said. "So, please, don't try me, I will put them right outside with you."

I opened the door without responding to that nonsense. When I got downstairs I put on my clothes and shoes and sat down on the couch. I looked at my keys and thought about leaving, but I was just too tired to go. I wasn't worried about Sasha's threat, I just didn't feel like taking the 30 minute drive home, so I laid down on the couch until I fell asleep.

The next day I woke up to the kids jumping all over me.

"Daddy, daddy," they yelled. "We want cereal."

"Okay," I said. "Go tell mommy."

"She told us to get out of her room and locked the door," said KJ.

"Then she told us to come wake you up and ask you for whatever we want, daddy," said Layla.

"I'm hungry daddy," added Brittney.

"Ok, let's go get some cereal," I said, following them to the kitchen.

"Daddy," said Layla. "Why do you have your shoes on?"

I looked down at myself and saw that I was fully dressed. "I must have fallen asleep with my clothes on baby."

"Why would you do that?" asked Brittney.

"I guess I was too tired to take them off," I replied.

"Oh," said Brittney. "We thought that maybe you were going home."

"Daddy lives here with us, don't you daddy?" asked Layla, staring at Brittney.

"I still have my own place Layla," I replied unsure of how to stop the conversation.

"Well you're going to be moving in soon. Mommy told me you didn't need your other place anymore because you live here. You sleep with mommy. So that makes us a family, right daddy?" she questioned.

"Sure baby," I replied. I watched, as a huge smile spread across her face. "Sure."

I didn't know what was going on with Sasha, but I hoped that the episode from last night was just a one-time thing.

"Good morning baby," said Sasha as she came downstairs holding Korey in her hands. She leaned over to kiss me before passing me the baby.

"Good morning," I replied.

"I hope the kids didn't wake you," she smiled, grabbing two bottles from the refrigerator.

"It's okay," I replied looking at her strangely. "I figured you were tired."

"Well, I feel great this morning," she said, kissing each of the kids. "Noelle is still sleeping but I know she'll be awake shortly, so I'll warm her bottle too."

"Ok," I replied, looking at her dressed in a nice pair of stretch pants and halter top. She leaned into me and kissed me again. "Thanks for last night baby, I hope I didn't scare you too badly," she whispered in my ear.

I laughed because I was hoping that last night was a joke and I was glad that she just verified my feeling.

"No baby," I said. "I kinda liked the aggressive bad girl you turned into last night. But don't ever tell me to sleep on the couch again."

She laughed before going back up the stairs. "I'll try not to, Kent," she said once she reached the top level. "So behave."

I smiled after she went in her room and closed the door. It looked as if everything is going to be fine, after all. Once I finished feeding Korey, I headed upstairs to finish where we left off last night.

Gabrielle

"Tomorrow's the big day" I said sadly to myself while looking in the mirror. I picked up the air freshener bottle and hit the glass. It didn't break right away, so I hit it again with every muscle in my body. It still didn't break. I sat down on the closed toilet seat and tried thinking of everything that I was losing if I went through with the surgery.

Now that I could no longer have children, who would want to marry me? I'd lost Benjamin already because I couldn't control my anger. I was probably going to lose my job because I hadn't been to work in a week.

I stood to look at myself in the broken mirror again. "Look at me," I yelled. "No one was going to marry me anyway."

I couldn't help but think back to my childhood days where my friends would tease me about how ugly I was and how no boys in the neighborhood liked me because I was a little on the chubby side. It wasn't until the age of twelve that I realized that they may have been telling the truth. There was this boy, Mario, in my class that I had a huge crush on. He was very popular. The girls would always talk about how he liked to play the kissing game with girls that he liked on his block. Well, one day, while I was visiting a friend that lived on Mario's block, he came over with a bunch of other girls and boys from the neighborhood. They went on playing the game in which Mario had kissed most of the girls already. When it was my turn to be kissed, he hesitated. One of the other boys teased him and said that he had to kiss the fattest ugliest girl in the world. I tried not to pay him any attention because I wanted my kiss from Mario. However, instead of kissing me, he turned to the boy and said, "I'm not kissing her because she'll probably get pregnant and say her ugly kids are mine." Everyone laughed. I didn't want to cry in front of everyone so I laughed too.

That was pretty much how most of my teenage days went. No boys wanted to go out with me, which meant no kissing for me. Whenever someone made fun of me, I laughed it off. It wasn't until high school that I learned how to use my good qualities to get in good with the boys. I was always very smart, so I started helping the football and basketball players out with their homework, even giving them answers to test and quizzes at times. This worked in my favor because I got in good with the popular kids and close to the boys.

After getting cool with most of the boys, they accepted me as one of them. They would invite me over to watch sports, chill at their homes and even into their bedrooms.

As my body began to fill out, the boys started to notice me more. They still didn't pursue me. I was still considered the home girl until one day I was dared to kiss Stephen, one of the players, during lunch. I was never one to turn down a dare, but I was hoping not to get the same reaction that I had received from Mario a few years back. I walked over to Stephen and leaned in close to him. As soon as he turned his head, I stuck my tongue in his mouth and kissed him. After 30 seconds, I heard everyone laughing, screaming and pointing but I was surprised that he was still just sitting there silently.

I walked back over to my table, where a few girls were still laughing. They each gave me high fives and congratulated me on choosing the cutest one at the table. It wasn't until sixth period that I received a negative response from the girl that was known to be Stephen's girlfriend. She walked up to me and started calling me all kinds of ugly names. She talked about my weight and how ugly I was. I again started laughing at her because I had the upper hand this time.

After that day, I quickly became the girl most girlfriends hated but the boyfriends loved. I snuck around with them behind their girlfriend's backs and they liked it because they knew that I wouldn't tell a soul about what we did behind closed doors.

Being the girl behind the scenes followed me into my college years and adult life, as I started seeing married men. I didn't care what anyone said or thought about me because I was getting what I wanted from them, with no strings attached.

I had got accustomed to being unattached until I met Benjamin. I felt that he was the one from the first day I met him, so I had dedicated the last three years to being with him and only him.

I didn't feel like a fool, knowing that he was cheating on me because I knew that this is what men did. I was his woman and he had made this known to his family and friends as no one in the past had done before. For this reason, I just knew that he would marry me and provide me with the life that I so desperately wanted. He loved me for who I was and I would be a fool to lose him over a petty argument.

I grabbed the phone and dialed his number.

"Hello baby," I said as soon as he answered.

"What's up?" he replied.

"I miss you," I said softly into the phone.

"Oh really?" he retorted, unmoved. "I figured that you would call sooner or later."

"I was hoping that you would stop by later if you aren't too busy," I said seductively.

I could feel him smiling on the other end of the phone. "I'll try to stop by in about an hour," he replied.

"I'll be waiting for you in the bedroom, so just use your key to come in."

"Oh really?" he replied. "See you in a few."

I went back into the bathroom to clean up the broken glass. I wanted the place to be spotless when he arrived, so that he could see that I was trying to please him. I fixed my hair and grabbed one of my new pieces of lingerie from the bottom drawer. The baby pink negligee looked so nice on my skin, as I stared at my body in the mirror. I put on some cherry flavored shimmer gloss that I picked up from Victoria's Secret last month and added a little make-up to my eyes for the complete sexy look. I lit a few candles and put fresh sheets on the bed and positioned myself on top of the covers to await Benjamin's arrival.

An hour later, Benjamin still hadn't arrived. I didn't want to call him because that would only aggravate him, so I turned the television on to watch the Desperate Housewives finale to keep my mind off him.

****

"This has to be the dumbest girl, I've ever been with," said Benjamin to one of his friends, as he took two puffs of the blunt before passing it. "I mean, she's so fucking book smart and has plenty money but she just don't get it. How does she expect me to act like everything is good after she pulled that stunt on me last week? But you know what, I'm gone play dumb right along with her. I need that new Benz that she going to get next week out of her." He laughed and hi-fived his friend. An hour later, he headed to Gabrielle's house. He was three hours behind the time that he told her he would arrive, but he really didn't care.

He used the key to get inside and stood in the living room for a few minutes before heading to the bedroom. "This is going to be funny," he said to himself. "I already know." He laughed softly as he headed to the bedroom.

When he entered he was a little surprised by the candles and music that was playing. Gabrielle was asleep, but he could tell that she was wearing some lingerie. He took off his clothes and got in bed with her.

"Hey baby," she moaned. "I'm sorry that I fell asleep."

"That's okay," he said. "Well, now that you're woke, why don't you take care of me the way I like it?"

"Ok," she replied. She slowly moved down towards the edge of the bed and noticed that he had already removed his underwear. He smelled funny but she decided not to say anything that would make him mad because she needed the company anyway.

After she finished, she heard him snoring so she climbed back into her spot and closed her eyes. The tears started rolling down her face, so she tightly closed her lips to avoid the whimpers from coming out.

Kyndal

"The tears I cried at the service last week were definitely tears of joy," I said to my mom. "I'm really looking forward to starting over for real this time, Mama."

"That's good to hear, Kyndal," she replied.

There was a knock at the door.

"Okay, I have to go now, Mama," I replied.

"Who's coming over Kyndal?" she asked.

"A friend of mine," I replied trying to get her off the phone.

"Is it that guy that got you to come to his church Kyndal? Now, don't go falling in love too fast," she warned.

"Bye Ma, I'll call you later," I said quickly, hanging up the phone.

I took one last look at myself in the hall mirror before opening the door.

"Hi Gerald," I greeted him with a huge smile.

"Hi Kyndal," he replied, giving me a hug. I noticed that he liked to pat my back every time we hugged, which really irritated me, but I didn't say anything.

I led him to the dining area where we took our seats.

"Mmmmm," he said. "It really smells good in here."

I smiled, happy that I'd chosen to make my famous Mostacolli dish. "Thank you," I replied.

"Are you sure you can cook?" he joked. "I'm prepared for the Tuscany pasta from Pizza Hut."

I playfully hit his arm as we laughed.

"Well, you know, I'm more than just a beautiful face," I said as I walked to the kitchen.

"I see," he said.

As I prepared the plates, he went to the bathroom to freshen up. I was extremely nervous because I wasn't really sure how to feel about having

146

a man around so soon. I mean, I was kind of feeling Gerald even though we hadn't talked about any private matters yet. When he returned from the bathroom, I watched as he turned the dimmer up on the lights a little bit. That was a little odd to me, but I figured that he might have wanted a little more light while we ate dinner.

"So Gerald," I said, "How long have you been a member of World Outreach?"

"For over 12 years now," he said. "And I absolutely love it there."

"That's good," I replied.

"Pastor Graves is by far the greatest pastor I've encountered. He believes in winning souls and it's amazing how many young people he has helped become true believers of the word. He is gifted."

"That's great," I said while reaching for the bread. He quickly passed it to me.

"It looks like you were one of the winners last Sunday," he smiled.

"Indeed," I replied. "I needed that word more than you know."

"I'm sure. But remember that asking God for Salvation is the first step to living a good life, as long as you believe."

"Amen." I said. "If you only knew my story than you would know that I don't have any reason not to believe."

"Well, praise God, sister Kyndal," he said. "I'm sure God knows your story, which is part of the reason that He led me to you."

"Oh really?" I smiled, raising one eyebrow questioningly.

"Yes sister," he continued. "We may not know the exact reason He led me to you that night. But I work according to the voice that I hear from above. He guides me in all the things that I do. You see, I can feel your troubles even though you don't show it. But Kyndal, you have to ask yourself. 'Does God trust that you can reach the next level on your own, or with help from another person?' "

I paused for a moment before responding, "Well I'm not sure. But I trust that He will guide me."

"Kyndal, I'm not sure if you understand what I'm saying to you and I'm also not aware of what's going on in your life. But remember that the next level of your life can be reached by meeting the right person."

I smiled as I thought of his reason for being here. I was glad that God had sent such a positive person to me but I wasn't quite sure how to handle him just yet.

We enjoyed the rest of our dinner, as we talked more about our years in college and what we enjoyed doing in our spare time. It was hard to believe that we had not crossed paths before because we shared so many interests. He loved to volunteer and mentor the youth. He loved poetry and the arts. He said that he was always busy working on some projects for the church, which left little free time for his other interests. I found that he also had a sense of humor behind all the preaching, so we were able to share laughs between his serious talks.

When the night ended, he thanked me for dinner and asked if it was okay if we met for lunch on Wednesday. I agreed.

When Wednesday arrived, I made sure to put on the perfect dress and shoes that would show off both my conservative and sexy side. I even grabbed my special set of pearls that Michael had given me on our trip to Paris. I smiled at myself in the mirror because, even though I had lost a few pounds, my curves were still there.

"Don't you look nice," said Dr. Gordon when I arrived at the office that morning.

"Thank you," I said as I headed straight to my office. I cleared my desk and set a reminder to call Karen to check on her because her 90-day check in date was coming soon.

At 10:30, I received a call from the front desk, "Ms. Kyndal, Ms. Graves is here to see you."

"Okay," I replied shocked. "Can you just send her to my office in five minutes," I replied.

"Sure," she said.

I wasn't sure how to respond to Melissa's visit. Of course, she was just like the rest of my clients, all of whom I would receive with open arms, but I also felt nervous because I was just at her father's church asking for salvation. How would she look at me?

I checked myself one more time and tried to hide my nervousness when she came in. "Hi Melissa," I said as she walked in. She looked absolutely beautiful, dressed in a beautiful lavender two-piece pantsuit. Her hair was straightened in a blunt cut and her makeup was flawless.

She smiled at me and turned around to show herself off. "I bet you didn't know that I cleaned up pretty good myself," she joked.

"It's good to see you, Melissa. You look beautiful."

"Why, thank you, Ms. Kyndal. You look lovely today as well."

"Thank you," I responded. She walked over to my desk and sat down in the chair directly across from me.

"I know that you're wondering why I came back here. But I just wanted to say 'thank you' for all your help even though I wouldn't allow you to help me." She laughed. "I don't know what you must have thought of me coming into this place, dressed like that and not accepting the help that you were trying to give. However, every person has his or her own way of dealing with issues and, I guess, mine was pretty bad. But I thank you."

"That's why I'm here," I replied.

"Well it's good to know that a place like *Moving On* exists for young girls that need help moving on after a hard time in their lives. That is part of the reason I'm here today. I told my father about you and this place and he wants to give more recognition to it amongst the members of his congregation. He would like for you to come speak to the congregation one day if you wouldn't mind.

"Thank you Melissa, we really appreciate your consideration but I'm not sure if I'll be able to do that just yet. I'll speak with Dr. Gordon and see what we can work out. "

She seemed a little disappointed by my response, but I wasn't prepared to change my answer.

"Okay," she said. "Well, I just want to be able to help in any way that I can, if possible. But I will understand either way."

"I'll let you know soon," I replied. "So how's everything going with your father?" I asked.

"I can't say 'great' just yet, but it is definitely good. He has accepted me back and so has my mother and the congregation. It feels good to be home with the people that really love you," she smiled.

"That's good to hear, Melissa," I replied. "How about your friends?"

"My friends?" she smiled with a little uneasiness. "Well, those that were true friends are happy that I chose to come back, but others have not been as forgiving. However, the one that matters most has forgiven and is willing to move forward."

"May I ask who that person is?" I asked.

"No, you may not," she laughed. "But he is definitely a righteous man of God."

We laughed before she stood to leave. "Thanks again, Ms. Kyndal, for being my ear. I hope to hear from you soon."

"No problem, "I said, rising from my seat. "You will definitely hear from me."

She left the office and headed to the parking lot, where I saw her get into a silver Mercedes. She put on her sunglasses and pulled off.

I looked at my clock and saw that it was 11 o'clock. I grabbed my cell phone and saw that I received a text from Gerald. It read, 'Hey sister. Please join us at Intermezzo Café on Warren Ave at 12. See you there.'

I was a little sad at first because I didn't know who else was going to be joining us but then I smiled at the thought of him introducing me to his friends already. That made me feel a little more special.

When I arrived, I tried calling Gerald but he didn't answer, so I went inside. I was surprised to see the large group of people that were seated in the back room. Marcus waved for me to come over and told me that Gerald was still working at the church and asked him to make sure that I was taken care of until he arrived. I was a little upset by this because I didn't know anybody. They all seemed to be enjoying their individual conversations.

As soon as we were seated, Marcus started grilling me about Gabrielle. I told him that she was involved but he didn't seem to be bothered by that. He pressed for more information until I joked that he was on a date with me asking about my friend. I smiled at the thought of Gabrielle dating someone like him. He was very nice, but I knew that she wouldn't be interested in him, not only because he seemed a little too nerdy, but he didn't meet her color requirement either.

Gerald hadn't arrived by 1 o'clock, so I excused myself and headed back to the office. The moment I reached my desk, he called and apologized for missing the luncheon. He said that he was ministering to one of the members and didn't want to leave the session unfinished. I told him that was fine and that he owed me dinner one night this week. He agreed.

On my way home, I decided to stop by Gabrielle's to talk to her, since she hadn't gone through with the surgery, as planned. She said that she wasn't ready to deal with the fact that she couldn't have kids just yet, so she would reschedule it for a later date. I was really feeling bad for her these days because I couldn't really do anything to help her and I knew that she didn't want to hear me "preach to her." I called to check on her regularly. She would answer, but our conversations always seemed a little distant. I was happy that she hadn't gone back to seeing Benjamin.

I decided to stop and grab her a bouquet of roses from the flower shop on Livernois & Davison. The florist told me that I should try giving her some multi-colored roses to cheer her up because everyone loved them. I grabbed a half dozen and headed to her house with Noah.

Kent

"Are these for me?" Sasha asked, as she looked down at the box of chocolate-covered cherries I placed in front of her.

"Yes baby," I replied. "These last few months have been wonderful and I wanted to show my appreciation for you. I really love you Sasha, and I'm looking forward to our future together." I pulled the small box from behind my back and handed it to her. She smiled at the rectangular box and hesitated before opening it.

"Kent you didn't!" she exclaimed in anticipation before opening it. However, suddenly, the look on her face went from surprised to frightened.

"Baby, I just wanted to give you something special," I said to her pulling the tennis bracelet from the box. She sat silently for a moment before replying. "You could've saved that money and paid a bill around here if you wanted to do something special!" she yelled before jumping to her feet.

I sat looking dumbfounded with the tennis bracelet in my hand as she walked into the kitchen. I had just spent the whole afternoon trying to find her the perfect gift with the cash I had available. Sure, there weren't any diamonds in it but the lady at the store said that my lady should love it because it was a gift from the heart. "Baby," I yelled into the kitchen.

"What Kent?" she screamed back.

"You don't like it?" I questioned. "I can take it back and get you something different if you want. "

"You can just take it back, Kent. What would make you think I would want something like that? I mean, you've never seen me wear a bracelet before, have you? I don't even like jewelry. But you wouldn't know that because you've never taken the time out to ask what I like! Oh how could I forget, we were just 'bed buddies' for the last six years. You're so fucking stupid, Kent. Stupid."

"Baby," I replied. "I'm sorry. I didn't mean to upset you. I'll take it back." I placed the bracelet back into the box and made sure to check that the receipt was still in my wallet.

"Come here, Kent," she yelled. "I need you to go to the store for me to grab me a few things because I just don't feel like going anywhere now." She pulled the list of household items and groceries off the refrigerator and handed it to me. "Oh, and take that stupid bracelet back while you're out because you're going to need that money to pay for those things."

I leaned in to kiss her, but she quickly moved past me and went upstairs to grab her phone that was now ringing. I looked down at the list, grabbed my keys from the counter and walked out of the front door.

****

"Hey Christina," Sasha said when she answered the phone.

"You sound like you're out of breath," said Christina. "Hope you and Kent ain't over there making another baby," she laughed. "Well, if you were, I'm glad I interrupted you because you don't need any more kids."

Sasha joined her sister in laughter. "Girl, you must be crazy. I wouldn't have another baby, if GOD paid me. Furthermore, I really wouldn't have another one with Kent."

"I thought that everything was going well between the two of you," said Christina.

"Well, everything that looks good on the outside doesn't always tell the true story, sister. I mean, we're doing okay. Kent has really opened up to me and showed me a different side of him, of which I wish I could enjoy. But there's just something about him that makes me want to hit him every time I see him."

"Now, that sounds crazy. You wanted him to love you and now that he does, you hate him. Sister, you have got to get it together!"

"I know," replied Sasha. "I was really hoping that this whole love thing was going to work for us. But now I don't know."

"That's what you get for seeking a magic solution instead of waiting for the real thing to happen. Maybe you should try drinking some of the stuff you gave him, then you'll be in love for sure," she joked.

"Girl, I'm not messing with that stuff. But it clearly does work. Kent hasn't seen or called another women since he drank that stuff. It's like, now that he's giving me all that mushy love stuff, I don't want it."

"So, what are you going to do now?" asked Christina. "He's going to be following you around for years because that stuff doesn't wear off easily. Look at mommy and daddy! Daddy still doesn't know that, he's been under a love spell for 30 years. I laugh every time their anniversary comes around and he says I must've surely been hit by the love bug because I'm still so in love with your mother."

"Yes, daddy has no clue," said Sasha. "But he loved mommy anyway. He just had that one slip up with his ex and she couldn't take it. She gave him the double dose of Love."

"Well I hope that things work out for you and Kent because you two make a very nice couple. Not to mention that you wanted to have six kids of your own but now you don't have to have but one more to complete the package."

"You're silly, sister!" Sasha joked. "I hope it works out too. But our love has never been like mom and dad's. I just hope that it can grow to be like that eventually. I'll try being a little nicer to him."

"You'd better," said Christina. "Especially if he's willing to love you, knowing that you're evil as hell."

"Girl bye," said Sasha. "I'll talk to you later."

They disconnected the call and Sasha went downstairs to prepare dinner. Layla joined her in the kitchen shortly after.

"Mommy," she said. "Where did daddy go?"

"He went to the store honey," she replied.

"Is he coming back?" asked Layla.

"Yes honey. Why do you ask?"

"Because I heard you two fighting during my nap and when I woke up he was gone." Sasha looked down at her daughter and dropped down to her knees. "Mommy and daddy just had a little disagreement, that's all. But he's coming back. Don't worry, sweetie."

"Is daddy going to stay with us forever mommy?"

"Yes," Sasha replied. Hearing that, Layla happily ran into the living room and found the cartoon channel she liked to watch.

"I hope so, Layla," she said to herself looking at her daughter. "He should, if all goes as planned."

When I returned home from the store, it was almost 8 o'clock. I walked into the kitchen where I could see that dinner was waiting for me on the stove. After putting the shopping away, I went to the bathroom to wash my hands. Suddenly, Sasha walked up behind me.

"Hey baby," she said. "I'm sorry about what happened earlier. That was really disrespectful and ungrateful of me not to accept your gift. I think it's time that we get to know each other on a different level, Kent. I mean, I would like for you to tell me your likes and dislikes and I will tell you mine. I think that might be helpful, since we haven't really done this before."

"Okay baby," I replied. "Whatever you like. I just want you to be happy." She kissed me on the cheek and left the bathroom. After washing my face I headed back downstairs to the kitchen to get my plate from the stove.

"Baby," yelled Sasha. "Why don't you come in here and watch television with me while you eat. I joined her as she turned to *Real Housewives of Atlanta*, one of her favorite shows. A part of me wanted to jump up from the couch and go upstairs to watch the game, but for some reason, I couldn't move. After I finished my dinner, we cuddled on the couch, as she watched a movie on Lifetime—another station that I didn't care for but I didn't object.

"Sasha baby," I said to her. "Let's go upstairs and make love."

"I can't Kent. I'm too tired and I'm still watching this movie. We can do it tomorrow," she replied.

"Okay," I replied. "I guess I can wait until tomorrow for you, my love."

I went upstairs to bed by myself that night and went to sleep while Sasha stayed downstairs, and fell asleep on the couch.

Gabrielle

"Surprise!" screamed Noah when I opened the door for him and Kyndal.

I smiled when he handed me the roses and gave me a big hug and kiss. "I love you," he said before running off to my room to find his video games that I had stashed away in the bottom drawer.

"Hey boo," said Kyndal giving me a big hug and kiss. "How are you doing these days? I hope we didn't disturb you?"

"I'm fine," I replied. I took the flowers to the kitchen to unwrap them. "Thanks, these are beautiful!" I yelled from the kitchen.

"I know," she replied. "I've never seen anything like them. I almost wanted to grab some for myself, just because. You know about my crazy love with flowers."

"Yeah I know," I said, laughing from the kitchen. "Remember, you used to say that, if a man doesn't give you flowers by the sixth date, he must not be that into you, or he just wants me to hold out on giving up the booty a little longer."

I laughed at how silly I was back in the days. "Well it worked for many years, as I usually received them by the third date, if we made it that far."

"Hmph, I never really got flowers unless the guy I was seeing was sorry for something he did. Or they he needed a way to apologize after getting caught by the wife."

I walked into the dining area, where Kyndal was seated, and placed the bouquet in the middle of the table. "I hope Benjamin doesn't trip when he sees these," I said, immediately realizing my mistake, as I hadn't told Kyndal that I was back seeing him.

"Benjamin!" she yelled. "I hope that you didn't go back to that piece of trash. You've got to be kidding me, Gabby!"

"Girl, hush," I said, walking away. "He's not that bad. I made him mad that day, so that's why he was tripping when you got here. I've never seen him act that way before. Plus, I was starting to get lonely and I needed some company."

"I guess you don't believe in being by yourself from time to time. But, I guess, if you like being miserable with the person you're with, I'm all for it."

I decided it was best if I changed the subject because I didn't want to hear her rag on how bad of a man Benjamin was. Besides, I was better off with a bad man than sleeping alone at night, like she was.

"Speaking of the person you're with, how are things with you and Gerald going?"

She smiled," I'm not sure. He's a really nice guy and not to mention extremely attractive but this is the first man that I can't quite figure out. I mean he's really cool and we talk a lot but he hasn't made a pass at me yet. At least not the kind I'm used to."

"He must be gay," I replied flatly.

"I hope not," she said quickly. "That would be such a waste of a good man."

"Well you know most of those church brothers that look nice and spend all their time in the church are gay. So I wouldn't be surprised."

"Please stop," Kyndal said, laughing. "I don't want to think about him like that. Plus I know he's not gay. My gaydar hasn't gone off with him yet. But we did have a conversation about relationships and he told me that he was waiting for his wife to be intimate with, but he's not a virgin. How does that work?"

"Sounds gay to me," I said. "Haven't you two been hanging out a lot lately?"

"I don't know if I would call it hanging out but he invites me to a lot of group functions and stops by sometimes during the evenings to talk for a little while, but nothing serious. It's kind of like we're just friends and that's okay with me."

"So you mean to tell me that he hasn't tried to kiss you, spend the night or anything?"

"Um no," said Kyndal. "The only thing we do is hug and not the intimate type of hug either. He gives me that annoying friendly hug with the back pat."

"He's gay," I said, matter-of-factly. "He's just trying to play the role with you. But don't fall for being the beautiful girl on a gay man's arm like Puff's baby mama."

"He's not gay," said Kyndal defensively. "I just think he's really into his religion and he's trying to go about things the right way."

"If you say so," I replied. "However, I don't expect you to wait around for a guy that's not into you like that. You know you bore easily."

"I do not. I actually would prefer a man that wanted me to wait with him."

"How stupid does that sound? A man that wants his very sexual woman to wait with him!" We both laughed. "I mean, you may be the wifey type, but you're not Mary Magdalene. And you are far from being a virgin too."

"Please stop, you make me seem like such a freak. I can do without for periods of time. It's been almost a year already."

"You're right, Kyndal. I'm just joking. But we both know that, when you get a man, you can get wild. You'll be calling me with all those wild sex stories before the year is out trust me."

"I may not be calling you until I'm married, if I'm waiting with Gerald," she said, still laughing.

"We both know that is not going to happen. Just ask him if he's into having casual sex, I bet you'll be over him next week."

"You're supposed to be my supportive friend. How dare you think of me that way!" She teased, still laughing.

"I know you all too well Kyndal. You're not a slut or hood rat that runs around screwing every Tom, Dick and Harry, but you do like to have sex and there's nothing wrong with that."

"Exactly!" she replied. "So how's your sex life going with Benjamin?" She changed the subject.

"It's still quick, almost so quick, that I can't remember when we have sex. But I've gone back to using other methods."

"And you call me the freak! I've never even touched a toy."

"Who's talking about toys?" I said. "I've still got action calling me regularly."

"Who Jeff or Mike?" she asked.

"Wouldn't you like to know?"

"Oh I get it. You use the black guys for great sex and use the white boy... for what again?"

We laughed until Noah came back into the room.

It felt good to be laughing especially after the last few days had been filled with me running out on lunch and late at night to satisfy my burning desire to have as much sex as possible before the surgery. I couldn't stop thinking about the information I'd read on line about how different it feels once they take your womanly goods out. I wanted to make sure that every pleasure point was hit before it was removed. All my boys from back in the day were coming in handy, married or not. I was living my old life again and I was pretty satisfied. I knew that I couldn't have kids so I didn't worry about using a condom either. I wanted it all, all the time, and there was nothing anybody could do to stop me.

"When is your surgery now that you rescheduled?" Kyndal asked.

"Later next month, but I may push it back even further," I replied.

"Why would you do that?" she asked.

"Because I still have a few things to do before they take my guts out, that's why," I said trying to joke with her but she was looking at me seriously.

"I think you should take this a little more seriously, Gabby. Your health, and maybe even your life, is at risk."

"I know mama," I replied. "I'm going to take care of it. Just not right now."

"Have you told Benjamin about the surgery yet?"

"Why would I do that? He doesn't need to know. He'll probably be happy anyway."

"What? I just can't believe you're with a person that is so not good for you and think that it's okay. You'd be better off with Marcus," she said before laughing.

"Marcus?" I laughed. "He doesn't even have a chance."

"Maybe you should give him one, since he asks about you all the time. It's actually getting pretty annoying because I see him more often than Gerald, but all he wants to do is talk about you, Gabby," she said, batting her eyes at me.

"I honestly don't know why. He was really cool in college but that's it. I don't see him as anything more than a friend."

"You never know Gabby. You might just be missing out on your husband."

"I don't think so," I replied. "I seriously don't think so."

I was a little sad after they left because they always made my home feel like a home. Noah's a very smart and good kid. I loved spending time talking to him, especially since Kyndal said that his dinosaur stories were starting to annoy her. I loved every moment of it. He would probably be the closest thing that I would have to having my own kid anyway.

I pulled the sheets back on my bed and hopped right in. Just as I was about to close my eyes, the phone rang. "Hey Operator, there's a fire on the west side of town that I'm going to need you to gear up for. You have thirty-five minutes to get dressed and slide down that pole before I send the truck over to come get you," said Jeff.

"I'll be there in twenty-five, so have it ready for me," I said jumping up from the bed. I quickly opened the closet and pulled out my chest full of sexy costumes that he loved and grabbed the firewoman dress from inside. I was glad that it was spandex because I didn't have time to iron it and when Jeff said 'be on time' he meant it. I grabbed my 5-inch red patent leather pumps and my keys and ran to the elevator.

That was exactly how I stayed sane during the four weeks before the surgery. Jeff and Mike definitely kept me busy. I wasn't really feeling Benjamin too much anymore because I really didn't need him. I figured that, as I was never going to get married or have babies, why deal with him and all his drama. I'd recently heard that he had another kid on the way anyway. I will say that it kind of hurt at first to know that he was just out there popping babies with no worries and still didn't want to give me one, no matter how much I tried to convince him. I just added it to the load of other things that I would need to cry about one day. But for now I'm living my life the only way I know how and that's behind the scenes.

Kyndal

It's been four weeks and I still don't know what's going on between Gerald and me. I really enjoy his company and I love the way that he has introduced me to new knowledge about God and religion. He's even taken the time to teach me how to pray correctly. He is truly an awesome man of God.

But tonight, I planned to ask him how he felt about me because I needed to know and I really wanted to know if he was gay or not. That thought still hadn't left my mind since I'd had that conversation with Gabby. I mean, what man didn't want to kiss me or hug me if they were in my presence? There had to be something wrong unless I wasn't taking the whole religion thing as seriously as he did. I knew that there were lots of women at their church that said that they were virgins, but I could tell they weren't. I always stayed quiet whenever that conversation came up because I didn't want to lie to anyone and tell them that I wasn't going to have sex until marriage. I just couldn't tell that lie.

When he arrived at 7:30, I was dressed and happy to see him. He seemed extremely happy when he walked inside my place.

"Don't you look happy," I said to him. "What's got you smiling so big tonight?"

"God?" he replied. I should have known he would only get so happy if God had something to do with it.

"Well praise Him in advance because your face is really lit up tonight," I said.

"I'm just happy that He has turned some things around for me and now I can move forward with my life according to His will."

"And what exactly does that mean?" I asked, taking a seat next to him.

"These last four years, I've been praying for a wife with all my might because I just needed to have a partner to share my life with. It's hard going home to a lonely house at times, but I never detoured because I knew that God had someone great for me. He's been working on her as well. And I'm glad that it's almost time for us to make it official."

"Oh really," I said sadly. "Who is she?"

"I can't tell you just yet but I will, once I confirm that she feels the same way about me. I'm still waiting on the Lord to tell me when and how to proceed.

I was extremely confused because I knew he couldn't have been talking about me. Still, why wouldn't he tell me who the heifer was since I'd just been his comfort friend these last few weeks? I wanted him to just get up and leave from my couch. But I also wanted answers.

"So is that why you haven't kissed me or hugged me yet?" I asked stupidly.

He just looked at me for a moment and smiled. "I'm sorry Kyndal if I led you on in any kind of way, but I felt that you needed a friend and I was here to be just that for you," he smiled at me again.

I didn't return the smile. "Are you gay?" I asked.

The smile he had left his face. "I'm sorry that you have to question my manhood on the basis of me not pursuing you the way other men have in your past. But please, believe that I am very secure in my manhood and, for that reason, I was fine with just sitting here with you talking and laughing and not displaying any sexual attraction towards you. I am not saying that you aren't a very attractive woman that any man would be pleased to have. But that's not the type of woman that I'm looking for. I know that women like you like to play games with men and love, but what I'm looking for is a woman that's much more stable and mature.

The type of woman that I love will love God just as much as I do and know that all of our strength and life blessings come directly from Him and not people of the world. The woman that I will marry will have cherished GOD all of her life and not just at a moment of despair. The woman I'm choosing is the woman that was already chosen for me by God."

I was astonished by his forwardness and eloquence. I knew that, if I were a weaker woman, my feelings would have probably been hurt by his words, but I wasn't, so his explanation made me respect him even more.

"Well it's good to know that you'll be receiving everything that you prayed for. You have my blessing and hopefully I will still have your friendship."

He smiled, "You see, Kyndal, you are an awesome woman of God too. I just hope that you will realize your gift before it's too late. The man that receives you will have a good and loyal woman as well because you respect God and know what you want. I hope that you will continue to stay faithful in prayer because all that your heart desires will be given to you before you know it. But don't rush it Kyndal, life is worth the wait."

He hugged me but this time it was a heartfelt hug that I truly felt was real and sincere. He left shortly after and I showered before going to sleep.

Before getting into my bed I headed to the window and pulled the blinds open. I got down on both knees, clasped my hands together and looked up at the sky.

"Lord, I come to you today in hope of receiving a listening ear. I want to thank you for your mercy, your grace, your favor and loving kindness. I want to say thank you for keeping me under your wings and showering me with all the blessings that you have seen fit for my life and circumstances. I promise to continue to be thankful, loyal and faithful to you Lord. I will continue to listen to your voice as you guide me daily. Lord please continue to guide me, as I know that my journey is not over but just beginning. Lord, as you may already know, I am not here to ask you for material possessions, as such things come and go. Today, I'm asking for your help in making my foundation stronger. I've surpassed so many hurdles, and I've accomplished goals that I couldn't have imagined I would.

However today, I feel that my foundation is weak and I'm looking forward to making it a solid one with your help, Lord. At this point, I don't know what I'm doing wrong because I work hard daily. Every day, I try to work on myself in areas of parenting, career, goal setting, finances and forgiveness, and even love. I know that you are thinking, *Love?* But yes, love. I'm willing to try this again because I'm ready. Yes Lord, maybe that's it—love. I'm going to try it again…. Amen."

I rose to my feet, walked over to my bed and got in. When I closed my eyes that night, I knew that it would take some time before my prayer was answered, but I was willing to wait it out because I knew that what God had for me would eventually come. I just hoped he would take me seriously and think that I was special enough to send me someone as special as the woman he'd sent to Gerald was—an awesome man of God.

Kent

"No matter what I do, she's never satisfied, Mom. I try daily to show and tell her that I love her, but she continues to push me away. How am I supposed to marry her if she won't even accept the love I'm trying to give her every day?"

"I don't know, son," she replied. "I do know that you love her, though. And I know that you made a promise to me that you would try. But have you prayed about it?"

"Prayed?" I said, looking at her in wonder. "This has nothing to do with prayer, Mom. That's stuff that women do to make them feel better about life. I believe in reality and the reality of this situation is that Sasha just doesn't love me."

"I don't believe that, son. She's still with you and the kids every day and she acts as if she cares for you whenever I'm around. Maybe she just needs a little more time to digest everything that has been happening between the two of you. You know, it has to be hard dealing with three other women's children in her home all the time. Not to mention the stress of going to work and taking care of everyone on top of that."

"I take care of myself, Mom. Or did you forget that I still have bills to pay at my own home?"

"I don't know why you still have that place. You're never there and that money could be used to take care of the house that you're living in. That's probably why Sasha's mad. You're still holding on to your bachelor's pad which to her may mean that you are not fully committed to a future with her."

I thought about what my mom was saying and decided that I would talk to Sasha about that later, to see if that was the reason behind her being angry with me all the time. If so, I would let my place go and move in with her.

"Son, I think it's time that you get your life back in order, starting with finding a job, then spending more time with me in church. Everybody asks about you all the time. Pastor Graves's daughter just returned from her life full of sin, so I know that my son should be willing to do the same."

"Mom, I don't think so," I laughed. "That whole church thing ain't for me. Plus, you can pray for me. Starting with a prayer about me finding a job."

"Consider it done son. But under one condition—if you go home and tell Sasha that you are willing to give up your place and it makes her happier, you must promise to go to church with me before this month is out. Do we have a deal?"

"Yes Mom, we have a deal, I promise!" I wasn't sure how the whole thing would play out because Sasha hadn't seemed pleased about any of my attempts to make her happy during the last few weeks. I figured that this would be no different but also was hoping to find something that would change her attitude. I didn't want to go to church with my mother, but I was willing to do whatever it took to make Sasha happy because it was really beginning to stress me out.

On my way home, my Pops called and asked me to meet him down at Flood's to watch the game. He teased me about calling to ask Sasha first, but I figured that she should be okay with me going out with my dad, so I didn't bother to call.

"Hey son," my father greeted me when I entered the bar.

"Hey Pops," I replied, sliding into the chair next to him.

"Has it been about three months since I've last seen you?" he asked. "Oh, I forgot! You're a family man now, so no chasing skirts with your Pops on Wednesday nights anymore, huh?" he teased and we both laughed.

"No Pops, you know, it's not like that. I just haven't had the urge to go out anymore lately."

"Where's my son, the party maker? What have you done with him you lame?" he laughed as he drank more of his beer and signaled for the bartender to bring another round.

"I'm not lame dad, just trying to stay in the cool zone with Sasha."

"So how is that going son? I never would have thought that you two would be serious. She's too much like your mother," he joked.

"Me either, but something happened after she had the baby and I just felt that I should be there with my family. I love her, Pops."

"Love her? What the hell do you mean son? You never loved anybody outside of that Taylor girl but she wasn't the one for you anyway. Too loose," he said shaking his head laughing.

I was starting to get irritated by his rude comments but I wasn't ready to leave just yet. "Pops, I'm really thinking about popping the question."

"What the hell is wrong with you son? Did she slip something in your drink or are you just that damn stupid. Marriage is not a joke and this girl is not the one for you! Trust me. You said that you weren't getting married after that mishap with that Taylor girl. Why the change all of a sudden?"

"I just love her, Pops. I just think that it's what's best for us and the kids?"

"Oh, the kids! I forgot. Your most precious jewels," he joked. "Boy you better go clean your eyes and your ears because the kids are going to be okay whether you're married or not. I almost felt that way about your mama, but I woke up as soon as she showed me that she wasn't the one for me. When a woman starts being evil towards you for no reason, even if you're trying everything in your power to make her happy, leave her before you lose all your sanity. You can't buy sanity, son. It's all you got. And crazy women will try and take that from you. Don't be the fool."

I hadn't told Pops about what had been going on at the house for fear of him teasing me or tell me what to do. I knew that my mom was still a little bitter about her and my Pops breaking up while I was young, but I didn't know that she too had an evil side that ran him away. She talked badly about my father all the time. It was almost 30 years later and she still didn't want anything good for him. I just couldn't understand all that bitterness. But I just figured that he had hurt her in some way.

I knew that I would have to have a talk with Sasha soon to determine if I was going to fully commit to moving in with her as well as proposing to her.

When I got home, Sasha was waiting for me on the couch. "Where the hell have you been Kent?" she screamed.

"Out with Pops baby. What's wrong?" I asked.

"You're such a fucking liar. I know you were probably out with one of your little whores!" she yelled, throwing the remote control at me.

167

I caught the remote just before it hit me in the chest. "Baby, I'm not lying. I wasn't with anyone else. I haven't been with anyone else since I've been here with you."

"Why don't I believe you Kent? You lie all the fucking time, that's why! Why didn't you call me?"

"I thought about calling you, but I figured that you wouldn't mind since I was out with Pops and I was coming home anyway."

"Home? This isn't your fucking home, Kent. You just sleep here!"

"Is that the problem baby? If that is what bothers you, I can change that," I replied.

"Yes, it's a problem," she said. "You shouldn't keep paying bills there when we have more bills now that you're here."

"So you want me to be here permanently now right?"

"Yes, if that's what you want to do," she said softening up.

I walked over to her and kissed her cheek, "Baby I want to be here with you forever. I just wanted to be sure that we were on the same page," she smiled. I pulled her closer to me and kissed her lips softly. She straddled me and continued to kiss me with such passion that I was almost ready to explode. I picked her up to carry her upstairs, but she stopped me and told me to make love to her right there. I pushed her up against the wall and slid her panties off with one of my hands while still holding her up with the other. I buried my head underneath her night gown and went to work. She moaned and continued to position my head in the direction she wanted it to go. I could feel her trembling above me, which meant that she was getting ready to explode. "I fucking love you Kent!" she screamed.

"I love you too baby," I said as I tried to capture all of her juices with my tongue. It had been a while since she last said 'I love you', so I really wanted her to enjoy the moment. I kept going until I could tell that she couldn't take it anymore. However, instead of cuddling with me on the couch afterwards, she went directly upstairs to the bedroom and got in the bed. I was hoping that she went to shower, as she usually does, but I found her sleeping twenty minutes later instead. I shook my head as I thought about the many nights that she had done the same thing over the past two months. Tonight would be no different than the others.

The next afternoon, I received a call from my mother, asking if I'd spoken with Sasha about moving from my place to hers. I told her that I had told Sasha and she was really happy with the news. She asked me what day I was going to church with her, since that was the part of the deal, so I told her Tuesday. I didn't think there was service on Tuesday but when she responded that Tuesday was prayer service at her church, I tried to back out.

"Kent, A promise is a promise, and you promised me, son," she said softly into the phone.

"I know Ma. But I really don't want to go," I tried to get out of it.

"Now, you don't have a choice, do you son? You can't lie to God and your mother," she laughed.

"Okay Ma, I'll see you next Tuesday," I replied. "Should I ask Sasha to join me?"

"That's up to you, son," she replied. "But I feel that you may want to enter this first prayer session on your own, so that nothing or nobody can block you from speaking to God about what's going on in your life."

When we hung up the phone, I felt like my mom had tricked me because she knew Sasha was going to be happy about me moving in. She probably wanted for us to be together more than Sasha did because she didn't want to see Sasha go through the same thing she went through with my dad. She would always say that I should marry the mother of my child, no matter what. She was embarrassed by the fact that I had four of them and wasn't with either of them. She said that she didn't raise me to be such a whore. I never responded because she didn't raise me at all. She gave me to my father at the age of five and I felt as if she never looked back. She would come visit me every weekend but never wanted to take me home with her because she said that my father didn't deserve such freedom. She would always talk about how he took her life away from her and how she wasn't able to do anything after having his child. I got tired of hearing her reasoning behind giving me away to my father because it didn't make any sense.

I would always hear people talk about how the relationship with a son's mother should be the best and the most secure, because she would be the first woman that he would fall in love with and that would determine how he treated women later in his life. I always wished that my mother would come and rescue me from my father's house because he didn't know how to show his love for me or anyone else.

There were times that I cried because I missed my mother. Still, whenever I would call her to come get me, she would always say that my father didn't deserve any freedom and made me stay there. She thought that she was punishing him, but I was the only one being punished.

That's when I decided not to care too much about anyone or anything. I became pretty much emotionless. My father told me that was the best way to be, especially with women. Whereas, my mother told me that women needed emotions to survive. I couldn't find a balance then, and now that I am trying so hard to show Sasha how much I care for her with no reciprocation, I'm starting to feel that my father was right.

Gabrielle

"Girl you have got to come hang out with me this week Kyndal," I said into the phone. "You're really missing out on all the fun I've been having lately."

"Fun!" she laughed. "Girl, please! If your idea of fun includes running around with all those married men, I'll pass."

"Well that is my idea of fun, especially when meals and drinks are included," I replied.

"Gabby, this is not the time for you to be partying like crazy. The surgery is scheduled for next week right or have you pushed it back again?"

"Not yet, but I'm thinking about it. I've been having way too much fun to be on bed rest for more than two days after the surgery."

"That's why you should be resting now and not partying," said Kyndal.

"I'm not trying to hear that Kyndal. So anyway, I met this new guy named Travis and he is so fine. He plays in the band down at Floods every Friday night. He invited me to come to see him, but I don't want to go alone."

"Well you may as well call somebody else because I'm not going down to that old man festival. I vowed that the last old man that I dated would be Michael because now I'm looking for someone to grow old with."

"Whatever Kyndal. You know that you will always love you some old men, because their money will last longer than that any younger guy can give you."

"This is true," she said laughing "But I'm at a different place in my life where I've come to realize that money isn't everything when it comes to finding true love. I'm willing to try something different this time round. I now realize that, while I was looking for money, I may have missed out on my husband."

"Wait a minute, I don't think I'm talking to the right person," I joked. "Did Kyndal just say that money isn't everything? I can't believe it! The world must be coming to an end or that whole church thing is paying off."

"You can say whatever you like. I just want to find a good man that is willing to love me for who I am and I'm willing to do the same. I'm not saying that I'm willing to date a bum because we both know that's not happening, but I am willing to grow with someone. So I'll open a few new doors."

"Listen to you. I'm so proud of you," I laughed. "Not! Since your options are open now, that's even more reason for you to join me at Floods."

"Girl no, that place is filled with nothing but old men chasing skirts and I'm not drinking anymore, so that's definitely not going to work for me."

"Okay Kyndal," I said sadly. "I was hoping that we could have one last drink together before my surgery next week, but that's okay."

Kyndal remained quiet on the other line for a few moments before she finally agreed to come.

"Good," I replied. "You need to get out of the house anyway and find you a nice piece of meat to clean up some of that mess you've got all bundled up inside of you."

"I'm fine," she replied. "I can do without."

She went on to tell me about what happened with Gerald and his revelation of finding his wife. I still thought he was gay but she seemed to believe that he was really going to be proposing to his mystery girl soon. I told her that he was just like any other man, leading women on with no intent of committing to them. She said that she was fine with them being just friends and, for some reason, I believed her. I knew that she wasn't quite ready to date again, but I was hoping that she would get out of the house a little more often than she was these days. Still, I couldn't really worry about her because I had my own problems to deal with. I'd been having so much fun these days that I hadn't had time to sit and think about the surgery scheduled for next week, which was good because I didn't really want to think about it anyway.

I looked over at the clock, which now read 7:30, and ran to my room closet to open the chest. Jeff told me that he wanted to be the guy in the front row of a burlesque show, so I grabbed my black leotard, thigh highs and pink flamingo wings and ran out the door. I was ready to put on the best burlesque show that he'd ever seen tonight.

"Where the hell do you think you're going?" screamed Benjamin when I reached my car.

I tried unlocking the door to throw the bag inside, but he grabbed my arm before I could open the door.

"Let me go," I yelled.

"No, you're going to answer me damn it! Where the fuck do you think you're going?" he repeated, yelling louder.

"Out," I said as he spun me around. He held my face with one hand as her poured the contents of the bag out on the sidewalk. I'd already dropped the wings on the ground but the sight of the lubes and flavored gels made the display even worse.

"Oh, so you're going to play dress up and fuck somebody else, huh?" he said clenching my jaws harder. "You nasty little bitch!"

I tried to pull away, but his grip was too strong. Suddenly, I felt a burning sting across the side of my face as he sunk his nails into my skin. I screamed, so he pulled my hair and pushed me on the ground, face first.

"All this time, I thought you were a good woman, but you're just like the rest of the tramps I've dealt with. You thought that I didn't notice that you were cheating on me, didn't you?" he yelled, as he kicked me in my side.

"Benjamin stop!" I yelled as I balled up on the ground. He smiled at me and started kicking me more intensely. "You slutty bitch! How dare you think that you were good enough to be my wife?" he yelled as he kicked me some more. I tried to scream, but no words came out. He yelled more obscenities that I couldn't understand as he knelt down and pulled my hair. The last thing I remembered was him spitting on me before I passed out.

I don't know how long I'd been lying there before the ambulance showed up. All I could hear was someone saying that I had blood coming from between my legs and they needed something to stop it. When I arrived at the hospital, the doctors surrounded me, sticking me with different tubes, while removing my blood-covered clothes. While they were attending to me, I heard one of them say, "She is pregnant, but the fetus has almost bled out. Her uterus is enlarged, so we're going to have to perform the surgery now. Has anyone called her family?"

"Yes, we were able to get a hold of the emergency contact from the ICE number she had stored in her phone. She said that she was her sister and is on the way."

"Gabrielle," the doctor finally spoke to me. "Can you hear me?"

I didn't know whether to say 'yes' or 'no' because I just wanted to die at that moment. "Yes," I finally replied.

"Your fetus has died. The tumors in your uterus are now bleeding, so we're going to have to perform surgery immediately," he said.

"Okay," I managed to say. "Okay."

I could feel the tears sliding down the side of my face but I couldn't move. Ten minutes later, I heard Kyndal's voice in the room. I could hear her crying, as the doctor started explaining to her what had happened. I closed my eyes because I couldn't take it any longer. I didn't remember opening them until the next day.

"Gabby," I heard Kyndal say. "Can you hear me?"

"I nodded my head 'yes'. I tried to turn my head to face her, but the pain was unbearable.

"Don't try to move," she said. "Relax, I'll call the nurse."

She pushed the button on the side of my bed to alert the nurse. Two minutes later, the nurse was at my bedside.

"Hi Gabrielle," she said in a gentle voice. "How are you feeling?" she asked.

I tried to move my mouth to speak, but the pain in my jaw stopped me. She noticed and told me to relax.

"You've been through a lot of pain sweetie, so you're not going to be able to move for a few days. I'm going to give you some painkillers and muscle relaxers to ease some of the pain." She reached over to the nightstand to grab the small cup of water and pills. She told me to sit up just a little in order for me to be able to swallow. I took the pills and tried to relax.

"I'll be back in one hour to check on you, but if you need anything in the meantime, just press the button to the right of you." She signaled for Kyndal to meet her in the hallway.

I overheard her asking Kyndal if she wanted to wait until later to tell me about the miscarriage, or if she wanted to tell me alone. Although I couldn't hear Kyndal's response, that exchange confirmed what I'd overheard last night before going into surgery.

When Kyndal entered the room, she looked a little sad. She walked over to my bed and began rubbing my hair. "Gabby, I have something to tell you," she said. "Last night, when the doctors brought you in, they found out that you were pregnant." She paused and I could tell that she was trying to stop herself from crying, but I couldn't move my jaw to speak. "But you miscarried after all the bleeding. I'm sorry Gabby." I tried to mumble that it was okay but my words were muffled. She continued to cry and say how sorry she was. Strangely, I managed to remain calm.

Kyndal said that she had to leave for a little while after my aunt arrived. I was hoping that she wouldn't call anyone in my family because I didn't want them to see me like this. Furthermore, I didn't want them to know that Benjamin was the one responsible for all this. I wasn't sure how much Kyndal had told her already, but I was glad that I wasn't able to speak clearly, as my aunt would have definitely wanted an explanation.

"Gabrielle," she said when she walked into the room. "Oh my God, look at your face baby!" She gently touched my face. "How could he do this to you?"

I was shocked. I couldn't believe that Kyndal would tell her what happened. She didn't even say anything to me about what had happened.

"The people at the front desk of your apartment called me this morning because they found your keys and purse outside your car. They told me that one of the tenants heard you screaming in the parking lot and called the police. The woman who called said that she wished there was more that she could have done, but she couldn't help you. She said that the way that he was beating you was monstrous. She said that no woman deserved to be treated that way and that she was sad that he got away but that she would be looking out for him."

It was only then that I realized that other people would know what really happened to me. I couldn't lie about it because someone would know the truth. I hadn't even thought about Benjamin, and I really didn't care what happened to him. If the police caught him, I probably wouldn't press charges because he still needed to be there to take care of his kids.

"I hope that you're going to do something about this, Gabrielle. He needs to get whatever punishment is coming to him because this probably isn't the first time he's done this. Why would he do this to you?" she asked. I shrugged my shoulders thinking about the events that took place last night. He couldn't have known that I had been sleeping with Jeff and

Mike for the past two months. *Oh my God, Jeff, he's going to be so mad at me for not showing up last night*, I thought. I'll give him a call later and tell him I was in an accident. I hadn't told him or Mike that I was in a relationship, hell it shouldn't matter since both of them are married anyway.

"Gabrielle, I hope that you will learn a lot from what has happened to you. These crazy men are definitely not worth your life, honey. It could have been a whole lot worse if that lady hadn't seen what was going on and had called the police," she continued. "Your mother and father would surely be rolling over in their graves if they knew the type of life you've been living. You think nobody knows, but people talk about you messing around with all those married men. I really hope that you change your ways before it's too late, Gabby. I really hope so."

She leaned over the bed and kissed my forehead. How could she kiss me after saying those things to me? Sure, I wasn't the good girl, but I definitely didn't deserve this. Hell, I was the one lying here in pain after the man I loved beat me and made me lose my baby.

I couldn't believe that I'd been pregnant. I'd been trying to get pregnant for the last two years, albeit without Benjamin's knowledge or consent, but nothing worked. It was probably for the best because I wouldn't even begin to guess who the father was after all the going back in forth between Jeff and Mike. They surely weren't going to leave their wives for me.

Damn, I would never be a wife now that I couldn't have any kids. Moreover, my good girl reputation within my community would cease to exist. I'd be known as the girl that was beaten in the parking lot by her boyfriend. I pinched myself just to see if I was really living this. The pain was there so this was definitely real.

I looked over at my aunt who was now sitting in the chair across from me, looking through her Good Living Magazine and I started to cry. I held back the muffled sounds only to allow the tears to run down the side of my face. For some reason, I wanted to feel the pain that I was in, but the painkillers wouldn't allow that to happen.

When the nurse came in later that day and asked if I needed more painkillers, I declined. I wanted to remember the pain that I was in so that I wouldn't forget that this happened to me in the future.

Kent

The following Tuesday came sooner than I expected. Sasha started an argument with me this morning about going to church with my mother and not inviting her. I asked her if she wanted to go and she bluntly refused, adding that I might want to rethink turning my keys in to my place the next day and went to work.

I'd tried calling her all day to apologize, but she never answered my calls. After picking the girls up from school and dropping them off, I made one last attempt to make things better with Sasha.

"Baby, come here!" I yelled up the stairs.

"What do you want Kent? I'm doing something," she yelled through the closed bedroom door.

"I want you to come and talk to me," I replied.

"We have nothing to talk about, Kent. As a matter of fact, why don't you just stay at your place tonight after you leave church with your mom, if that's who you're really going with," she said.

"What?" I asked, walking up the stairs. I opened the bedroom door and sat down on the bed next to her. "Baby, there's no need for you to be this mad at me. I love you and I asked if you wanted to come with me, so I don't understand what the problem is."

"The problem is that I don't love you, Kent. I am tired of you. I'm miserable every day that I have to look at you. I just hate you and I want you out of my life for good," she said before storming off into the bathroom.

I didn't understand where any of this was coming from, so I asked her, "Is it your time of the month baby? We were fine yesterday."

She hit the door and screamed, "Oh, you think this a joke, huh? I'm dead serious Kent. I don't love you and I want you gone. Get your things and leave my place and don't ever come back."

"Baby, just come out of there so we can talk about this," I pleaded. "You don't mean that. I can stay home if you want me to."

"No, get the fuck out of my house Kent! I'm serious. Get out!"

I looked down at my phone to see that my mom was calling. I didn't want her to hear us arguing so I didn't answer. I knew that I couldn't break my promise to my mom, so I walked downstairs, grabbed my keys and left.

I felt a little relieved when I walked outside and got in my car. I would just call Sasha later to see if she really meant what she had just said to me because this was starting to become too much for me to deal with.

There were hundreds of cars in the church parking lot when I pulled in. "Damn, this many people go to church on Tuesday!" I said aloud. It wouldn't be hard for me to find my mom because, this morning when we spoke, she told me that she would be in the second row to the left, wearing pink. I felt kind of nervous seeing that everyone was bowed in front of their chairs praying. I couldn't remember the last time that I had been to church, let alone prayed. I didn't know how. When I found my mom, she instructed me to be seated two chairs down from her and to get right down on my knees to start praying before the pastor started to speak. I got down on my knees and started looking around at the other people that were praying. I tried not to laugh, but I never would have thought that I would be amongst hundreds of people praying. My mother waved her hand at me with her eyes still closed and signaled for me to start praying. I closed my eyes and spoke these words:

"Hey man, I mean God. Or Heavenly father whatever they call you. As you know, I don't do this often. I'm here today because my mother won her bet for me to come to church with her. I said that I would come on Tuesday, not thinking that there was actually going to be a prayer service on a Tuesday. Go figure! Well, she got me and she's kneeling right here next to me, watching me pray. I know this may be funny, right, because I'm supposed to be praying, but I don't even know where to start. There's a lot going on in my life right now and I just wanna ask you—why me? I did everything right. I graduated from high school and college and I even got a good job right afterwards. So, why me? Why did everything have to come crashing down for no reason. First, I lost my job and then my house and I have five kids to take care of. I've never admitted this to anyone, but I'm struggling. Struggling to make it, struggling to provide, and struggling to hold on to all the things that make me a man.

I really don't know what to do about Sasha because I love her, but for some reason, things aren't going right between us. My mom keeps saying that things will get better and that I just need to pray about it. I have kids to take care of and this isn't helping. Man, you know what, I'm just ready to give up. But I can't! So, Lord if you can hear me, please help me. Yeah, that's right, I am asking you to help me."

Before I could say 'Amen', the pastor's voice came blasting through the mic. "Rise to your feet and say 'Thank you Lord'. Thank you. How many of you thanked God for your life today? Lord, I tell you. How many of you are thankful for your breath, for your home, for the food that you received this morning, and will eat this afternoon and tonight. Just say 'thank you Lord' where you stand. If you believe that He is the almighty God. That He is the creator of all things that give breath, say 'thank ya Lord'. 'Thank you Lord'!" As he continued, my mind drifted back to the encounter I had just had with Sasha. I wanted to be thankful that I had her in my life, but at this moment, I couldn't help but feel a little sad.

As the pastor continued with the service, I continued to think about all the things that I would be facing in the upcoming months, if I didn't find a job. It wasn't until I heard him say,

"The work of the devil is among us today and I want to call him out. He is attacking your mind, your body and your spirit and I want you to break free from his hold. Tell him, 'Devil you are a liar and my life belongs to the Lord.' I repeated the phrase along with the rest of the congregation. 'The devil still has his reigns on you, my brother and my sister, but I want you tell him that no weapon formed against me shall prosper and it is he that strengthens me that allows me to release you right now today, in the name of the father, the son and the Holy Ghost. Say it now!" he yelled at the congregation. We repeated every word of the phrase.

"Now, a few of you may need some help shaking the devil off, so I want you to grab the hand of your neighbors on both sides and yank them as you call out all the things that you feel are attacking you."

That's when I felt my mother step in between the lady sitting next to me and grab both my hands. She started speaking in tongues, which I couldn't understand, but I began to yell out the names of the things that I felt were attacking me the most, "the world, the economy, my family, my friends, my finances, my addiction, women, Sasha," I yelled. "Sasha" I yelled again.

The pastor said "Keep it going, keep it going, keep it going, release those demons from the flesh. I can feel them rising in the church today. I can feel the miracles that are on the way." I closed my eyes and remained silent for the rest of service.

"Son, I'm so proud of you," my mother said after pastor ended the service. "I know that God is working on you because I could feel his presence in this house today. Please know that you were here for a reason." She kissed my cheek and turned to talk with her friends. I headed to the aisle to leave, but right before I made it to the end of the aisle, I bumped into a woman wearing a blue dress. "Excuse me," I said to her and smiled. She smiled back and said "No worries, praise God."

I decided that it was best that I go to my own place to sleep that night. When I sat down on my bed, I felt more relieved than I had in the past two months. I took off my suit and got into bed without showering.

I closed my eyes and couldn't help but reflect on the message from the service. "Thank you Lord," I said aloud and went to sleep.

Kyndal

"Thank you Lord," I repeated over and over again as Pastor Graves ended prayer service. Today's service was most definitely needed. I needed to pray for myself and especially for Gabrielle. I was thankful that God didn't allow her to be taken from me because I don't know what I would've done if I lost her. I prayed that God would release the evil spirits that were surrounding the people I love. "Thank you Lord," I repeated.

As everyone cleared the church, I saw Gerald in the front row. I wanted to speak to him, since we hadn't spoken to one another since the day he announced that he was getting married. The church was crowded. I tried my best to wait for a chance to head down the main aisle.

"Excuse me," I said in unison with the man that bumped into me. He smiled at me and I couldn't help but smile back. "No worries, praise God." I said as I hurried to the front of the church.

"Hey Kyndal," Marcus greeted me before I could reach the front row.

"Hey Marcus," I replied, trying to move past him.

"It's good to see you," he said catching up to me. "How's everything been?"

"Good," I said trying not to sound irritated.

"Maybe, one day, you'll bring Gabrielle," he said, sounding hopeful.

I stopped at the mention of her name. I turned to him and said, "Marcus, please pray for Gabrielle. She's in the hospital."

"Why? What happened?" he questioned.

"I'm sorry, I can't say. But just pray for her," I said, as we reached the front aisle.

"Kyndal," called Marcus as I walked in front of him. Gerald turned around as he heard my name.

"Hi Gerald," I said smiling and waving.

"Hi sister," he replied. Although he was smiling, he did not approach me. I noticed his reservation, so I looked around him to see Melissa, who was just ending a conversation with another woman. She smiled and ran towards me when she saw me. "Ms. Kyndal, it's good to see you!" she exclaimed sincerely.

"It's good to see you too, Melissa," I responded.

"What are you doing here?" she asked.

"I've been attending services here for a few months now. We just haven't crossed each other's paths."

"Oh it looks like you two already know each other," said Gerald.

"Oh sure we do," said Melissa playfully hitting him. "Kyndal is an old friend that helped me through some trying times. Praise God."

I smiled at the thought of trying times. I would have never thought Melissa to be the person standing in front of me today. "That's right," I smiled.

"Well that's good to hear. Kyndal is an old friend of mine from college," he said.

"Old friend," I thought. Who was he calling old friend, when not too long ago, he was sitting on my couch, enjoying dinner with me. I tried not to look as uncomfortable as I felt. "Well, it's definitely great to see both of you," I said trying to exit the conversation.

"We just got engaged," said Melissa showing me her ring.

I stared at the ¾ carat diamond on her ring finger and smiled. "That's great," I replied nervously. I felt a little awkward looking up at Gerald. "Congratulations," I managed to say.

"I'm honored that God blessed me with such a perfect, awesome woman of God," he said as he turned and smiled at Melissa. She blushed and leaned into him.

"He's just too much," she said to me.

"Well congratulations again," I said turning away from them.

"Excuse me honey," I heard Melissa say to Gerald.

"Kyndal," she called after me. I turned around to see her coming towards me. "I just wanted to thank you once again for everything. I'm so happy that God is continuing to bless me. Gerald is a great man. He kind of reminds me of my own father in so many ways. I've always loved him, but it wasn't until I returned that I found that he shared the same feelings. He doesn't know about the things I've done while I was 'out, living in the world'. I plan to share those memories with him one day, but I don't feel like talking about my experiences with anyone right now. Can you respect that?"

I shook my head in agreement. It wasn't my responsibility to tell Gerald that the perfect woman that he'd been praying for wasn't so perfect. "Everything that we've ever discussed is completely confidential, Melissa. Your secrets are safe with me, but I hope you won't keep them from Gerald or your family, as that will hinder you from fully moving on."

"I totally understand Ms. Kyndal and I thank you again," she hugged me and went back to the front, where Gerald greeted her with a huge hug.

I watched them laugh together and, regardless of how I felt about either of them, I was happy for them. They probably were the perfect fit.

I headed towards the back of the church, expecting to see Marcus, but he was nowhere to be found. I hoped it was a good idea to tell him to pray for Gabby. He seemed to care for her a lot more than as just a friend, which I didn't understand, but hey, who was I to judge?

I walked out to my car and headed home. I called the nurse at the hospital to see how Gabby was doing because she still couldn't speak, since her jaw was still swollen. The nurse told me that she appeared to be doing fine and that she had a visitor. I figured that it was her aunt or uncle, so I didn't ask for any details.

I walked into the house and headed straight for my bedroom. I showered, sat in the chair next to the window, stared up at the stars and started to pray.

"Dear God, if you are listening, please continue to watch over my family, my friends and the people I have yet to meet. I will continue to worship and praise you daily because you are deserving of all the glory and the praise. Please continue to work on my heart, my mind and my spirit. Continue to allow me to be a blessing unto others. I thank you in advance for your mercy, your favor and loving kindness as I live my life according to your will. Thank you Lord. Thank you."

Gabrielle

"Do you have a patient by the name of Gabrielle Jacobs?" Marcus asked the lady at the front desk.

"Yes, she's in room 316, but visiting hours will be over in 30 minutes, so make it quick," she advised.

He held the balloons and flower arrangement tightly as he ran to the elevator. Once he reached the third floor, he asked the nurse which way room 316 was, and she pointed to the left. He walked into the room, where, it appeared, Gabrielle was sleeping. He put the balloons in the corner and walked over to her bedside.

She jumped at the sight of him and sat up immediately. "Marrs? Wha r ya ha?" is what managed to come out of her mouth.

He laughed. "I think you're trying to ask me what I am doing here. Right?" She nodded 'yes'. "Well, Kyndal told me that you were here, so I wanted to come see you. I'm sorry if I scared you or invaded your privacy, but when she told me to pray for you, I just wanted to make sure that you were okay."

She looked down at the covers. He placed his hand on top of hers. "I just wanted to be here for you," he said as he smiled at her. She thought about moving her hand away, but kept it there instead. "Here, I brought you something pretty to look at," he said, grabbing the flowers from the table.

She smiled and muttered "Thank you."

"I know that I don't have that much time today, so I just wanted to stop by to offer my blessings. I'll stop by tomorrow, after work, if that's okay.

She turned her head and smiled, not wanting to say 'yes'. She looked at him smiling at her, and mumbled 'okay'.

When he left, I felt so relieved. I was going to kill Kyndal for sending him here to see me like this. How could she tell him what happened to me? I picked up the phone to call her and placed it on my ear. The phone rang twice before I remembered that I couldn't speak. I reached over to get my cell phone that my aunt had brought with her when she arrived. The battery was low but I still had enough juice to text her.

"Kyndal how could you send Marcus here? I'm gon' kill you if you told him anything about what happened last night."

It was several minutes before I received a reply: "What are you talking about? I didn't send Marcus anywhere. He must've come on his own after I told him to pray for you. And I still don't know what happened. Please tell me."

I reread her text and couldn't believe that she hadn't told Marcus to come. I felt both uneasy and happy at the same time. I looked over at the flowers and the balloons and smiled again, even though my face was hurting.

I hit the reply button and said: "I'll tell you tomorrow. Hopefully, the swelling will go down tonight."

She replied: "Ok Gabby, I hope so too. I love you."

I replied, "I love you too. Good night."

The next day, when the doctor came in to check my cervix, he said that I was healing fast and that I could possibly go home in a few more days. That's when I realized that I hadn't called my office.

"Hi John," I managed to say, still feeling the pain in my jaw.

"Hi Gabrielle," he replied. "I'm sorry to hear about your accident. Your friend Kyndal called yesterday and told us it would be awhile before you would return."

"Thanks John," I replied. "It will probably be about 2-3 weeks before I'm fully healed from the surgery. I'm sorry I left the team with so much unfinished work. I hadn't planned to be out until next week. However, Cassie knows where all my files and charts are stored and I can send her my password to access anything you need. As a matter of fact, I can do some of the work from here when I get my laptop later."

"Oh, no, Gabrielle. Please get your rest. Bill will be handling all of your duties and I'm sure he'll call if he has any questions."

"Bill?" I asked, irritated by the sound of his name.

"Yes," John replied. "He said that he has been following all of your charts and responsibilities for a while. So he knows how to do your work

185

with no problem. We're trusting that if you allowed him to follow you, he'll be good. So go on now, Gabrielle, and get your rest. Everything will be fine here."

"Okay John," was all I managed to say. After we ended the call, I tried my best not to throw the phone across the room. "That lying snake!" I yelled. "This had been his plan all along."

I placed the phone back down on the receiver and poured a glass of water.

"Pour one for me too," said Kyndal as she cheerfully walked into the room carrying a colorful bouquet of tulips, her favorite flowers.

"Ooh, those are pretty!" I exclaimed as she came over to the bedside to hug me. I was still in so much pain, but I managed to sit up.

"Thank you," she replied. "I couldn't help myself. I saw them downstairs in the shop window and had to buy them. You know I haven't been getting any flowers lately and you've been in need of them, so why not?" She laughed while placing them next to Marcus's arrangement.

"These are cute too," she noted, touching the carnations.

"Marcus brought those yesterday," I said.

"Marcus?" she said. "I can't believe he came here last night."

"Me either," I replied. "I woke up and there he was leaning over my bed, smiling at me. He scared the shit out of me!"

She laughed, "I would have been scared too. That's rather extreme. All I told him to do was pray for you because you were in the hospital."

"Scary, but sweet," I managed to say. "Better than any of those other bastards I've been dealing with. Neither Jeff or Mike has tried to call me once since I've been in here."

"Where's Benjamin?" she asked.

"I don't know," I said flatly. "I've tried not to think about him since I've been in here. I can't believe that he did this to me, Kyndal."

Kyndal got up and walked over to me. "What happened?" she asked.

I told her as much as I could remember from that night. I told her that my aunt said that a neighbor heard me scream and called the police. I told her what my aunt had said about her knowing about my affairs with married men.

It wasn't much longer before I broke down. Eventually, I had to ask her to leave, so that I could get my head together. She left and I fell asleep shortly after.

"Gabby," Marcus whispered as he stood over me.

"Marcus," I said sitting up in the bed.

"I brought you some food from Bean's and Cornbread for lunch. I figured you may be tired eating hospital food."

I just looked at him for a minute before responding. Why was he being so nice to me? "I actually, haven't been eating anything these last few days."

"That's not good," he replied. "I got you some gumbo, bread and some red beans and rice. I figured you couldn't eat much because your jaw was swollen."

I touched my jaw and thought about how bad I must be looking. Instinctively, I rubbed my hair down and straightened my gown. "Excuse my appearance," I said.

"Don't worry about your appearance. You've been through a lot. You still look fine to me though," he said smiling.

I smiled back. I didn't know what I looked like because I hadn't looked at myself in the mirror for the last two days.

He prepared my plate for me and sat down next to me on the small bed. We sat and ate as if we were old friends. He talked about his work place and some event that was happening at the church. However, while he was talking, I couldn't help but wonder why he was here.

He cleaned up and said that he had to go back to work, but would be back tomorrow. I told him that I was fine with that and would look forward to seeing him again. I forced myself out of the bed and walked over to the bathroom. I turned to look at myself in the mirror and was shocked at my reflection.

My jaw was still swollen and my already dark skin was badly bruised. There were black rings around my eyes and my lips were extremely chapped and dry. My hair was flat and looked stringy from not being combed. I almost didn't recognize myself. I touched my face and the tears began to fall.

The message alert sounded on my phone, so I moved as fast as I could to get to my bedside to grab it.

It was a text message from Benjamin, which read: "I apologize, baby. I hope you're okay. I love you."

"Love," I said to myself throwing the phone down. "If only people knew what that word really meant."

Kent

"I know what I said to you the other day was wrong Kent and I'm sorry. I was really mad and I didn't mean it," said Sasha.

"I know you were mad Sasha. But I still can't understand why. I was only going to church with my mother. I have been nothing but nice to you but every time I turn around you're yelling and throwing things at me. I don't know how much more of this I can take."

"I said I was sorry Kent," she said getting up from the couch. "The kids miss you and I love you."

"Do you?" I asked. "Do you really love me Sasha? Because you have an odd way of showing it."

She just stared at me with no response.

"All I've been trying to do is keep you happy. All I get in return is you pushing me away. Do you really want this to work Sasha?"

"I told you that I did, didn't I?" she replied somewhat angrily.

"Yeah, you did. But I'm starting to feel like you really don't. At times, it's hard for me to recognize the loving person you used to be once, because you can get really evil. Have you noticed that you yell and scream at me more than you tell me that you love me?"

"Now, you're just being ridiculous Kent. I tell you that I love you all the time, but if you need to hear it more often, then, I can do that for you, I guess."

"This is still a joke to you, but it certainly isn't for me," I said getting up from the couch. "I didn't turn the keys in at my place because I'm going to be staying there for a while."

"Oh no, you're not!" she yelled coming towards me. "Sit down, Kent."

I stood looking down at her. She wrapped her arms around me and began to hug me tightly.

"I'm sorry, baby. I'm really sorry. Can you please stay here with us? We need you."

"I'll always be here for you, Sasha, but I think that we both know that this is not going to work."

"It will, Kent, I promise," she said sweetly, still hugging me.

"I love you Sasha I just think that we may need some time apart."

"No we don't, Kent," she said sadly. "What about your promise to Layla? What will she think if daddy's not living here anymore? You promised her Kent, and I will not allow you to break a promise to my child."

I sat back down on the couch. I couldn't stand to break my daughter's heart. I thought about how happy she had been since I'd been here. She always made me promise that I was going to stay here with her and mommy every day. I thought about all the broken promises my parents had made during my childhood and how I felt afterwards. I didn't want to break my daughter's heart, so I turned to Sasha and said, "Alright I'll stay, but you have to promise to work on how you treat me because this isn't going to work if you continue on like this."

She agreed. I left the house and went to the store and to my place to pick up a few things. I decided to keep my place for the time being, just in case Sasha changed her mind and kicked me out again.

"Girl I don't think the spell is working anymore," said Sasha to her sister Christina.

"What do you mean? That spell has been around for over 30 years."

"Tell me about it," said Sasha. "Kent has really been acting funny lately. It's like he has fallen out of love with me in three days. Today, he threatened to leave if I didn't start treating him better. I don't know what could've happened to him, but I guess I better start acting right."

"Hmph, you should've been acting right the whole time. Let a man tell me and show me how much he cares about me all day, I'd be all into him. That's the thing that we women want most, and here you are, got the man under a damn love spell and you choose to treat him like trash. The spell probably only works if the love is real. It worked for mommy and daddy because their love was real from the beginning. Kent may love you, but you don't seem to love him. You just want him for your own selfish reasons. That's why the spell isn't working!"

"Whatever Christina! You're just jealous because you don't have anyone."

"Jealous?" she laughed. "I don't think so. To be honest, your life isn't anything to be jealous of. You have a man that you don't love willing to love you, but you can't stop being a bitch to receive it. You think that, just because you got those kids, everything is supposed to be perfect. Have you looked around lately? There are a lot of happy baby mothers in the world living happier lives than yours is. I'm not trying to be mean, sister. I just want you to see that what you have right now is truly not meant to be. But good luck," she said before hanging up the phone.

Sasha held the phone, disgusted by what her sister had just said. She walked upstairs to her bedroom and opened the top drawer to retrieve her photo album. She opened the album and started looking through pictures of her family from her childhood. Every photo showed her mother and father smiling happily, surrounded by the kids. She turned the page to a photo of her, holding her Wedding day Barbie and Ken doll, smiling. She thought about the day she received them as a gift from her father after getting all As on her report card. He told her that, one day, she would marry the man of her dreams and they would have children and live happily ever after.

She closed the album and grabbed a second album from the drawer; it was a recent album, with pictures of her and Layla growing up with her and the family. Kent couldn't be found in one single picture. She threw the book back in the drawer and headed downstairs as Kent and Layla came through the door.

"Hey babe," he said as Layla ran into the kitchen to the refrigerator.

"Hey," Sasha replied. "Kent can I ask you a question?"

He took off his jacket and sat down on the couch. "Sure."

"Are you in love with me?" she asked.

"I, um, I think so," he replied. "Why you ask me that?"

"Because I want to know if you have any plans for us to get married one day."

"Well, I've been thinking about it. But we still have to work on a few things," he said.

"Kent, I don't want to hold you up. I don't want to marry you. I think it's best that you leave because this isn't going to work."

"Sasha what are you talking about?" Kent replied. "What's wrong with you now?"

"There's nothing wrong with me. I just think you should move on," she said.

"Mommy, don't make daddy go please!" cried Layla.

"I'm not going anywhere sweetie," he said. "Go upstairs so mommy and daddy can talk."

"There's nothing else to talk about Kent. Please leave now."

Layla ran to her room crying, as Kent got up from the couch. "Are you sure Sasha?"

"Very much so," she replied. I thought I saw tears forming in her eyes, but she turned to go upstairs before I could say anything else. I put my jacket back on and walked out the door.

Kyndal

"Mom, I'm really thinking about relocating."

"Oh here we go again, Kyndal," said my mom. "Where and why do you wanna move this time?"

"Do you always have to have such a negative reaction when I talk about moving someplace else?" I asked before continuing." I'm thinking of moving to Texas or Florida, somewhere hot with more job opportunities for me."

"I guess that's a good enough reason to move because the economy here is pretty tough right now. But are you sure this doesn't have anything to do with that church guy you were seeing getting married."

"No!" I snapped. "We were just friends and I don't really care if he's getting married. He wasn't my type anyway."

"Uh huh. Sounds like you're mad to me," she laughed. "So how are things going at the church, honey? Have you decided to join yet?"

"I haven't Mom. I mean I really like it there but I'm not sure I'm ready to call it home."

"Maybe your purpose was to go there to receive salvation, if nothing else. I'm really proud of you Kyndal, because it really does take a strong woman to stand up after facing so many troubles in the past."

"Thanks mom," I said. "I'm still a work in progress. You know what's funny, I'm a counselor to young women trying to move on and I'm still facing issues of my own moving on. How does that work?"

"There's nothing funny about that. Life is full of tests and trials and sometimes you have to go through them in order to help others. I don't believe in the blind leading the blind."

We shared a few moments of laughter before my mom said, "Honey, I really think that it's time that you go out like you used to and have some fun. You always enjoyed being the life of the party and I don't want you to become a bump on a log like me over here."

"I hear you mom. But I really don't think that life is for me anymore. I'm a mom and I just don't have time."

"Promise me you'll make some time to at least try it once a month."

"Okay, I guess, I can try it once a month. However, don't get your hopes up of me meeting a man."

"I'll keep my fingers crossed on that one, Kyndal," she teased, before laughing. "Life is so much better when you have someone to share it with, honey."

"Yeah, okay mom," I replied smiling. "I'll call you later."

"Bye sweetie," she replied. "I love you."

I picked up the desk phone to call Karen to confirm our 1 o'clock appointment. She told me that she wasn't going to be able to make it because she had to have a conference with one of the students' parents. She said that everything was going good for her at her new job and that she had decided to move to the suburbs to get away from the drama in the city. When I asked what drama, she told me that she had to let the guy go that she was dating because he had too many problems for her to deal with. She said that she was going to give up dating for a while but asked me to join her for drinks at Floods on Friday. She told me that she enjoyed the live band there and that the food was great as well. I agreed to meet her there at 7 for dinner.

I scanned my calendar for appointments and checked my email for client updates. I received an email from Melissa with an invite for their engagement party. I looked at the picture of them together and smiled, but I couldn't help but think about my engagement photo with Michael. I quickly closed the email and wrote the date down on my desk calendar.

Ring. Ring. I reached over and grabbed my cell phone.

"Hey girl," said Gabby sounding extremely cheerful.

"Hey," I replied. "Don't you sound happy?"

"Girl, I am," she replied. "Marcus just told me that he got us tickets to go to the *How Sweet the Sound Show* in Chicago next week."

"Wow, that's great. Look at you and Marcus!" I teased.

Marcus had visited Gabby every day that she was hospitalized, bringing her gifts and flowers. Sometimes he would even bring in his laptop for the two of them to watch movies together. She said that she didn't really like it at first, but since she had been home, he had been there every day as well. I was glad that he was there to help her because there were still a few things that she couldn't do around the house. When she told me that he'd done grocery shopping for her and prepared dinner, I told her she'd better keep him or I would gladly hook him up with one of my lonely clients. She laughed and told me that she was definitely going to be keeping him around for a while. She said that they hadn't even shared a kiss over the last few weeks, but I could tell that she was really into him.

"I know," she replied. "Who would have thought?"

"I would," I said jokingly. "You claimed what you wanted early on in life, so God saw fit to send that man of God your way. I'm just glad that you accepted him."

"Me too," she said. "Maybe yours is on the way."

"I hope so, but I don't know about that," I said.

"Well you have to let someone in first, Kyndal," she said. "I'm not telling you to go out and fall in love, but you should try to just have some fun."

"Fun?" I said, "I just had this talk with my mom a few minutes ago."

"Great minds think alike," she joked. "But for real, I know you're all into church and stuff right now and I'm probably not the best person to give relationship advice, but just have some fun for a little while, Kyndal. Remember, your old 'no strings attached' days."

I laughed as I thought about the line I used to say to men during my 'having fun' days. "I don't think the world is ready for the 'no string attached' days again," I responded, laughing.

"Maybe you should try it just once," said Gabby.

"I'll pass," I said. "I'm starting to think about my life long term these days. You know 30 is right around the corner and I plan on being married with two kids by then."

I paused at the mention of having kids and wished I hadn't said that last comment. I knew that Gabby was still trying to come to terms with the fact that she couldn't have children and I didn't want to upset her. "I'm sorry," I said.

"Don't worry about it," she replied quickly. "It looks like I'm going to be having more fun this year than I've ever had. I've booked trips all over the world for every 3rd weekend of every month. I'm going to be too busy to think about not having the life I planned before 30. Plus, I have Noah and the other bundle you'll have soon to spoil."

"Nobody said anything about soon," I laughed. "I have to find a man first,"

"No, you just need to get some first," she joked.

"Whatever," I replied. "But you know what, getting some doesn't sound like such a bad idea! Now who can I call?" I joked.

"Umm, nobody from the past," she said. "You know that they'll be all in love again, and you don't want any of them anyway."

We laughed. "Have you ever thought having a one night stand?" said Gabby.

"Girl no!" I said. "That's not my style."

"Mine either, but I wanted to live my fantasy through you," she laughed.

"If God could hear this conversation, what would He say?" I asked.

"He'd probably say 'take the shackles off that thang Kyndal and get some'," Gabby teased.

"Oh sweet Jesus, please don't strike my friend down right now," I joked. "You are definitely crazy. I don't know what Marcus is going to do with you once he realizes how much of a freak you are."

"He's gonna love it, trust me. But I think I'm gonna wait this one out, Kyndal." Gabby said calmly.

"What? Is there a bad connection in the phone," I said joking. "I don't think this is my friend I'm talking to anymore. Especially not the one who wants me to go out and have a one night stand."

"You're silly. But I'm serious about this, Kyndal. Sex with random men hasn't gotten me anywhere in the past but broken, cold hearted and, oh yeah, hospitalized. This time, I want things to be different, if this Marcus thing plays out."

"That sounds good and I'll definitely keep you in my prayers," I laughed. "In the meantime, I'll work on having a little bit of fun myself. I'm going out with one of my past clients on Friday to Flood's for dinner and drinks."

"Drinks?" asked Gabby. "I thought that you weren't drinking anymore."

"I'll just have a glass of wine with dinner."

"Well, it's good to know that you're getting out" she said.

"Yeah, it's been a long time," I agreed.

I could hear Marcus entering the apartment in the background. Gabby told me that she would call me back after dinner. I told her to have fun all night for me.

Kent

"Son, it's good to see that you came back to reality," said Pops. "You really had me thinking that you were losing your damn mind." He laughed and signaled the bartender to give us another round.

"I'm good," I replied. He turned back to talk with one of his other friends.

I can honestly say that it really felt good to be back out on the scene again. Sasha was still going through whatever she was going through and I didn't care. I was happy to be back at my place without all the bickering, but I was really missing my kids. It was hard the first few weeks after I left. Layla would call me, crying, asking me to come back. I couldn't understand why her mother would allow her to do this, being that she was the one responsible for me leaving. I explained to Layla that our life would be no different because I would still see her every day that I picked her up from school and that she would come and stay with me on weekends. It took a while for her to accept this but she was starting to come around.

Angela had stopped by the house and informed me that she had a new man but she was going to be sending in the papers to the child support office because her child was not going to go without or be put in last place. I tried to convince her that I was going to take care of my child regardless of my circumstances, but she, of course, got nasty and started yelling at me for no reason. I told her to do whatever she felt was necessary and escorted her out of my place. When I walked her to the front door, I could see her new man waiting outside, with both kids in the car. She walked over to the car and kissed him, after which she turned around and smiled at me. I guess, she must've wanted a reaction but I could care less, so I closed the door. That was about a week ago and I still haven't heard from her.

"Son, what's new with you?" said Pops.

"Nothing much," I said. "Still job hunting and taking care of the kids in the meantime."

"What? No new women in your life," he joked.

"No! And to be honest, I'm really not trying to find one."

"C'mon now son! You with no women is like a squirrel with no nut," his friends joined him in laughter.

I decided that it was best not to reply, because once Pops got started with his lame jokes, there was no stopping him. I honestly hadn't even thought to call another woman the three weeks I'd been home alone. For some reason, I was still very sexually attracted to Sasha, but I didn't want to be in her presence for long. It was as if, whenever I was around her, I was instantly horny. But she would always reject me and tell me to go and screw someone else.

Today, I attempted to do just that. I called Krystal from my old workplace. I wasn't surprised when I called her and she agreed to let me come over. When I got to her place, she was dressed in an all red lace gown with black stiletto pumps. She didn't waste any time guiding me to her room where the candles were lit and slow music was playing in the background. She told me to sit down in the chair next to her bed so that she could take care of me. I was enjoying every moment of her seductive lap dance so when she slid down to the floor to unzip my pants I was completely embarrassed by the fact that ol' boy wasn't as ready as I should've been. She looked up at me and smiled and continued to remove my manhood from my boxers. She went to work. However ol' boy refused to stand up. Now I was pissed. This had never happened to me before. I had just left Sasha's one hour ago, where he was at full attention, refusing to go down. Krystal finally stopped and walked away from me. I just sat there dumbfounded for a few minutes until she came back over to the chair and asked me what was wrong. I told her that there was nothing wrong and that I could get him to wake up. After about five minutes of trying, with no success, she handed me my jacket and asked me to leave. She told me never to call her again and, if I did, to take some Viagra before I came over.

I couldn't understand what the hell was going on with me. I figured it must have just been her, but she was looking sexy as hell so that couldn't have been the reason. I needed a drink after that so that's how I ended up with Pops at the bar.

"There are a lot of beautiful women in here tonight," he said.

"I see," I agreed, scanning the room. The band was definitely doing a great job. The dance floor was packed and people were dancing on the other side of the bar as well. I ordered another drink, but this time I decided to get something a little stronger. I ordered a shot of 1800 silver and took it back with no problem, then ordered another one.

"Hey Son, don't hurt yourself," said Pops," I'm not going to be able to drive you home because I'm leaving with one of these young cuties tonight."

I laughed and walked over to the dance floor. I watched the ladies do the ballroom hustle for a few minutes until the band switched it up to a different song. The men grabbed the ladies' hands to dance and, even though I liked to dance, I decided it would be best if I walked around for a bit. I headed to the back of the bar where the men's restrooms were. When I turned to my left, I saw Karen. She must have seen me too because I saw her turn around to go the other way. I figured it was best that I didn't go say anything to her so I went into the bathroom instead.

Kyndal

"Kyndal, I have to go," said Karen.

"Why?" I asked "The party is just getting started." We had just finished dinner and I saw that they were dancing in front of the club where the band was playing, so I wanted to dance a little. I think I had one too many glasses of wine because I was definitely feeling free.

"I know, but I'm just tired and I need to get up to tutor in the morning," she said. "Sorry, I don't want to be the party pooper."

"Oh, go ahead then. I'll be fine. I think I'm going to stay for a little while."

"Are you sure?"

"Yes, I'll be fine. I won't stay long and I'll call you tomorrow to let you know that I made it home safely."

"Okay," she said heading towards the front exit. She seemed to be in a hurry. I hoped everything was okay. I wasn't going to let her spoil my night out. I was use to going to the club alone, so I didn't need a partner to stand and talk with.

I made my way to the front of the club, where several men tried to either grab my hand or hips to get my attention. I refused them all. I just wanted to be free tonight. The dance floor was packed, so I went to the bar to order another drink. This time, I ordered a watermelon tini. I don't know what I was thinking ordering alcohol. Alcohol always made me angry or horny and I didn't need to be either one of those tonight. I sipped the drink slowly, while telling myself that I would not finish it all. Before I knew it, the drink was gone and I was on the dance floor. I liked to dance alone, so I turned down every guy that tried to dance with me. While dancing, I noticed a nice looking gentleman standing directly in front of the floor trying not to be obvious that he was watching me. When he finally turned his gaze to meet mine, I smiled at him. He smiled back and bit his bottom lip. I walked over to him and said, "Don't do that. You don't know how long it's been." He leaned into me almost as if to kiss me and said, "I can take care of that."

I smiled and walked away.

Kent

"Damn, who was that son," said my Pops from behind.

"I honestly don't know," I said still smiling. I turned around and watched as she walked to the back of the bar area. An older guy offered her a seat, which she accepted. He tried speaking with her, but she flagged him away. I could tell that she was one of those women that knew that they were very attractive but wouldn't give most men the time of day. I didn't feel like playing her game, so I stayed in front with Pops and his horny friends.

"You better go find out who she is then, son," Pops suggested. He was wasted and so were his friends. I was feeling really good, but I didn't feel the need to chase her. "I'm good," I said to Pops.

Thirty minutes passed before she made it back to the dance floor. I watched as she danced seductively in front of me, still not allowing any men to dance with her. I got up from where I was sitting and walked over to her and started dancing. She pulled me in close until her butt was rubbing against me. She was obviously buzzing because she couldn't keep her eyes open. I grabbed her waist, but she stopped me.

"I'm sorry but I really don't dance like this," she said trying to pull away. I pulled her back to me so that we were facing each other and said," Do you have some flat shoes in the car?"

"What?" she said quickly disturbed.

"Let's take a walk by the water," I continued, still holding her close to me.

"What?" she laughed. "Oh no. I don't know you."

"I know, but we can get to know each other," I replied.

"I'll pass," she said.

"If not tonight, maybe some other time," I said.

She reached into her purse and handed me a card, saying that I should call her on her cell number listed on the card and walked away. After that, she headed to the front exit and left.

I looked down at the card and stuffed it into my pocket. I wasn't into calling people that gave me their business cards, so I knew that I wouldn't call her.

Kyndal

"Gabby," I almost yelled into the phone.

"What's up Kyndal?" she said still sleeping.

"I was definitely a hot commodity last night girl," I joked.

"Ooh weee," she said getting up from the bed. "Let me go into the other room to hear this."

"Marcus spent the night?" I asked.

"Yes, but nothing happened," she replied. We were watching a movie in my bed and we both fell asleep. He tried to get up to leave at 4 a.m. but I told him to lie back down and promised not to take advantage of him."

"Well, I wanted somebody to take advantage of me last night but I just couldn't do it," I joked.

"What?" she laughed. "What happened girl?"

"I went out with Karen and we had a great dinner A nice tall handsome guy was flirting with me from across the room the entire time, he even paid the bill for us."

"Now that's what I'm talking about. Kyndal back in action." We laughed.

"It actually felt good to be back in action. I will admit that I kind of missed the nightlife a little. But anyway, his name is Jason, we weren't able to talk much because he was with his group of friends. We exchanged numbers and he said that he would call me for lunch."

"What did he look like? Did you smell money girl?"

I laughed at the phrase I used to say in my younger days. "Yes, I smelled money girl. On top of that he was nice and clean, cut just like I like em'."

"Sounds like another winner to me," she said.

"But that's actually not the one that I was excited about meeting," I replied.

"Ooh there's more men," she teased.

"Yes. Girl, you know when I drink liquor, I start dancing really freaky."

"You mean like a stripper," she joked. "But go ahead."

"Anyway, I was on the dance floor, dancing alone, when I noticed this guy staring at me, but trying not to be noticeable. I smiled at him, and he smiled back. Then he bit his bottom lip and I don't know what took over me but I walked over to him...."

"You walked over to a man, I can't believe it."

"Let me finish," I said cutting her off. "So I walk over to him and say, 'you don't know how long it's been and walk away'."

"What did he do?" she asked.

"He didn't do anything. Pissed me right off because I just knew he was going to follow me."

"Wow. What happened next?"

"Almost nothing. After I cooled down for almost an hour, talking to some random old guy, I went back to the dance floor and then he came over to dance with me. I was so horny I wanted to give it to him right there on the dance floor, so I told him that we had to stop. But this fool asked me if I had flat shoes in the car," I laughed.

"For what?" asked Gabby.

"He suggested taking a walk by the water."

"What a perve!"

"Exactly. I was thinking he was either crazy or he must do this all the time. Who asks a stranger to walk with them at 11 o'clock at night?"

"Weirdo," Gabby replied. "You didn't give him your number did you?"

"I did," I replied. "I actually want him to call me because there was something about him that I want to know more about. I dreamed of him last night girl."

"Oh my god, you having wet dreams about him already!"

"If that's what you want to call it," I laughed. "Just kidding."

"Uh huh," snapped Gabby. "Sounds like you wanted to take that walk to me."

"Girl please! I watch too much *Law and Order* to do anything like that. But I wouldn't mind taking a walk with him someday," I said.

"He'll call you tomorrow," said Gabby.

"I want him to, but I don't want him to at the same time," I replied. "I already know what's going to happen, so we'll see."

"I want him to call you, so that you can give some of that booty up," she said. "Please call her Mr. Perve. She needs you."

"Whatever," I replied.

"Mommy, mommy," screamed Noah from downstairs. "I'm hungry. It's time for breakfast," he yelled.

"Kiss my baby for me Kyndal," said Gabby.

"I will. We were going to stop by later, but I'll call first to see if you still have company."

"Okay, just call me," she said before hanging up.

"What do you want for breakfast?" I asked Noah once I got downstairs.

"Dinosaur pancakes," he said. I laughed because he wanted everything dinosaur these days.

"I'll try," I said. I went into the kitchen and prepared breakfast for the two of us.

After we were done with breakfast, I got dressed and walked outside to the mailbox. I was almost down the road when I saw Gerald jogging in my direction. I waved and hoped that he wouldn't come over to talk to me because I didn't feel like talking and I needed to get back to the house with Noah. However, by the time I made it to the mailbox, he was just a few feet away.

"Hey Kyndal," he said sounding out of breath.

"Hey," I replied smiling but trying to make him see that I didn't want to be bothered.

"Is everything okay with you?" he asked.

"Sure I'm fine and you?" I replied.

"Blessed as always," he said. "Are you and Gabrielle coming down to Jubilee this Friday," he asked.

"Umm, I don't think so," I replied, looking down at the mail in my hands.

I started walking back and he followed, "I know things were a little bit awkward at the church that day,"

"Not really," I replied noticing there was a letter from my father inside.

"I didn't know you knew Melissa or I would have told you about her earlier," he said.

I was still focusing on the letter from my father, which showed that he was in Harrison Correctional Facility. "There was no need to," I replied. "We were just friends. "

"Well, tell me how you know Melissa," he said.

I looked up at him, trying to think of a way not to lie to him but not tell him that she was one of my disturbed clients that was trying to get her life back on track. I didn't want to tell him that the woman he held on a pedestal had tried drugs, lived on the streets and had a baby that died during the past year. I looked away from him and back down at the letters. Finally, I said, "She's an old friend. I have to get going."

"Okay," I heard him say as I walked faster to get to my front steps. "I still hope that you can make it out this Friday, It's going to be nice."

"I'll try," I said as I opened the door. I loved the poetry sessions at the Jubilee, but I wasn't going to make any promises to return this Friday. I was hoping to receive a call for a dinner date from one of the two new men I had met yesterday.

I sat down on the couch and opened the letter from my dad, which read:

"Hey Kyndal, I hope everything is okay with you and Noah. I feel bad that I haven't really met or spent time with my grandson in all these years, but I'm going to change all of that once I get out of this place. I'm never coming back here again. I promise. Anyway, I spoke with your mother the other day about all the things you've been going through lately. I'm sorry about what happened to Michael. I was really hoping that he would be a great man for you because you deserve it.

I know I haven't always been here for you when you needed me and I'm sorry for that. I hope that things will change between us once I get out of this place because I'm ready to change my life. I promise. I just wanted to tell you to keep your head up because you've come too far to go down the wrong road, Kyndal. I'm proud of you. I wish that I could take some of the credit for you being the smart young lady that you are, but I know credit is given to those worth giving it to, and I may not be worthy. But I am still your father and that will never change. Kyndal, I love you. Stay strong. Love, your daddy.

I closed the letter and bowed my head. I was having mixed feelings about the letter. I was happy that he had reached out to me and that he seemed apologetic about not being there for me as he should have been. However, I was a little uneasy that he was always saying 'sorry' and 'I promise', but it never seemed as though he really meant it. I know my mom must have told him that Dr. Anderson said that he may have been the root of my mistrust and failed relationships with men. My mother could be very straightforward when she wanted someone to listen to her. This was both a gift and a curse that I too had been blessed with.

In a way, I was happy that my mom had told him because I had never had the guts to tell him exactly how I felt about anything.

I looked over at my phone to see the text message alert going off. It was a message from Jason.

"Hey beautiful, how are you?" he said.

"I'm fine and you?" I replied.

"Just watching a little basketball right now. What are your plans for the evening?" he asked.

"I don't have anything planned," I replied.

"Well maybe we can do dinner later. I'm only in town until tomorrow, so I wanted to see you before I left."

"Ok. I'll see what I can do," I replied not wanting to sound too eager. "Where are you from?" I asked.

"Originally from Michigan, but I live in between Arizona and Georgia throughout the year. I travel a lot."

"I see. What kind of work do you do?" I asked.

"Let's talk about it over dinner. Is 8 o'clock cool?"

"Yes," I replied.

"Meet me down at the Book Cadillac hotel at 8."

I hesitated for a few minutes before sending a reply. Then I figured, what the heck, it's been a while and I want to have some fun! Moreover, he evidently had the kind of taste I liked. "Ok," I finally replied.

"See you later, beautiful," he said.

I decided not to respond because I didn't want him to think that I was too eager about anything. I could tell that he was definitely a man that took control and made decisions for himself. This was something I had always been attracted to in men. However, I was a little on edge about meeting him at a hotel, but that was probably a better place than inviting him to pick me up from my home.

I called my mom and asked her if she would be able to watch Noah later that evening. She agreed and started questioning me about Jason. I told her as little as I could get away with before she finally allowed me to end the call.

I went upstairs to my bedroom closet and searched for something nice to wear. I was used to dating men like Jason, so I figured he would want to see me in something simple, yet sexy, but not too revealing. He seemed like the sexy black dress type, so I went to the back of my closet, which housed all the 'just in case' new dresses and found a perfect black tank, slim fitting one.

I arrived at the Book Cadillac Hotel at exactly 8 o'clock. I hated waiting on people, so I always arrived on time, for the first date, at least.

I walked inside the building, where I was greeted by the coachmen. I walked over to the bar and was happy to see that he was there, waiting for me.

He rose from his seat at the bar and walked over towards me. "Hello, beautiful lady," he greeted me before leaning over and kissing me on the cheek. Jason was 6'4 and well built. He was nicely dressed in a pair of slacks and a button up. I could tell that he had good taste in cologne because he smelled great. It was the kind of scent that made a woman want to stay next to him all night.

He took my hand and led me to the dining area where we were to be seated. The hostess showed us to a dimly lit area towards the back of the restaurant.

"So how was your day today?" he asked.

"It was actually pretty good," I answered. "And yours?"

"Busy, as always. My phone never stops ringing, so please excuse me if I have to answer during dinner. People don't realize that businessmen have lives too," he laughed.

"No problem," I said. "Business may come first, but you must always make time for pleasure, or you'll grow old and lonely before you know it," I joked.

"Well I definitely don't plan on doing that," he said. "That's where meeting beautiful ladies like you comes in."

"It's been with me all my life, so you're going to have to work a little harder Mr." I said.

"Good sense of humor," he said. "I like that. So tell me, why are you single?"

"Long story short, I'm still waiting."

"Nothing wrong with waiting, but hopefully, I made it just in time," he smiled at me with believable eyes. I could tell that his words were sincere and not just lines. Right before I could ask him anything else, the waiter appeared.

"Could we start with a nice bottle of wine?" he asked.

Jason looked over at me and told the waiter to bring a bottle of Brunello di Montalcino 1979-'89. The waiter smiled and said that he would check to see if they carried those years.

"That's fine wine," he said. "I'm sorry I didn't ask if you preferred white or red wine."

"I see that you're a man that likes to take charge and I'm fine with that. I do prefer white wine because I have yet to find a red that suits my taste. But I'm willing to try anything once."

"Yes, please keep an open mind when you're with me. We'll get along better that way," he joked.

The waiter came back to the table with the wine and poured a glass for the both of us. I actually enjoyed it. "I like it," I said to Jason.

"Of course you do," he said. "I only choose great things. That's why I chose you?"

"I see you're quite the charmer," I said.

"I wouldn't call it that but I do have a sense of charm. I believe in, see it, like it, have it, make it mine. Life is so much easier that way."

"So, is that your plan for me, or do you tell all the women that?" I joked.

"I've actually chosen a few, but they weren't ready to be chosen, so we didn't make it to the last step. But, this time, I prayed and I just hope it's right."

I was flattered, but still a little on edge. I hadn't even asked him what he did for a living, how many kids or baby mothers he had or where he was born and he was already proposing to me. I figured there must be something wrong with him because he was definitely playing all the right cards tonight.

We enjoyed the rest of our dinner, after which we set drinking wine and talking about our careers. He told me that he was a scouting agent for the NBA, which required a lot of travel. He didn't have any kids and he owned two homes, one in Arizona and one in Georgia. He wasn't married. However, he was ready to settle down.

I thought I saw him frown a little when I told him that I had a son. He said that he had dated women with children, but it never really worked because they couldn't travel as much with him as he would have liked. He said that he didn't want to have any children for this reason. I was a little taken aback at this comment, but I figured, I'd give him the benefit of doubt because, at least, he made it known upfront. Although I didn't have to have any more children, I certainly wanted a man that would accept mine.

After about an hour of talking, he asked if I wanted to go listen to some music at the jazz lounge in Harmony Park. I agreed. He left me seated at the table and walked over to the hotel lobby entrance and asked valet to bring his car around.

When we walked outside, I smiled as I looked over at the silver A8L W12 parked right in front. He walked around and held the door open for me, even though the valet was there as well. "True gentlemen," I said to myself.

Once we arrived at the lounge, I noticed that he was a little more reserved than he had been at the restaurant. We ordered drinks and found a booth open in the back of the club, out of the view of the band that was playing.

"I see you like sitting in the back," I joked.

"I do," he said sternly. "I don't like people gawking all over me. It's what I've become accustomed to."

"Oh so I'm with a very special person, I see," I joked, trying to lighten the mood.

He laughed, so I figured that it worked a little. We stayed in the club for another 45 minutes before he was ready to go. We drove back to the hotel, where he waited for the valet to bring my car around. I was relieved and surprised that he hadn't tried to ask me to come up to his room. He just said that he would call me tomorrow.

On the way home, I tried to call Gabby, but she didn't answer, so I called my mom instead.

"Kyndal," she answered sleepily.

"Yes mom, it's me," I said.

"Don't come get Noah tonight. Let him stay until morning. He's sleep already," she said.

"Okay," I said.

"Was your date good, honey?" she asked.

"Kind of," I replied. "I'll tell you in the morning, after church."

"Okay," she replied. "Good night and be careful."

I hated driving home alone at night when I had things on my mind. I needed to tell someone about my date. Although I wasn't extremely happy about it, I just wanted to tell someone. I tried calling Gabby again, but she didn't answer. The wine was really having an effect on me now. I looked down at my phone as the text message alert went off. It was from Jason. It read: "Hey beautiful, I hope you made it home safely. I really enjoyed your company tonight and I'm looking forward to us really getting to know each other. I'm glad I met you."

I smiled and hit the reply button, "I had a good time with you tonight as well. Good night until next time." He was nice and all, but for some reason, he reminded me of every guy I'd dated in the past. I wasn't sure if I wanted to deal with the men that wanted to control me because they had money. However, I still loved a strong focused man and Jason was definitely that.

Once I got home, I kicked off my pumps, turned the TV to VH1 Classics Body and Soul and poured another glass of wine. I rarely drank at home, but I was really feeling myself tonight. My life was back on track and I was ready for someone to explore my body again.

I sat back on the couch and closed my eyes. I allowed the Eric Benet's words to take over my mind. I instantly recalled the other gentleman that I had met the night before. I could see his smile and his smooth brown skin. I wanted to taste his lips this time when he pulled me in close to him. I could hear him say "Let's take a walk," but this time I agreed.

Ha ha ha. I burst out laughing. I still couldn't believe that he asked me if I had flat shoes in the car. I turned off the television and headed upstairs to my bedroom to shower before going to sleep.

Gabrielle

"Marcus, unlock the door please!" I yelled. I still couldn't understand why he always locked the door whenever he took a shower at my house. I could hear him cutting the water off and grabbing the towel from the towel holder.

"Marcus," I said again. "I only want some tissue."

"Just give me a few more minutes, Gabby," he said laughing. I laughed too.

I really enjoyed spending time with Marcus over the last month. He was very easy going yet fun at the same time. We hadn't attempted to have sex, yet which was fine by me, but I started to wonder why he hadn't tried. We slept in the bed together four days a week now and he hadn't tried to rub or touch this big ass of mine once.

I know that he's a 'church man', but I have yet to know a man that didn't want to at least grab on my ass from time to time. He says that he's really attracted to me, but wants to allow me time to readjust and get to know him. At first, I laughed because that's something that women say, but it kind of made me feel good, knowing that he wanted to get to know me first as well.

I honestly can't remember the last time I waited over one week to have sex with anybody. But what the hell, I really don't have anything to lose by not having sex with him. I'm just reaching the point of being physically attracted to him anyway. Moreover, although he's knows about my surgery and the fact that I can't have kids, he's still around, which I find reassuring. I thought that such news would scare him for sure, but he said that he was fine with adopting kids, if he had to.

"Gabby, why do you always do that when I'm in the shower?" he asked, coming from the bathroom with the towel wrapped tightly around him. I looked at his chest, which housed a few muscles and it looked good with the oil he'd applied to it. He turned to the side and I was able to see that his package wasn't small at all, as I'd imagined. There was a hump there, which meant this skinny little nerdy guy was actually working with something.

"I ummm, ummm," I stuttered. He must've followed my gaze and turned in the opposite direction. "I just like to be able to roam around the house freely with no restrictions," I said.

"Is that right?" he said. "Restrictions are good from time to time. You don't want to unwrap gifts before it's your time. It's like ruining the surprise."

I laughed because he was still corny as hell. "Surprise huh?" I said as I walked into the bathroom to grab the tissue. "I just hope it's a good one."

"Just get ready for the luncheon Ms. No Restrictions. I'm looking forward to introducing you to everyone," he said.

"I wonder if Kyndal's coming," I said aloud.

"I hope so," said Marcus. "I really miss talking to her."

"She said that I stole you from her. Now she doesn't have anybody to talk to," I laughed.

"Why don't you call her and tell her to join us?"

"I can do that once I'm dressed," I said pulling the blouse over my head. I noticed Marcus peeking into the bedroom from the dining room. I wanted him to get a full view of all this body he's been passing up at night.

"I see you looking in here Marcus," I said. "I'm not shy, so you can join me in here if you like."

"I think it's best that I stay away for now," he said. "Wouldn't want to tease myself."

"Why would it be a tease?" I asked.

"Just get dressed we'll talk about that later," he said.

I dressed and applied my make-up as best as I could. I always loved to go to the MAC counter to get it done before going out, but I didn't have time this morning and I didn't want Marcus to think that I was putting on a show for his friends.

When I looked into the living room area to see if he was dressed, I saw that he was in the kitchen, slicing fresh fruit. I smiled. He was such a good man. Any woman would be happy to have him. I just hoped that I could get to that place before I lost out on a good man.

I tried calling Kyndal but she didn't answer.

After service, we headed to the church ballroom for the Leadership Luncheon. Marcus held my hand the entire time as he introduced me to his friends. Once we were seated, I noticed that there were two seats left at the table. When I asked Marcus who they were for he told me that Gerald and Melissa would be joining us. I had yet to meet the fabulous Melissa that Gerald had chosen over Kyndal. Although Kyndal said that she wasn't mad, I could tell she was a tad bit jealous. She never even talked about the girl Melissa outside of saying she was surprised by Gerald's choice.

When they finally arrived at the table, I was kind of disappointed. Here stood the handsome Gerald, dressed very nicely, while his fiancé looked as if she was dressed in her friend's clothing. Her two-piece designer suit was nice, but I could tell that she didn't choose it for herself. I looked down at her shoes and was even more disappointed by the expensive grandma shoes she was wearing. Out of all the years of me attending church, I have never seen a pastor's daughter look like this. They were either all glammed up or homely looking. Melissa was both. I could tell that she wasn't used to wearing make-up because her shadows weren't blended and her lipstick was wrong for her coloring. In my view, only old women wore dry red lipstick. The only thing right about her was her beautiful hair.

"Hello," she said to me. "I'm Melissa."

"I'm Gabrielle," I replied. Marcus told her that I was here with him and that Kyndal was my best friend. She asked where Kyndal was and after I told her that she wasn't attending, she looked a bit relieved. Gerald finally came back to the table and entered into the group's small chat before the speaker walked to the podium.

The topic was about change and how to use those around you for inspiration if needed. I was amazed at how young and successful most of the speakers were. They were all very informative about their career and life choices while giving all the praise to God. I really enjoyed the luncheon more than I had anticipated.

"That was wonderful," Marcus said to me after we said our good-byes to everyone.

"Yes, it was," I agreed sincerely.

"I don't know if I told you already, but you look lovely today," he added.

"Thank you," I replied.

"I'm really happy that we are getting to know each other," he said.

"I am too. I thank you for being here for me, Marcus. It really means a lot to me."

"I plan to be here for a long time if you'll allow that," he said opening the car door.

I smiled because I wasn't sure how to respond just yet. I was really feeling him, but I wasn't sure if I was ready to be more than just friends. I sat silently, thinking about the last two months during which I'd shared most of my days and nights with Marcus. As badly as I wanted someone like him to share my life with, I just couldn't allow myself to let go.

At times, it felt like I was still holding on to Benjamin, for whatever reason. I couldn't believe that he hadn't attempted to call or text me since the last time. I felt sorry for him, as I thought about how he must have been struggling to take care of those kids and get around without me. I think I just needed closure from him in order to move forward with Marcus.

"Do you want to go down to the river walk for a little while?" asked Marcus.

"No, I think I'll just go home and lie down for a while," I replied softly.

"I'm kind of tired too," he said. "Do you mind if I stay over for a little while?"

"I kind of just want to relax alone," I said, regretting saying it as soon as the words left my mouth.

"Okay," he replied. "I hope I didn't say anything wrong."

"No, you're good. I just need to sort through a few things, but I'll call you later."

"Okay. Have a good nap," he replied.

I undressed as soon as I got into my bedroom. I slipped on a pink chemise and pulled my hair back into a ponytail. I took my cell phone out of my purse and sat down on the bed. When I reached Benjamin's number, I felt a slight chill—mixed with a little excitement—run through my body. I hesitated before pressing 'Send'. After the phone rang, I didn't know what I was going to say to him so when he answered, I just held the phone for a few moments.

"Gabby," he yelled into the phone. "I know you're there."

"Yes, I mean, hi Benjamin," I finally uttered.

"Hey," he said. "What's up?"

"Nothing much," I replied.

"Why didn't you respond to the last text message I sent to you over a month ago?" he asked.

"I don't know," I replied.

"Hmph," he said. "Well is everything good with you?"

I couldn't believe that he just breezed over the fact that he almost killed me and still couldn't say 'I'm sorry'.

"I'm doing better," I responded.

"I wanted to come see you. But I figured you didn't want to see me just yet."

"You never tried," I responded. I was starting to feel a little rumbling in my stomach. "I do need to see you Benjamin."

"Oh really," he said. "Why is that?"

"I just need to talk to you face to face," I said.

"I can come now if you want me too," he replied quickly.

"Okay that's fine," he said. "I'll be there in fifteen minutes."

Right after I hung up the phone, the phone started ringing again. It was Marcus. I decided not to answer it. I tidied up the kitchen area and cleared my bedroom of all evidence that another man had been here. Exactly fifteen minutes later, Benjamin was ringing the bell. I buzzed him up, sprayed the last bit of air freshener around the living room area and opened the balcony window.

When I opened the door, he greeted me with a great big hug and kiss, which took me by surprise.

"You look nice," he said while touching my face and rubbing my hair. He grabbed my hand and led me to the couch.

"Thank you," I nervously replied. I hadn't witnessed this side of him since we'd first started dating.

"I've missed you so much, Gabby," he said, grabbing my face again. "I love you," he said before kissing me.

He continued to kiss me passionately. I kissed him back out of comfort. I heard the door open and Marcus walked inside. Before I could push Benjamin away, Marcus said, "I'm sorry to interrupt you, but I left my keys in your nightstand."

Shocked, I quickly stood to my feet, "Marcus," was all I managed to say. He walked right past me and went to my bedroom to obtain his keys.

Benjamin got up from the couch and glared at me. Once Marcus came out of the room, he walked to the front door. "It's good to see that you're happy again, Gabby." With that, he closed the door and left.

I wanted to go after him, but my feet didn't manage to connect with my mind.

"You fucking whore!" yelled Benjamin, breaking me from my thoughts. I moved quickly to the other side of the couch. "You're still sleeping with other men and have the nerve to call me over here right after one leaves! Didn't you learn your fucking lesson?"

"Get out of my house Benjamin!" I yelled. He came towards me instead, with his fist raised.

I grabbed the lamp that was closest to me and started swinging it at him. "You dirty little bitch!" he yelled.

Marcus came running back into the apartment. He grabbed Benjamin from behind and pushed him over the table. He turned him over and started punching him in the face. I dropped the lamp and ran to the other side of the room. "Stop, please stop!" I screamed.

I watched as Marcus pounded Benjamin's face in. Benjamin had balled himself up into the fetal position and wasn't fighting back. Finally, Marcus got up from on top of Benjamin after kicking him one last time. "That's what you get for beating up on women. Now get the hell out of here before I call the police!"

Benjamin staggered to his feet at the mention of the police. He looked over at me but then walked slowly over to the door. "Don't ever think about coming back over here again," said Marcus following behind him. He closed and locked the door after Benjamin left.

"Marcus," I said moving towards him.

"Don't say anything to me, Gabrielle. I see you like abuse, so you can continue to chase after dirt if you want to. But remember that, next time, I won't be around to pick up the pieces."

"Marcus, it wasn't what you think," I said before he cut me off again.

"It's never what anyone thinks. However, I have two eyes and I know what I saw. I cared for you Gabrielle, but I guess, you didn't feel the same way. Thanks for showing me," he said before opening the door to leave.

"Marcus, it wasn't what you think. I just needed closure."

"Closure?" he repeated, handing me his set of my keys, "Well I guess we both got closure today. Goodbye," he said before walking down the hall to the elevator.

I stood with the door open crying, hoping that he would come back, but he didn't. I closed the door and picked up the phone to call him, but he didn't answer.

After three attempts, with no success, I called Kyndal.

"Hello Gabby," she answered the phone cheerfully. "I've been waiting all day for you to call."

"I messed up," I cried. "I messed up bad."

Kent

"Sasha do you feel bad about what you did to Kent now?" asked Christina.

"No," Sasha replied. "I felt that it was necessary at the time and sometimes I feel that it can still work out between us but I want him to want it."

"I honestly think that he was trying. You just didn't hold up your side of the deal."

"Whatever Christina. You'll never understand. I do love him, but there's just something stopping me from being completely in love with him."

"I can name a few reasons for you. He's lied, cheated and had several kids with other women since you've been together. He's still living life as if he's a single man with no obligations. Those are all the things that I would be mad about if I were you. I really like Kent, but you don't have to accept or deal with all that to be in a relationship with someone. Sasha, I love you and I feel that you deserve better."

"I do sister, I do. It's just hard to let go for some reason. I mean, he hasn't been here for a few weeks and I miss him. I know that the kids do too. I don't want to be alone."

"Sometimes it better to be alone than to be miserable and unhappy. I'm not saying you're miserable, but you can't honestly say you're happy either. Sasha, just be glad that the spell is wearing off and let it go."

The doorbell rang. "Christina, Kent is here. I have to go," said Sasha hanging up the phone.

"Hey Sash," I said when she opened the door.

"Hey," Sasha replied dryly. "Thanks for coming over. I need you to watch the kids while I run a few errands. I'll be back in an hour or so."

"Sasha, are you okay?" I asked.

"Yeah, I'm good. Why you ask that?" she replied.

"You just seemed a little down these last few times I've come over."

"No, I'm good. Maybe just a little tired, that's all."

"Okay, well I'm here if you need to talk about anything. We are still friends."

She smiled and grabbed her keys. She leaned over to kiss the kids and gave me a kiss on the cheek as well. I instantly became aroused. I couldn't understand how this was happening because I'd tried to get down with a couple of women over the last three weeks but I still couldn't get it to work. I was becoming really frustrated with this because I know that there's nothing wrong me. Hell, I even tried taking one of those Viagra pills before going to Ashley's house, but that shit still didn't work.

I looked down at him standing so tall and erect in my pants now, all because of a kiss from Sasha. This was about the fourth time this had happened to me. Every time she hugged me or gave me a kiss, he would stand up, but not when it was time to get down with other women. What the hell had she done to me? I wasn't really attracted to her anymore, but he seemed to get happy whenever she was around. I walked into the bathroom and pulled my pants down to stare at him in the mirror. "What the hell is going on?" I said to myself. I stood there for about five minutes staring at it until it finally went back down. I wasn't going to say anything to her or anyone else because they would surely think I was crazy or something.

I pulled my pants up and washed my hands before going back downstairs to play with the kids.

"Daddy, can we play dress up?" asked Layla.

"Daddy's too big for dress up honey," I said while tickling her.

"No you're not," she said laughing. "Okay let's play Mr. Wizard the magician."

"Ok, how do we play that?" I asked.

"I'll be the magician and I'll make you disappear."

"But I don't want to disappear. Do you have any other type of magic tricks?" I asked.

"Hmm, let me see. Oh I know. I can get the magic potion that mommy uses sometime," she said getting ready up to run upstairs. I stopped her before she made it half way. "Come here Layla, how about you make me disappear instead."

"Okay," she said happily. "I can use the potion next time."

We played different games for over an hour before she got tired. She finally laid down on the couch while I rocked the baby to sleep. An hour later, Sasha arrived and woke all three of us up.

"Thanks Kent, you can go home now," she said softly.

"What if I wanted to stay?"

"No, I think its best that you go."

I moved Layla off my chest and rose from the couch. I grabbed my keys and left.

After I got home, I showered and ate the leftovers from the night before. I grabbed my wallet from the table. While looking for my old college buddy's business card, I pulled out the card of the young lady that I had met a couple weeks back. "Kyndal" I said to myself. I placed the card on the table and pulled out my cell phone to call my buddy. He didn't answer, so I left a voicemail. I lay back down on the couch and flicked through the channels. Nothing was on and the sports updates were all reruns. I placed the remote back on the table and picked the card up again.

She had an inviting smile. I laughed at the fact that she was a counselor but, that night at the club, she was dancing and drinking like she didn't have a care in the world. I picked up my phone again and started to dial her cell number. I figured it was best to send a text instead.

"Hello Ms. Kyndal. Are you ready for our walk?" I didn't expect her to reply because she seemed like the snotty type, but she was very attractive and she seemed to be interested in me that night.

A few minutes passed before she replied: "Sure, Is Friday Good?"

Damn, I guess I may have been wrong about her. She was definitely ready and I liked the fact that she didn't hesitate to tell me when she would be ready.

"Friday's great!" I replied. "How about 9 o'clock?"

"No, 7:30 or 8 is better. I need to have some daylight left when I meet you there. Lol. I already think you're crazy."

I laughed before responding, "8 is cool. And I'm not crazy at all. See you tomorrow."

She didn't reply. At least she had a sense of humor.

The phone rang as soon as I placed it on the table. I looked down at the caller ID and saw that it was Angela.

"Hello Angela," I said.

"Hi Kent," she said sarcastically. "I need you to keep Noelle for me Friday night."

"I'm sorry Angela, but I already have plans," I said.

"Well, you better break those plans because you don't have a choice. I'll drop her off around 7."

"No you won't," I said, getting angry.

"Yes, I will and you better open the door if you know what's good for you."

"Angela I," was all I could say before she hung up the phone. I didn't feel like arguing with her so I didn't call her back. I just had to find someone to keep Noelle while I went out for a little while.

I grabbed a pair of slacks out of the closet and put on a T-shirt. I grabbed my keys and headed down to the sports bar inside Greektown Casino. The bar wasn't crowded at all, so I grabbed a stool next to the lottery machine. I told the bartender to send over a shot of Remy and a Heineken. I looked over at the machine and couldn't help but think of taking a chance with picking a few numbers. I didn't have anything to lose. My luck hadn't been all that great lately. I chose the numbers 5,8,31,45,19,32 and 69. I watched as the numbers displayed on the screens around the bar. When I saw the number 5, then 31 and 19, my heart started to beat a little faster. Maybe my luck was changing after all! Finally the number 69 was displayed. I jumped up from my seat and yelled, "There we go." I gave my ticket to the bartender, who gave me $60. I was in a good mood now, so I decided to stay to watch the replays of the baseball highlights.

Tonight was one of those nights where I would easily pull out my phone and call one of my lady friends to arrange for some fun after drinking. Thus, out of habit, I pulled out my cell phone, but finally decided it was best not to call anyone with the problems I had been having lately. Just the thought of me not being able to perform was driving me crazy. I needed to call a doctor first thing tomorrow.

"Damn," I said to myself as I thought about my date with this new girl Kyndal. She was sexy as hell from what I could remember. I would probably just have to refrain from making this one of those 'getting down on the first night dates'.

Kyndal

"Girl guess who finally called," I said to Gabrielle as I fixed myself a plate of her chicken salad.

"Who?" she said walking into the kitchen.

"That 'let's take a walk' guy from Floods."

She laughed, "Oh yeah Mr. Pervert himself."

"You silly! Well he didn't actually call; he sent a text message," I said, walking to the table to sit down.

Gabrielle grabbed her salad and sat directly across from me. "Okay, so tell me what happened."

"Well you know I'm starting to get irritated with this whole 'let's date via text message' thing that I've been running into lately with the few guys I've met over the last three weeks."

"This is the new millennium form of dating, girl, so you better get used to it!" she teased, laughing.

"I guess, while trying something new, I'm really going to have to learn new things. However, I still love to hear a man's voice upon first contact."

"Why so you can tell if he's intelligent or not? What difference does it make?"

"It makes a helluva difference to me. I need to be able to communicate with you and you can only say so much via text message. My phone only allows 120 characters. But anyway, he texted me and asked me if I was ready for our walk yet."

"Perve," she said. "Damn he can't even ask you out on a real date."

"I thought it was kind of cute, seeing that that would be the only way I would remember him since we didn't exchange numbers and I don't even remember his name."

"So let me get this right, my sophisticated friend Kyndal is going out with a stranger she met three weeks ago to walk by the river, a body of water, with a pervert and she doesn't even know his name. Sounds like a Law and Order: SVU case waiting to happen."

"I know right," I said before laughing. "You make it sound so bad."

"It is bad, Kyndal. I want you to have fun, but not risk your damn life doing so."

"I know. I don't think he's crazy, Gabby, or I wouldn't be going out with him. There was just something about him that night."

"Did you forget that you were drunk and horny that night? That's all it was, because he obviously isn't your type. Did he even offer to buy you a drink that night?"

"No he didn't," I agreed, recalling the events from that night. "But I was already drunk. He didn't say much either, now that I think about it."

"Hmmm," she said, looking at me like I was crazy. "And you're serious about going out with him. What happened to Jason? Now I like him."

"Jason is fine. We talk almost every day. He's in Atlanta now and he said he'll be back to Michigan in two weeks. He's been sending me flowers and emails every week since he left," I said, smiling, just thinking about him.

"Now, see, that's the type of man I need for you to continue to date. I like him."

"I do too, but he's not tangible enough for me. I want him here and I still feel there's something he's not telling me."

"Like what?" she questioned, pouring us both a glass of the Sangria she made.

"He says that he's not married and has no children, which is fine. However, he seems to be unavailable in the late night hours when I call sometime."

"He is a working man. Maybe he's sleeping."

"Maybe, but something in my gut is telling me that he has some other things going on in his life."

"Just try asking him before you start assuming things, Kyndal. I think that he's a good guy and you really don't need someone all up in your space right now anyway, so the long distance thing may be just what you need to get over everything else. Who knows, he may turn out to be the one for you?"

"Who knows? But tonight, I'm looking forward to getting to know Mr. 'let's take a walk'."

"Uh huh? Just take a walk Kyndal."

"You should already know I'm not one to give anything up on a first date. Not a kiss on these lips or the ones below."

"Okay," she said before getting up. "There's a first time for everything."

After my lunch with Gabrielle, I headed back to the office to meet a new client. Her name was Passion. It seems as though her mother named her correctly because she was a recovering sex addict. She told me point blank that she was addicted to sex and that she had to have it with whomever, whenever. She told me a few stories about her past, but what caught my attention was the number of men that she had slept with within the last year. She said she had slept with over 500 men, both protected and unprotected. She said the reason for her wanting to get some help was that one of the men she had unprotected sex with in the past was HIV positive and had syphilis. Apparently, he had provided her name to the department of health, where they sent someone out to pick her up for testing. The tests confirmed that she had contracted syphilis, however, the HIV test came back non-reactive. The doctor told her that she needed to come back for testing in three months, just to be on the safe side. She said the last two months of living knowing that she could possibly have the virus was driving her crazy. She wanted to live a better life for her and her three children, but she needed help in order to do so.

When I asked her if she was having sex with anyone presently, her answer was yes. I couldn't believe that she would be willing to put someone else's life at risk. When I asked her why she would continue to do this, her response was, 'he's going to have whatever I have anyway. We've been having unprotected sex for over three years and he's the father of two of my kids.' I almost wanted to yell at her for not thinking of how selfish she was being, not thinking about her children's lives if, in fact, the test came back positive for HIV later. I told her exactly how I felt about her choices and advised her to speak with her partner about getting tested before coming back to the next session. She said she would try and left before our time was up.

I hoped that she would return to get the help she was going to need to move forward with or without the next test results. However, I wasn't really convinced that she would return.

When I arrived home later that evening, I ran straight to the closet to find something to wear. I didn't want to look too sexy or made up, so I decided it would be best to wear something simple. I pulled out a pair of jeans that I knew fit my shape perfectly. I prepared a hot bubble bath and poured the last of the Moscato that was left in the refrigerator.

After I bathed and dressed, I looked at myself in the mirror. I'd lost a few pounds, but I was still in great shape in all the places that mattered. I checked the time, noticing that it was already 7 o'clock. I went downstairs and turned on the news. After watching the depressing stories for five minutes, I turned the television off and went into the kitchen to grab a snack. I chose the fruit salad and grabbed some crackers from the cabinet. I was feeling really nervous but I didn't know why. Before I could get back to the couch, I dropped the fruit salad, which splattered all over my jeans and T-shirt.

"Damn," I yelled at myself, running back upstairs to my closet. It was now 7:20 and I didn't like to be late on first dates. I scanned the closet but everything seemed too dressy. As I reminded myself to purchase more casual clothes at a later date, I grabbed a purple pair of leggings and a long bohemian styled top. I didn't like what I saw at first when I looked in the mirror. All my curves were hidden and now I just felt regular. The clock read 7:37. I grabbed a pair of flat gold sandals and made a quick dash to the bathroom mirror to freshen up my make-up.

"Lovely," I said to myself in the mirror. I grabbed my keys and ran out the door.

"Kyndal, pull it together," I said softly to myself while driving. "He's just some regular guy."

I laughed at how I never really felt this way about anyone before. Maybe I felt this way because he was a total stranger. I was still trying to remember if he told me his name the night we met. I' vowed to find a way to pull it out of him before the night was over.

I drove around for ten minutes before finding a space to park. When I finally found a spot that was close enough to walk, I sent him a text telling him that I was there. He replied that he was walking into the GM building at that moment.

Once I reached the building, he walked out and greeted me with a soft 'hello' and a smile. He had the nicest smile that I had ever seen on a man. We walked inside without saying much to each other while staying close. When we made it to the escalator to go down to the lower level, he reached for my hand. Before I knew it, we were holding hands. It felt awkward because I barely knew this man and it usually took a man a few dates before they were willing to hold your hand.

"You look nice tonight," he said.

"You look nice too," I said easing my hand from inside of his. He was wearing a nice pair of slim fitting jeans and a T-shirt. He actually looked like a model. Once we made it down to the lower level, he turned towards me as if to kiss me, I quickly turned my cheek and said, "I don't kiss strangers."

He smiled again and said," It was only going to be a friendly kiss on the cheek."

"But I don't know you," I replied laughing. "You must do this with all the women."

He laughed and we continued to walk towards the exit to the outside. The sun had gone down and the breeze from the water felt really good. The river walk was a little crowded, but that didn't seem to bother the couples that were out.

The first five minutes were like any other date, filled with the initial 'interview' questions and a few laughs. I was beginning to feel really comfortable with him by the time we reached the middle of the walk. Before I knew it, he turned to me and kissed me. Although that took me by surprise, it didn't stop me from kissing him back. It felt so good. The kiss was soft and so full of passion. I closed my eyes and when I finally opened them, I felt like I wanted him to do it again. It felt magical.

However, instead of following my first instinct to kiss him again, I pushed him away. "Why did you kiss me?" I asked him.

"Why did you kiss me back?" he asked. "You can't be kissing me like that." He said laughing.

"I didn't kiss you," I said, turning away from him, trying to keep a serious expression.

"Well. Let's see if you won't do it again," he teased, pulling me close.

I closed my eyes again and enjoyed the magic that was taking place between us. I never really enjoyed kissing, but for some reason, I didn't want this kiss to end. He must have felt the same way because he didn't stop either. There we were, two strangers, standing in the middle of a public walkway, kissing like we were the only two people there.

I pulled away again. I had to stop myself. I couldn't let him get the best of me, even though I wanted to give him all of me at that moment. I grabbed his hands and we continued to walk and talk. I asked him if he had kids and he said 'yes', but before I could ask how many, he asked me the same question. I told him that I had Noah.

When I asked if he had a boy or girl, he replied, "Both. They're like twins."

"Like twins? " I asked. "What do you mean by that? Are they twins or not."

"No, they're not, but they're the same age."

"How old are they?" I asked.

"Well, they're both six and…" he said before I cut him off.

"What do you mean? Do they have two different moms?"

"Yes," he replied. I immediately started walking away from him. He laughed and pulled me back into him, kissing me on the cheek while saying, "Don't judge me."

Even though I laughed at the comment, I couldn't help but think that he was one of those men that I talked about regularly—the kind that slept around a lot, having no self-control with women and leaving them with the children. He was the kind of man I tried to stay away from. I decided that it was best not to ruin the night by walking away, I was having a little fun laughing with him.

By the time we reached the carousel area, I was holding his hand again, laughing.

"You really shouldn't kiss people like that when you first meet them," he said as we positioned ourselves against the railing looking out towards the water.

"You kissed me," I said.

I stared out into the dark waters for a while as he held me from behind. I couldn't help but think of how good it felt to be this close to a man with so much passion. I hadn't felt this rush in a very long time. He pointed to the half-moon and raised my hand to look up. His touch felt great. I turned around to face him and our eyes met again. We both silently agreed to allow our lips to touch again. This time he ran his fingers through my hair. That was a No, No so I stopped kissing him.

"Please don't do that," I said.

Instead of doing as told, he went for my lips again and pulled my hair back with a little ruggedness. I didn't stop him, even though I'd never allowed anyone to pull my hair in the past. After a minute or so, our lips finally parted. He led me further down the walk to an area that was well lit, yet more private, at the same time.

He turned into me and said," I really can't help myself for some reason."

This time, I grabbed the back of his neck and took advantage of him. After a while, I finally managed to pull myself away and we agreed that we should go back inside to talk a little more.

Once we were inside, I excused myself and went to the ladies room. Once there, I pulled out my cell

phone to call Gabby.

"Girl, can I do it?" I asked as soon as she picked up the phone.

"Do what?" she said sleepily.

"Yes or no?"

"If it's what I think you're asking me, Hell No!"

"I Know. But he just keeps kissing me," I objected, smiling, relaxing my forehead on the mirror.

"You're kissing a fucking stranger Kyndal?" she yelled, finally waking up. I could tell she was getting excited. "Was it good girl?"

"Yes," I answered. "I'm scared I might let myself go all the way."

"You can't be serious, Kyndal. That's something I would do, not you. You better get it together."

"I know. I'm just going to tell him that I'm ready to go home."

"I wouldn't rush to go home, but I wouldn't give him any either."

"I won't. I mean, I'll try not to," I corrected myself, laughing.

"Girl, bye! Well if you gone do it, do it right. Put it on him, so he'll call you again."

"Trust me, they always call. So that won't be a problem."

"But for real, Kyndal, be safe. I'll call you in an hour to check on you."

"Okay. I'm not going to do anything, trust me," I said before hanging up the phone.

I walked back to the area where he was seated.

"I don't want the night to end just yet," he said. "How about we go to another little spot off the water that's a little more private. We can stop by the store and grab some wine."

"Okay," was all I managed to say as I followed his lead to his car.

When we arrived at the store, I decided to stay in the car. I wasn't sure if I was just being stupid or dumb for going along with this stranger's suggestion. But my mind was telling me that I wasn't being either, I was just having a little fun.

When we arrived at the Lighthouse, I opened the bottle of wine and quickly started drinking it.

"Are you okay?" he asked as we walked towards the lit area. I looked around, relieved to see there were two other couples there as well. Once we reached a secluded spot, we began kissing again, but this time his hands started to roam. He lifted my shirt a little to allow his hands to roam freely through my wetness. I could tell that he liked it because, he closed his eyes and continued to kiss me softly. I began moaning softly as he caressed the part of me that had been longing to be touched for almost a year now. His touch was soft and pleasant. He gently pushed me into the railing as he moved down toward my belly.

"What are you doing?" I asked with my eyes closed.

"This," he said as he pulled my leggings down along with my panties in one attempt. I knew this was wrong but I wasn't going to stop him from doing what I wanted so badly.

"Baby, we have to stop," I managed to say softly.

He did not react. Instead, he allowed his tongue to speak for him. I closed my eyes and tilted my head back as he allowed his tongue to slowly circle my clit. It felt so good that I began to rub the top of his head, telling myself to push him away to stop. Instead, I held him closer so that he could finish. He continued, allowing his fingers to enter me. I almost screamed as I felt my juices flowing freely. I looked up and saw a new couple entering heading our way. I was almost at my highest point but I didn't want to get caught either. I started moving his head up and down. Noticing that I was almost there, he started to speed things up with his fingers.

"Baby, baby, baby," was all I managed to say. As the other couple neared, the woman must have felt me looking at her as she screamed. "Get a fucking room," I didn't pay her attention as I was trying to release everything that was in me at that very moment. I let it all go. I closed my eyes and relaxed on the bench. He slowly pulled my pants back up and wiped his mouth. He leaned in to kiss me and I allowed him to.

"Baby, you taste so good," he said. I couldn't reply I was in a zone so deep that if I had been home I would have easily fallen asleep.

It was then that I realized what I had just allowed to happen in a public place. I felt both embarrassed and ashamed.

"Can we go now?" I asked.

"You ready to leave me already?" he asked.

"No, it's just that I can't believe I just did that and now my pants are all wet."

We laughed. As we walked back to the car he asked if I would allow him to come back to my place for the night. I declined.

I had already done too much. Letting him come back to my place would be a Law and Order: SVU case ready to happen for real. He took me back to my car but before he allowed me to leave, he pushed me up against it and started kissing me again. This time we were both hungry for each other, and the kiss held much more passion than before. He slid

234

his hands back into my pants; however, when I reached to grab his, I was slightly disappointed. I slowed the kiss down and said my goodbyes.

"I had a great time Kyndal," he said. "I hope we can do this again sometime."

"We will," I replied, confused by his lack of response. There had to be something hard growling in his pants after all of that, but when I took a quick unnoticeable look, I didn't see what I was hoping for.

He leaned in to kiss me but instead of kissing him back, I traced my fingers around his lips and said, "Until next time," and pulled off.

I looked back in my rearview mirror to watch him as he walked back to his car.

"I knew it was too good to be true. But damn I hope all that isn't being wasted on a small package," I said laughing before hitting the expressway.

Kent

"What the fuck is wrong with me?" I yelled reaching into my pants. I couldn't believe that I was having this problem again. I wanted her so bad that my whole body was ready to explode but ol' boy wasn't responding again.

I hoped that she hadn't realized what happened or wasn't happening when she reached for him.

"Damn!" I said hitting the steering wheel. "Today out of all fucking days!"

She was definitely hotter than any of the women I'd dated in the past. On top of that, she seemed just as sexual and ready for whatever as I was. I liked that. I really enjoyed her company tonight. I just hoped that she felt the same way because we had some unfinished business.

I looked at the time display on the radio and saw that it was 11:30. I picked up my phone to call Sasha.

"Hello," she said sleepily.

"I'm on my way back to pick up Noelle," I said.

"She's sleeping and I don't want you to wake up both the babies. Why don't you just come over and spend the night?"

"Ummm," I hesitated. I really didn't want to go over to her place like this but I didn't want her to get mad at me for not coming back as I promised to pick up Noelle. "Okay, I'm on the way."

"I'll leave the door open for you," she said.

"Cool," I responded.

As I headed down Jefferson to the expressway, I couldn't help but think about Kyndal. She was so soft and sweet. She seemed like a very smart woman with her life in order. I was definitely looking forward to getting to know her a little better.

I found myself smiling, thinking of all the passion behind the kisses that we shared tonight. "Damn," I said to myself. "That's one bad woman."

When I reached Sasha's place, I was happy to find that she had left the door open. However, when I walked into the living room I was surprised to see her sitting on the sofa dressed in a nice piece of lingerie.

"Hey Sash," I said looking at the pink gown she was wearing.

"Come here," she said seductively.

"Ummm I need to go to the bathroom first," I said heading towards the bathroom.

"Kent!" she yelled getting up from the sofa.

I walked into the bathroom and dropped my pants. Before I could close the door she was behind me rubbing my chest. "Go ahead and finish up, I'll be waiting for you," she said walking away.

I sighed a sigh of relief because I knew I would have to wash my face and brush my teeth discreetly. I turned the water on low in the sink and quickly grabbed the mouthwash. I grabbed the bar of soap and proceeded to wash my face.

"Kent!" Sasha yelled. "What are you doing?"

"I'm just trying to get rid of the onion and garlic taste from my mouth from the food I ate earlier," I yelled.

"Well, hurry up," she said.

I grabbed a towel from the hall closet and dried my face before going back to the living room, where I sat down next to Sasha.

"So how was your date?" she asked.

"It was cool," I replied.

"Hmph, she couldn't have been that interesting seeing that you came back early and didn't spend the night out."

"Whatever Sasha," I replied. I got up from the couch and moved to sit in the chair across the room.

"Well, her loss. But now I need you to take care of me, Kent," she said, spreading her legs.

I instantly got a hard on as I looked across the room at her. She walked over to me and began to kiss me. I positioned her right on top of me. She reached down, unzipped my pants and pulled all of me out. Before I knew it she was on top of me. I was more surprised at the fact that my manhood was cooperating than into the sexual performance itself.

We finished the first round downstairs and decided to take it upstairs to the bedroom. I made love to Sasha the entire night until she asked me to stop. Ol' boy was still standing proudly until I fell asleep.

"Daddy, daddy," yelled Layla as she hopped into the bed in the morning. "Are you staying here with us again?"

I wiped my eyes and looked over to where she was sitting. "Huh?" I said.

"Mama said that she knew you would be back," Layla added, laughing.

"Oh yeah," I said turning to look at Sasha, standing in the doorway, holding Noelle. She smiled at me and walked away.

I decided it was best that I didn't respond to Layla because I had no intentions of coming back to stay with Sasha. Last night was great, but it was just sex, in which I needed it just as much as she did.

I asked Layla to leave the room while I got dressed. I looked down on the floor and didn't see my clothes. That's when I realized I had left everything downstairs including my phone. "Damn," I said loudly. I rumbled through the drawer until I found one of my old long T-shirts. Right before I closed the drawer I noticed a small bottle of what appeared to be some erotic lotion. The label said it was Love Potion *Tata Remi and Palo Mayombe*. I threw it back in the drawer and headed downstairs.

Sasha and the kids were seated at the table, eating breakfast. I went straight to the living room and grabbed my pants. I pulled my cell phone out of my pocket and saw that I had no missed calls or texts. I placed it back inside my pants and went to the kitchen.

"Good Morning Kent," said Sasha.

"Good morning," I said going around kissing each of them on the cheek.

"Hmph," said Sasha getting up from the table. "All I get is a cheek kiss huh?"

"I wonder if it was just as good as the kisses that you gave that little tramp last night that texted you this morning," she whispered in my ear.

"What?" I said turning to look her directly. She smiled and walked away.

I went back into the living room to get my cell phone. I checked my messages and found a message from Kyndal at 12:30 a.m. which read," I made it home safely. I really enjoyed you tonight including the good kisses. Good night ☺ "

I smiled and placed the phone back on the table. I grabbed Noelle's things and dressed her quickly. Right before I got ready to leave, Sasha came back downstairs.

"There's no need for you to run away Kent. I know you're still going to run the streets with different tramps. That's why I don't want to be with you. But we can still make something work between us where I get what I want from you from time to time. Kind of like last night," she said laughing.

"Whatever Sasha," I said opening the front door. "You're crazy."

"You just don't know how crazy I am," Sasha responded softly to herself. "If I can't be happy with you, I'll make sure that you are not happy either."

Gabrielle

It's been two weeks since Marcus last spoke with me. I'd tried to call him, but he wasn't answering my calls. I hadn't realized how much I cared about him until recently. I think my feelings have grown past the friend stage almost to the point where I could see us being together long term. But I guess it's too late for that.

I picked up my phone to call him one last time. "Hello I'm busy right now. Can I call you back?" he said upon answering.

"Yes," I replied softly, glad that he was at least willing to talk to me. He quickly disconnected the phone.

Since I had returned to work, I couldn't stop thinking about him. At times, I would find myself thinking about all the corny jokes he told or the way he kissed me on the cheek from time to time. None of the men I had dealt with in the past had really shown any form of compassion outside the bedroom.

I looked over at John's office and saw Bill walking out smiling. I heard John say, "Congratulations again," to Bill as he walked away.

I got up from my desk and headed towards John's office. "Hey John," I said.

"Hi Gabrielle. How's everything going?"

"Everything is great," I responded.

"Well why don't you come in and have a seat," he said.

I suddenly didn't feel so well. I sat down in the chair directly across from him and tried to smile, but for some reason I knew this wasn't going to be good news.

"Gabrielle, we're glad to have you back in good health. While you were gone, we decided to do some restructuring of the teams. There are some positions that we will no longer need, so we're moving people around to other teams. Bill has been doing a great job handling all of your responsibilities. So good, that we have decided that it would be best to promote him in recognition of his ability to handle so much in so little time. In short, you and Bill will share responsibilities as Team Manager until further notice."

I sat silently for a few moments. I was relieved that I wasn't being fired while also feeling angry that I would now have to work more closely with Bill. "Okay," I said softly, trying not to show my frustration.

"I'm glad that you're fine with this. You two will make an awesome team."

"Sure," I said rising from my seat.

"Gabrielle, why don't you go over and welcome him to your team," he suggested, gesturing towards the door.

"Okay," I said leaving his office. I was really upset that Bill had gotten exactly what he wanted and that was my job. I don't know how John could say that we would make a great team, knowing that Bill had no respect for me. Knowing that it was best that I keep my feelings to myself, I walked over to Bill's desk and offered my congratulations.

He nodded his head in acknowledgment, but didn't respond. I took that as a sign to just walk away, because if I responded in any way to his ignorance, it wasn't going be nice.

When I reached my desk, I saw the text message alert going off on my phone. It was Kyndal asking me to meet her for lunch. I hadn't spoken to her since the night she went out on her date. I know that she had been dying to tell me about it but her sister was in town and they had recently gone to visit her father in jail.

I told her to meet me at the Java Café. I finished emailing necessary correspondence to the other team members before logging off my computer.

"Will you be back in 30 minutes, one hour or longer?" Bill asked sarcastically as he saw me leaving.

"Just know that I'll be back," I said with a smile and walked away.

Kyndal and I pulled into the parking lot at the same time.

"Hey girl," we said in unison hugging each other.

Once we were seated, Kyndal looked at me and said, "I really needed this."

"If you only knew. I needed this too," I agreed, signaling the waiter to come over. He walked over to the table and swung his hips towards Kyndal. "May I help you," he said in a feminine voice," We both looked at each other and ordered a double espresso and turkey sandwiches. Kyndal ended it by saying, "We need something strong!" He pouted his lips and walked away.

"That's a mess," I said.

"That's worse than a mess. He is too big to be gay wearing extra juicy lip gloss," she pouted her lips to mimic the waiter.

"Anyway, back to reality," I said, changing the subject. "This has been a crazy week for me already and it's only Wednesday."

"Okay, you know this lunch was meant to be an opportunity for me to share my news, but I guess, I'll let you go first Gabby."

"Thanks for being so generous," I teased, laughing, because she always liked to talk about her issues first, which usually left only the last five minutes of lunch for me to gossip.

"It's just that I still feel really bad about the whole Marcus situation. He won't even speak to me."

"Yeah that was bad," she said, shaking her head.

"But I just wanted to tell him that it wasn't what it looked like. I really care for him, Kyndal. Much more than I thought I would. But he's made it clear that he wanted nothing to do with me, so I'm just going to have to deal with it."

"I'll see what I can do for you," said Kyndal.

"No, just let it be. I knew it was too good to be true anyway."

"Aww, don't say that! Marcus was the kind of man that you deserve. I can tell he cares for you. He respects you and treats you like you deserve to be treated. Not to mention that he loves God, and, in my view, any man that loves God knows how to love a woman. And that's what you deserve."

"Thanks boo," I said softly. "But let's talk about something different. I'm tired of sulking and this espresso is kicking in."

"Ok, as you know, I went to visit my father. It was actually really therapeutic for me to see him in that environment. I know that sounds bad, but I don't think I would have been able to talk to him the way I did while I was there. I went there with intentions on asking him questions that I felt needed to be answered, most of which relate to my childhood. However, when I got there, I found myself asking him more questions about how he felt about his life at this moment. He really opened up to me about his addiction and some of the bad choices that he had made while on drugs. But the most important part was him telling me that he was sorry for ruining our bond and our family. He asked me to forgive him and I did. I felt that I finally got my closure. It really felt good talking to my daddy again."

"That's great to hear, Kyndal," I replied. "So, moving forward, how are the men in your life doing?"

"Well Noah's great! He's been spending a lot more time with his dad these days, which is good because it has allowed me time to do something for myself."

"That's good. So what are you doing with all this me time? Are you getting 'me' some satisfaction during your 'free-k' time?"

We both laughed. "Girl, sex is the furthest thing from my mind right now. I'm focusing on bettering myself while gaining a stronger relationship with God. However, I was so ready to give it all to Mr. Kent the other night but I'm glad I didn't. I woke up the next day thinking, 'girl, are you crazy?' Here I was, acting as if I was in high school, kissing a strange man in a public place and thinking of sleeping with him. Not to mention that he has kids with an s."

"How many?"

"I can only remember him saying two or three, but the thing that got me was that he had two kids that are the same age."

"What?"

"Yes girl. This fool even had the nerve to say they were like twins."

"Oh hell no," I replied laughing. "I told you not to go out with him Kyndal."

"I know, but I can't stop thinking about him either," she said, smiling, looking down in embarrassment.

"What the hell? You must be going crazy. What has happened to my friend? Don't let this whole 'trying something different' thing take you down, Kyndal. You've been through too much already."

"Gabby, you're getting too serious. It's just that the chemistry between us was so strong it was almost magical."

"Oh, here you go with all that 'fall in love like the storybooks' BS."

"No, I'm serious Gabby. When he kissed me, I felt something much stronger than passion. I felt a connection."

"Yeah a connection between his lips and your horny vagina."

"How about his lips were all over my vagina and it felt so good."

"What?" I asked, shocked. "Where is my real friend again?" I joked, looking around for the cameras.

"I'm right here. I almost couldn't believe it myself. He took all of me into his mouth right there at the lighthouse. It was awesome."

"So you gave it up at the freaking lighthouse Kyndal?"

"No, we didn't get that far, but I wanted too. I was a little ashamed, so I decided that it was best that I go home."

"He let you?"

"Yes he didn't have a choice. But we've been sexting every day since then."

"It looks like my freaky friend is back, but I'm not sure I want her back."

"Whatever. Although I really can't see this being anything serious, I still feel that I have to unlock the mystery now that I've had a taste, right?"

"I guess. Just don't fall in love, Kyndal," I said.

"You know that I don't do that easily."

"True. Whatever happened to Jason?"

"Jason's fine. He's still calling and texting me, but I'm getting bored. He said that he would be back next week sometime, so I hope that, this time, our time together will be a little more interesting."

"So, this is what you should do. Let Mr. Perve get you all excited and give it up to the big man with the master plan when he comes to town. That way, you won't lose."

"Girl, you're crazy!" she said laughing.

"Speaking of crazy, I have to get back to the office now that I have that crazy ass white guy Bill working as team manager with me."

"Isn't Bill the guy that's been after you since you started?"

"Yes, and while I was gone, he made his way to the top almost as if he's taking my spot. Now I have to be on top of my game all the way with no mistakes because I know he's watching me and ready to give me the boot."

"Yeah, 'cause you know they stick together," Kyndal agreed, grabbing her purse.

"I'll call you later, Missy. Try not to give it up to Mr. Perve for a while."

"I'll try, but it won't be easy," she joked, getting into her car.

Once I reached the office parking lot, I decided to send Marcus a text, "I really enjoyed the time that we shared together. Thanks for giving me so many memorable moments. Good bye."

Pressing the 'send' button kind of hurt, but I needed to release that whole situation in order to move forward.

Kyndal

"I'm really looking forward to seeing you again on Friday," said Kent.

"Me too," I replied running my fingers through my hair as I sat at my desk.

It had not even been a week since our last encounter and I already couldn't wait to see him again. Every day, I found myself daydreaming or smiling every time I thought of him and those kisses. I tried to put all those other thoughts of him being a player with multiple baby mamas behind me. I finally came to the conclusion that he would be just for fun. Hell, I didn't have to marry him.

Men do it all the time. They find a woman that doesn't quite meet their list of requirements and still lead her on by having fun with her during the late nights. They call it 'friends with benefits', but I used to call it a 'Jump-off'. I don't plan to have any long term commitments or fall in love with him. So that's just what I'll call him—my jump-off.

I'm long overdue for a little sexual healing, anyway, and he definitely knows how to wake my body up. I can feel him now rubbing his hands all over my body, while kissing and biting me until I beg him to stop. I may never say 'stop' with all this build up I have inside of me. I just hope that he meets my expectations in the bedroom because I really don't have room for any disappointments in that area.

"Kyndal," he said disturbing me from my daydream. "I have to go, but I'll call you later. Just keep it nice and ready for me, okay?"

"Okay," I said, sounding like a little schoolgirl, before disconnecting the call.

I hope he doesn't think I'm really this easy. He will have to put in some work like all the others. Who was I kidding? I didn't really care if we went to dinner or not. I just wanted him in my bed, doing all those nasty things he did to me that night at the lighthouse.

"Ms. Kyndal, your 2 o'clock appointment is here," said the lady at the front desk.

"Please send her in. Thank you," I said getting myself back in order before Passion walked in.

"Hello Passion," I said, greeting her with a smile. I noticed that she looked really sad.

"Hi," she replied dryly.

"How's everything been going since we last spoke?"

"Everything's fucked up! I listened to you and told my kids' father about the syphilis and he left me."

"I'm sorry to hear that Passion."

"Yeah right. You knew that was gonna happen. Now he has taken my kids and everything. Said he don't wanna be with me no more because now he has proof that I'm a whore."

"I'm really sorry to hear that Passion. But it's better that you told him…"

"Better for who?" she said cutting me off. "He was my everything. He paid all the bills and took care of the kids. Now I don't have nothing. Who's gonna take care of me now?"

"I understand exactly where you're coming from, but you need to take this time to really evaluate how you're going to live your life from this day forward."

"What fucking life? I don't have one without him and the kids. Since they left, nothing matters. I feel like I'm dead already. They might as well tell me I have the virus so I can hurry up and die."

"Passion, you have to remember that you still have a reason to live. Think about your kids. He may be angry now, but I am sure that it will soon pass."

"I don't think so. You don't know Rob like I do. I've done so much too him in the past that he doesn't care about anything I have to say to him right now. I haven't even told him that two of those kids may not be his. They might be his brother's. That's why they look so much like him. Not to mention that I still haven't told him about the HIV part. And you know what I'm not going to tell him. Don't make since for both of us to worry about dying. He's been great to my kids and they deserve to have a father who loves and cares for them. He's been more of a parent than I have been. The only thing I've been doing for years is running around sleeping with men—men that didn't care nothing about me. I've slept with over 500 men in the past year alone, and I'm only 25," she said before finally taking a breath.

"Passion, your past can be just that—your past. It will only affect your present and future if you continue to live the same way. Now, I think you need to tell Rob the full story so that he will know how to handle all that you've kept from him all these years."

"I'm not telling him nothing else," she said, rising from her seat. "See, you don't know anything, Ms. Kyndal. It's always better to not know that you're dying even if you're not. No one wants to live knowing that their days are numbered." With that, she walked quickly towards the door.

"Passion, please have a seat," I said rising from my chair.

"No thanks, and I won't be back!" She yelled, slamming the door shut, and ran out of the building.

I rose from my desk and walked over to Dr. Gordon's office. She wasn't there. I needed to talk to her about how to handle what I was told by Passion. I knew she would never come back and patient confidentiality was taken very serious in the state of Michigan. I just wish there was something that I could do to stop her from ruining the lives of others and her own.

I returned to my desk where I pulled out Passion's file. There was really nothing there aside from the few passages I had written after our first meeting. I grabbed a blue pen from the pen holder and began to write down all the information she had provided me about her life, her diagnosis and her family. Next to the word 'family' I wrote a question mark and drew a line towards her children's names and their supposed father. The phrase 'dying on the inside' kept flickering in my mind, so I wrote it down next to the Passions' name.

When I got home that evening, I thought about all the clients that I had counseled in the past. I kept thinking about how all of them, at one point, felt as if they were dead after a tragedy had struck them. I thought about all the pain that they had dealt with due to either love or not being loved. I thought about how I felt after Michael's death and my not wanting to continue living. One thing was consistent in all of our situations—we were all dying to be loved.

I opened my bible and read a familiar passage: "For God so loved the world that he gave his only begotten son. Whosoever believeth in him shall not perish but have everlasting life." After rereading this passage several times, I came to the conclusion that, no matter how fair, harsh or brutal the journey of finding love may be, in the end, we all sacrifice something. In most cases it's a part of our life, some dying on the inside from self-inflicted wounds, while others try to find different strengths and measures to keep holding on.

I bowed my head and said a silent prayer for all those that may have sacrificed their lives in hope of finding love.

"Dear God. As we face the many struggles of living in the world today, our greatest struggle has been the inability to find love. Today, I realized how big of a part this plays in most women's lives. At times, it feels as if we are trying to find the most desired treasure with no luck. But that isn't the case. The love that we need most is right here with you. You are the one that deserves all our love, God. You give us the strength to endure. You wrap your arms around us and comfort us during our time of need. It is you that we must learn to love wholeheartedly, with no expectations. It was you that gave your life, so that we could live ours. No real man would make this ultimate sacrifice. It is you that we need to learn to love God. It is you."

I declare that from this day forward I'm going to leave finding love, in God's hands.

Kent

"I love you daddy," said Layla kissing me on the cheek.

"I love you too baby," I replied.

"Are you sure daddy?"

"Yes. Why do you ask?"

"Because the kids at my school said that daddies don't love their kids as much as mothers do because they always leave them. They said that daddies can come and go as they please and don't really care about their kids."

"What?" I said, turning to face her in the backseat.

"They said that most daddies don't live at home because they don't love the mommies or the kids."

"That's not true, honey. I love you and your brothers and sisters more than anything else in the world. I love you guys just as much as mommy and maybe even more. I don't have to live with you for you to know that. I will never leave you or your brothers and sisters. You hear me?"

"Yes daddy," she said smiling. "I just wish you could come home."

"Layla, your house is your home. I have a home of my own. Don't think that because I'm not there with you every day that I love you any less. I think about you all the time and you know you can call me whenever you want to talk to me."

"I know daddy," she said, hugging me as I took her out of the car. I knocked on the door a few times before Sasha finally opened.

"Hey Kent," she replied dryly.

"Hi Sasha," I replied. Layla ran inside and I turned to leave.

"So you're not coming in today?" Sasha asked.

"No, I have a few errands to run."

"Well I need you to do something for me Kent."

"What is that Sasha?"

"Just call me once you're done with everything today and we'll talk."

"Okay," I replied.

I picked up my phone to call my mother.

"Hi baby," she answered. "I was just thinking of you."

"Oh yeah. What were you thinking?"

"I was thinking about how proud I am of you as a father. I wish I could say that about your father."

"Oh Mama, please don't start. Pops was a good father. He taught me a lot of things."

"Hmph. Yeah, I see he taught you how to sleep around with numerous women. He wasn't good for too much else. I'm just glad that you got your good parenting skills from me."

"Okay Ma, I don't feel like arguing with you so I'll take the compliment."

"There's never a need to argue. I know what I'm talking about. If it weren't for me, you wouldn't know how to treat your children or the women in your life. Showing respect and being able to care for those you love is learned. Those are two things your father knows nothing about."

"According to you, Ma. Pops has been a great father and, as I recall, I spent more time with him growing up then I did with you. Do you even remember my childhood? Because I don't recall you spending too many days with me while you were trying to punish my father! Do you remember that? Probably not, because you can only recall the good stories and times when you were there to celebrate my accomplishments. I used to find it funny that you were always the one bragging about how smart your son was, but never remembered you spending anytime with me doing homework. Do you remember the days that I called for you to come pick me up to spend time with you and you refused because you didn't want to allow Pops any free time? I do. I spent so many days wanting to be with you that I cried myself to sleep on many nights, until I realized that you weren't ever going to change. So, before you continue to bash Pops for not being a good father to me, you need to look in the mirror."

"Kent! I'm your mother. And you will not talk to me like this."

"I'm sorry, Mom. I really am. But I'm a fully grown man now and I'm tired of hearing you bash my father. I think it's time that you get over it."

"Kent! You have no clue and I refuse to allow you to speak to me this way."

"Again, I'm sorry Mom."

"Sorry you are son. Sorry you are," she said before hanging up the phone.

I felt bad for having spoken to my mother this way, but a bit relieved that I had finally told her about how I felt as a child growing up without a mother. She spent so much time bashing my father that she never took the time to think about her own neglect. I hope that I got my point across to her. I knew that I would have to do something special for her soon because I didn't like being at odds with my mother at all.

As I drove to the eastside of town, I decided to call Taylor to check on Brittney. I hadn't seen her in over a week due to her being sick with the flu.

"Hi Taylor, how are you and Brittney?"

"We're fine. She's doing a lot better now that the virus is gone. She's been driving me crazy all day asking if she can go outside to play."

"Well, let her go out and get some fresh air. It'll be good for her."

"Yeah you're right. I just have so much stuff to do around the house today that I won't be able to watch her outside."

"I'm in the area. I can stop by for a little while to play with her outside."

"Okay. That'll be good."

"I'll be there in 20 minutes."

I stopped by the post office first to send off an application for a job up north that I was applying for. I hadn't really decided if I wanted to move away, but I was willing to do whatever it took to get back to a steady level of income. I was barely making it and I hadn't figured out how long it would be before I got behind on most of my bills.

When I got to Taylor's house, they were sitting outside on the porch. Brittney ran to the curbside and waited for me to get out.

"Daddy, daddy!" she shouted, jumping up and down.

"Hey pumpkin," I said picking her up. "Looks like you're feeling a lot better."

"Yes. I think the sickness is gone. That's what mommy said."

"That's good. You can get back to school."

"Yeah, I'll be able to play with all my friends. I'm tired of staying in the house with mommy every day," she said.

We both started laughing.

"The feeling is mutual Brit," said Taylor.

Brittney ran inside the house to get her tricycle. I took a seat next to Taylor and asked how she was doing.

"I'm fine," she said. "Keeping busy with work. It's too bad that I had to use some of my vacation days to stay home with Taylor."

"You should have told me that. I would've kept her."

"You don't have a mother's touch," she laughed.

"How would you know? I learned to treat all my illnesses alone as a child."

"That's probably half of what's wrong with you now," she said.

"There's nothing wrong with me. I'm a good daddy. At least I'm trying to be. I can handle some of the parenting responsibilities on my own. Y'all just don't give me a chance."

"Yeah, I can see you now, trying to care for all five kids at one time. You'd probably lose your mind before we picked them up," she laughed. "As a matter of fact, how are the two new little ones doing?"

"They're fine. Just growing."

"And how are their mothers?"

"They're good for the most part, I guess."

"You guess, huh? Well dealing with a baby on your own is a hard work, Kent. I feel bad for them in a way. I'm not having another kid alone if I have anything to do with it. That was just too much work."

"You didn't have to do it alone, Taylor. Remember, you chose to leave."

"That was probably one of the best decisions of my life. But Taylor and I are fine now. I'm in a good place with my job and serving on the church board. I don't have any worries here."

"That's good. You shouldn't have any. Where did Brittney go?"

"I'll go check on her. You know she gets distracted easily. She's probably watching TV or something now?" she said, laughing as she went back inside the house.

A few minutes later, Brittney came to the door and said, "Daddy I changed my mind. I don't want to play outside anymore. I want to watch the Princess and the Frog. You want to watch it with me?"

"I'm sorry baby, I have to go."

"Okay daddy," she said, showing no concern. She almost closed the door in my face without saying goodbye.

"Wait a minute Brittney. Can daddy have a kiss?" She smiled and jumped to give me a hug and a kiss. I said goodbye to Taylor and headed to my car.

On the way home I couldn't help but think about what Taylor said about us not being together was the best decision of her life. That kind of hurt a little because I really loved that girl. I was both honest and genuine when I had asked her to marry me. I had stopped sleeping around with other women because I didn't feel the need. It wasn't my fault that two of them ended up pregnant after I asked her, she was partly to blame for cheating on me. It took about two years after our break up for me to get completely over her but I spent a lot of that time enjoying plenty women. None of them ever meant anything to me outside of sex. The only woman that ever came close to being meaningful was Sasha because we had built an everlasting friendship and now she was the mother of two of my children. But there was just something about her that wouldn't allow me to take the next step.

Women were just too damn confusing. That's why I only played bed games with them.

I smiled when I thought of my lighthouse rendezvous with Kyndal. Now that was a sweet girl, but I wasn't planning on doing much more with her then I had done with the other women. As a matter of fact, I needed to stop by the drug store to pick up some stimulators to ensure that "he" was going to act right tonight. We'd been sending sexy text messages for

254

the whole week and I planned to live out some of those things I said I would do to her. It's always good when a woman was able to stimulate you even when she isn't around you and that was exactly what Kyndal was doing. Even though I sent most of the messages, her responses were just as forward as mine.

I stopped by the dry cleaners to pick up my laundry. Just as I put my clothes on the back seat, I turned to see Karen taking her clothes out of her car.

"Hey Karen," I greeted her.

"Hi Kent," she responded dryly.

"It's good to see you."

"I wish that I could say the same, but it's not a pleasure."

"Wow. Is that how you're going to treat me every time I see you? I don't remember doing anything to you for us not to be able to be cordial to one another."

"Yeah, you would say that. But that didn't stop your crazy baby mama from jumping on me and stalking my house now did it."

"What?" I asked.

"Oh, I see. Ms. Angela didn't tell you anything! Well, the day that we went for that jog, I returned home only to be attacked from behind by that crazy tramp. The neighbor told me that she had been stalking my apartment and took some flowers that were delivered to me weeks before. Crazy chic."

"Wow Karen. I'm so sorry. This is the first I've heard of any of this. Why didn't you tell me?"

"What for, Kent? I wanted to be done with you that day and I'm glad that I'm done with you now," she said, walking away.

I stood there for a moment, thinking about how she must have felt after being attacked by Angela's crazy ass. The funny thing was that Angela had stopped calling me like crazy after that. I wonder if knowing that Karen was out of the picture triggered that.

I was kind of happy in a way because I hadn't had to deal with her for months now. I felt bad for Karen. She didn't deserve any of the things that happened to her while she was with me but I didn't miss her.

When I entered my apartment, I was greeted by the cinnamon spice fragrance that I placed in several spaces earlier that day. I wanted to make sure that my place looked and smelled perfect when Kyndal arrived. I planned to prepare a nice salmon dish with wild rice and bread pudding for desert.

I was a little surprised that she had agreed to come to my place right away. Maybe she wasn't such a good girl after all. I had about a good hour before she would arrive. I prepped the food for cooking and decided it would be best to shower first just in case she was running late. I wanted the food to be hot when she arrived.

Ring. Ring. The phone started to ring just as I was about to hop in the shower. I looked down at the caller ID and saw that it was Sasha.

"Hey Sasha, what's up?"

"Hey Kent. The kids and I are around the corner from you, can we stop by for a minute?"

"Ummm, no. I'm just getting into the shower and I was about to head out in a minute."

"We'll make it quick. Come open the door for us. I'm in the parking lot," she said before hanging up the phone.

"Damn!" I said to myself. I grabbed my robe from behind the door and went to the door.

"Hi daddy," said Layla. "We got a present for you." She pulled out a square-shaped box, decorated with a bow from behind her back.

"Wow, what is this?" I asked.

"Open it daddy," she said excitedly, grabbing my hand and leading me inside the house. Sasha followed closely behind.

We sat down on the couch, as I unwrapped the gift. Inside was a portrait of Layla, Sasha and baby Korey with the inscription that read, "Daddy's Angels". It was framed in a mahogany wood frame with the words *Family Means Everything* engraved on the bottom.

I looked at Sasha and the kids and said 'Thank you'. I gave Layla a big kiss and smiled at Sasha.

"See daddy, we are a family," said Layla.

"Yes we are," I said back to her.

Sasha smiled as she held the baby tightly in her arms. "This is very sweet Sasha." I said to her.

"Where are you going to put it?" she asked.

"I'll find a place for it," I said looking around the room. I looked up at the clock which now read 7:20. I only had forty minutes to shower and cook.

"What are you guys about to do now?" I asked.

"Can we stay here with you, daddy, please?" asked Layla.

"Yeah can we stay daddy," whined Sasha, mimicking Layla.

"Sasha. I told you that I have plans."

"Well, change them," she said laying the baby down on the couch.

"I can't Sasha."

"Yes you can. Just call your little girlfriend and tell her that you can't come."

"Sasha," I said getting angry.

"Daddy doesn't have a girlfriend mommy. You're his girlfriend right?" asked Layla staring at me.

"See, look what you started, Sasha!" I raised my voice at her.

"Oh please, Kent. You don't think that she knows about your other women?"

"Sasha, I have plans and I don't feel like arguing with you in front of the kids. Please leave."

"Oh so, now you putting us out Kent," she laughed as she grabbed the baby to get up. "I must've been a fool to think that you would choose to be with your family instead of one of your little tramps. I hope she enjoys the show because she definitely won't be enjoying nothing else tonight."

I didn't respond because I didn't feel like arguing with her and I was glad she was leaving. Layla was crying on the way out the door and I almost felt like asking Sasha to let her stay, but I didn't.

****

"Mommy, I thought daddy liked the present," she said once they got into the car.

"He did sweetheart, he just has other plans."

"But I thought the picture said 'family means everything'. We are family, right?"

"Yes we are, honey. We're just a special kind of family. We both love you and your brother and that will never change. You hear me?"

"Yes, mommy. I just wish we could be a real family," she said sadly.

"We are honey. We are."

They drove home in silence. After putting the kids to bed, Sasha went to her room and began crying. "Family!" She screamed looking at the portrait of her and her two children without Kent.

"I hate him! I hate him!"

Kyndal

Today had been one crazy day. After meeting with Passion again, I finally realized that I definitely didn't want to go down the road of destruction again with men. From what she had told me, it appeared that she had been having sex with numerous men trying to fill a void in her life. She said that she really didn't care about any of the men she slept with she just had to feed her craving for sex at the time. I was happy that she didn't have the virus. She said that she'd gotten a job so that she could live a better life for her kids.

During the session, I gained insight on my current life, in which I was trying to live a life far better than my past. I wanted something new, but I wanted that experience to be representative of my current state of being and my path of righteousness. I no longer wanted to fill the void of being lonely and lacking love with a person.

 As I thought about my dinner plans with Kent this evening, I knew in my heart that I was attracted to him for the wrong reasons, which would take me off the path that I was currently on. The sexual chemistry between us would definitely lead us to the one place that I didn't want to go—the bedroom. Even though I picked up my phone to call and cancel numerous times throughout the day, I just couldn't find the nerves to do it.

Now, here I am sitting here dressed looking at the clock, which now reads 7:45, debating on if I should go to his place or not. It was too late to cancel and I didn't know what excuse I would use for not coming because I don't like to lie or, worse, say 'I don't want to come to your house because I'm sexually attracted to you but I don't want to have sex with you'. Both would make me sound like a fool.

I kneeled down beside the couch and prayed:

"Dear God, I know that you know my mind, my heart and my body far better than I know myself. But I want you to know that when I vowed to give my life to you again, I really plan to uphold that promise. Living in the world can be very hard at times, in which there are things and people that make you want to go against what you truly believe God wants for you and plans for your life. I want to live my life according to your will Lord. I really need you to guide my mind and my body to do what's right

tonight Lord Jesus. I need your help Lord. Please keep me in your favor. Amen."

I grabbed my keys from the counter and headed to the garage. As I was pulling out I saw, Gerald and Melissa jogging up the street together. I waived at them as I drove by. I looked in the rearview mirror and smiled. It was always a pleasure to see two people who have decided to share their lives together happily enjoy each other's company. I wanted that and I vowed to have it sooner than later.

When I arrived at Kent's place, I complimented him on how nice it was. The aroma was soothing and the soft jazz music playing in the background was very relaxing. I could tell that he knew what he was doing in the kitchen as I watched him put the finishing touches on the salmon and wild rice that he prepared. I liked the fact that he had chosen one of my favorite dishes to prepare for me.

We sat down to enjoy dinner together and chatted about the debate over President Obama's decision to provide free health care to everyone. His views were very similar to mine in regards to feeling that everyone deserves it not just the poor. We shared a few jokes and laughed about things that were going on in the world.

I couldn't help but notice how handsome he was. I loved looking at his lips when he spoke to me. At one point I felt as if I was ready to jump across the table and devour them without asking. He touched my hand a few times from across the table which made it even harder for me to concentrate on not being able to throw myself at him right then and there. But to my surprise as my mind did its own thing my body stayed in place. I composed myself as a true lady.

Once dinner was over, he took my hand and led me over to the sitting area, but before I could sit down, "Submerge" by Maxwell—one of my favorite songs—came on. He must have felt it too because he pulled me closer into him. He grabbed my hands and slowly turned me around. Instead of kissing me, he twirled me outward. I answered moving my body side to side. As he pulled me back into him, we connected and moved our bodies slowly to the music. We danced closely for the first few minutes until he released me with a twirl. At one point, he touched my face and smoothed my hair back down. When the song was over, we stayed connected until I sat down.

He leaned to kiss me and I obliged. However, this time I interrupted him by asking where the restroom was. I closed the door behind me and sat down on the closed toilet. I smiled to myself as I thought about how strong the feeling was for this man. I hadn't felt this with anyone else before. I knew that it was going to be very hard to resist him but I didn't have a choice. Passion was not going to win tonight.

The rest of the evening consisted of us talking about life and the changes that we saw coming. He told me that he was 31 with five kids and currently unemployed, but he was looking and planned on getting his life back in order very soon. This piece of information was definitely enlightening, as I now knew that I would have to keep the straps tight because I didn't want to have any more kids and he was clearly a baby maker.

I used my sense of humor to get through the night, and before I knew it, the clock read 1:30 a.m. I thanked him for dinner and a good time and told him that I had to leave. He politely led me to the door.

Once we got to the door, he softly kissed me again and said that he would love to see me again. I agreed and left.

During the drive home, I found myself smiling more as I thought about him and his soft approach with me. I was thankful that he wasn't really aggressive about the whole sex thing. I thanked God for giving me the strength to get through the night and for allowing me to get to know Kent on a personal level.

Things were definitely looking up despite of all his baggage. I liked him as a person and I loved the changes that he had brought out of me on these last two encounters. I was feeling young and happy again. I just hoped that he could keep up the good work because I wasn't a believer in the saying too good to be true. I preferred "both good and true" together.

Gabrielle

"Marcus," I greeted, surprised to see him, as I opened the door.

"Hi Gabby," he said, heading towards the couch.

I hadn't seen him in weeks. I instantly got nervous. He'd been ignoring my calls and never responded to any of my texts and I didn't know what to expect from him.

"Gabby, I need to get this off my chest, so I may speak a little faster than normal. Please understand and bear with me."

"Ok," I said, moving to the spot next to him.

"Gabby, I know more about you than you think I do. I knew when I first laid eyes on you that you were the right one for me. There are some things that I, of course, had to deal with regarding your past, but when I came to you, I honestly thought that you were ready. I prayed and asked God to tell me when it was time, but instead of receiving an answer right away, I was advised to continue to get to know you. The day that I came to your place and found another man here—well, excuse me, that wasn't a real man—my feelings were deeply hurt because I expected so much more from you. I don't think that you know how great of a woman you truly are because you have been with the wrong men that haven't taken the time to show and appreciate you for the qualities that you endure. Your insecurities will lead you down the wrong path if you continue to pursue them."

"I'm not in—"

"Stop it Gabby. I didn't come here to argue with you. I came here because you need to know that I care for you. These last few weeks have been extremely hard on me, but it just wasn't the right time. I know you may not look at me as the most handsome man you know, but I can honestly feel that there was a genuine love growing between us during the time that we spent together. Even though I've tried, I can't stop thinking about you. I'm hoping that you feel the same way and will allow what we started to grow, blossom. Are you ready Gabby?"

The tears wouldn't stop falling. I smiled through them and said, "Yes!"

"Are you done with the past?"

"Yes."

"Are you ready to experience real love?"

"Yes," I said tears still flowing.

"It's going to take some time. But I think you're worth it," he said before hugging me.

I buried myself in his arm and the tears stopped. I felt a warm feeling on the inside as he held me. I knew that this was love and this is how it was supposed to feel.

"Thank you God. Thank you," I said silently while Marcus held me in his arms.

Moving Forward

"Longing for a child that will give him their all. Give it all. He wants it all..."
Forever Jones

Kyndal

Tonight is definitely going to be a night that Kent will never forget. I planned to take him out to a nice dinner and finish the night off with a little poetry at Jubilee. I love the way he enjoyed experiencing new things with me over the last six months. I guess, he's still "trying to hang in there," as he always teases.

He's been going to church services with me and even to bible study on Wednesdays. They say a woman that leads a man to the house of the Lord is a keeper. I just hope that he's not doing all of this just to see if I'll eventually open up to having sex with him. I haven't gotten this vibe from him yet, but I still have my reservations when dealing with men. However, I've come along way, and he has too, judging by the way he opened up to me.

Two months ago, I finally met one of his children's mothers, Sasha. She was polite and all, but I could tell there was something not right with her. She seemed to be a bit too reserved when speaking to Kent in front of me. Now I know how it is to be the child's mother, picking up the kid when another woman is around the father, but it was almost as if she was shooting daggers at him without saying anything. I asked Kent if he was still sleeping with her and he immediately told me that he wasn't. He said that they'd had one sexual encounter since the two of us started seeing each other, but nothing more. I wanted to believe him, but there was still something about that woman that I just couldn't figure out, but I knew I would uncover it sooner or later.

I called Gabby to see if they were still meeting us at the restaurant. I was so happy for her and Marcus. I knew that Marcus had picked out a ring and was planning to propose to her, I just didn't know when.

Life was finally looking good for the both of us.

The message alert sounded on my phone. It was a text from Kent. "I miss you already and I can't wait to see you tonight. beautiful," I smiled.

He had a way with words and I was glad that he wasn't afraid to express his feelings. At first, I thought that he was just conning me. But overtime, I had started to feel that he was really genuine when he expressed his feelings to me.

I grabbed a pair of gold sandals from the back of my closet and sat them next to the bed. I couldn't help but think about how much I was really falling for him. It has been extremely hard to resist him and not to have him in my bed at night. But I just have to do it this way.

I vowed to God that I would not allow another man to use my body for temporary pleasure. After working with Passion, and thinking about my past with men, I realized that I was using them as much as they used me, trying to fill a void.

I don't know what will become of Kent and me, but this is something that I'm going to have to commit to. I figured, if he stays good, but if he goes, I haven't lost anything.

I took one last look at myself in the mirror and smiled. I'm really proud of myself at this point in my life. Everything is going good for me at work, home and church, and even in my relationship with Kent. I have so much to be thankful for and I owe it all to the man above.

"Thank you Jesus," I said as I blew myself a kiss in the mirror and walked away.

Gabrielle

"Wow, you look gorgeous," said Marcus as he stared at me from the bedroom doorway.

"Thanks babe," I said as I turned around. "You look quite handsome yourself. Look, we're matching without even trying."

"That just means that we are really in sync."

I walked over to him and gave him a quick kiss on the lips. "I didn't hear you come in babe."

"I hope I didn't scare you," he said.

"Not at all," I replied. "Well, we'd better get going. You know Kyndal hates waiting on people."

He laughed, "Yes, she does. She better ask God to really work on her patience skills."

I laughed because that was definitely something she needed to work on. "Leave my friend alone. She'll be fine. God is working on her in other areas. Trust me." I laughed a little, as I thought about her and Kent.

"I believe you. I'm just glad to see her happy. She's really a great person," he said.

"Yes she is. Why do you think I love her so much?" I said playfully.

"I hope you love me just as much."

"I do, but in a different kind of way—a little more special."

"Good. I hope you remember that 'little more special' tonight."

"Hmm, are we talking dirty now Mr. Marcus?"

"Who me?" he said shaking his head. "Not at all."

"Don't let me find out you really Mr. Nasty and been holding out on me all this time."

"You'll find out sooner or later."

We laughed. Over these last few months I have really fallen in love with Marcus. It was definitely scary at first because I'd never experienced real love and happiness before. My guard was up at first, but Marcus just made it too hard for me not to fall. He has accepted me, flaws and all. We have even talked about travelling around the world in the next year or so. I'm definitely looking forward to it.

"Come on baby, let's go," I urged him, grabbing his hand.

When we arrived at the restaurant, I was surprised not to find Kyndal and Kent waiting in the lobby for us.

"I wonder where they are," I said to Marcus.

"Well, we don't have to wait for them. We can be seated," said Marcus.

"Okay," I agreed, following the waiter to a table set for four.

Kyndal and Kent arrived 20 minutes later. Kyndal was smiling from ear to ear and I suspected that Kent had everything to do with that.

"Hey girl," she said giving me a hug. "Hello Marcus."

Kent greeted us both as well, but he seemed a little bit more reserved than his usual friendly self.

"Hi Kent," I said trying to bring him in. "How have you been?"

"I've been great. I can't complain."

"Please no complaints at this table tonight," said Marcus.

"You won't hear any coming from me when I have this beautiful lady sitting beside me," Kent replied, giving Kyndal a kiss on the cheek.

Since Kent and Kyndal have been dating, Kyndal definitely seems a lot happier. She says that they are not having sex, but that's hard to believe because the sexual chemistry between them is very evident whenever I'm around. They are always kissing and groping each other. I know my girl and she is not one to keep her legs closed for long, especially when she's really into her man. She has always been known for her freaky ways. Come to think of it, she was the one telling the girls how to please their men on several occasions. And from what I've heard about Kent, he's not one to keep the dragon on a leash either, having five kids and all. I still don't see how she's doing it, but that's none of my business.

Kyndal says that she's on a new spiritual journey and she's really not going to engage in sex until she's married, but we'll see. She seems happy and I'm just going to let her enjoy it.

Speaking of enjoying sex, Marcus and I haven't engaged yet either. But I can wait. I still have my fair share of toys and he fulfills me in ways no other man has. I just hope that he can put it down when the time comes.

After dinner, the waiter asked if we wanted dessert and of course, Kyndal said 'yes'. She ordered strawberry cheesecake with vanilla ice cream for her and Kent. Those two haven't stopped touching each other since they sat down.

"Okay now kids, table manners are taught at the age of five. How old are you two again?" I said.

"We can't help that we love each other," said Kent.

Kyndal looked surprised. She smiled nervously but said nothing.

"We can't help it either' right?" Marcus turned to me and asked.

"No baby, we can't," I said giving him a kiss.

I haven't told him that I love him yet. But I really do. I've never felt this way about another person, especially without having sex with them.

He placed his hands on top of mine and began rubbing them.

"I love you," I whispered in his ear. He turned to me and said "I love you back."

Kyndal and Kent were oblivious to everything that was going on at the table outside of them.

"Okay kids, it's time to go to the 'real party'," said Marcus.

"I thought we were going to that poetry spot," said Kent.

"Yeah bro, we are. But it's still a real party," said Marcus.

"Okay," said Kent looking at Kyndal for confirmation.

""You're gonna love it," she said to him.

"It'll be something that you'll definitely remember," I said to him. "The spirit will surely be in the house tonight. I can feel it already."

Sasha

I thought for sure that when I told Kent to leave, he was going to come back like he always does. We've been doing this break up to make up thing for over five years now. I was also hoping that the spells would keep him from wanting another woman, but he is really stuck on this Kyndal girl. I was shocked when he started dating her, because she doesn't seem like his type. Don't get me wrong, she's pretty and nice, but why would she want to be with someone like Kent? I guess, every woman loves his gifts in the bedroom.

Kent has been seeing her for over six months now and he claims that they haven't been sexually active, but I don't believe him. He hasn't even come over once to take care of me, so he has to be doing something with someone else.

I'm really pissed every time I look at these damn kids of his when I'm by myself. Don't get me wrong, he's a good father, but I want him here with us. My sister constantly reminds me that I should have been a little nicer to him when he was here, but I really can't stand him even though I love him. He should be here with us, not running around with her. I get upset every time I think about the two of them together.

Christina told me that she saw them out last week at a diner and I wanted to go over to his house and slap the black off him, but I have to keep reminding myself that we aren't together. But we should be. I'm the one that has to deal with him and all of his kids. I've been here for him since he lost his job. I deserve to be the one he's taking all around town. I can't even remember the last time we went out on a date.

Maybe I should let go and move on with my life like Taylor, Missy, and even Angela's crazy self. They have all found a way to move on with their lives. But I can't. I wish I could just forget him, but it's not that easy. I know that I deserve so much better, but for some reason I'm still in love with him and tonight is going to be the night that I'm going to tell him how I feel about him.

I knew that he was going out with Kyndal because he told me earlier today when I tried to get him to stay home with me and the kids to watch a movie, he said that he had other plans. That really pissed me off.

I started an argument with him just before he left, but he still left. I told him that he would regret it.

I wiped the tears away from my face as I pulled into the "Triumph's" parking lot and waited for them. I didn't plan to say anything to Kyndal but Kent deserved to feel some of this fire tonight.

Kent

I pulled Kyndal into me before we walked out of the restaurant. "Baby, I really meant what I said back there. I really do love you."

"Ok honey, I um. I love you too," she said.

A feeling of relief came over me because I was afraid that she would respond differently. These last six months with Kyndal have been a breath of fresh air for me. She's everything that I want in a woman. She's smart, nice, kind and sexy as hell. I want her more than she knows, but I'm actually willing to wait for her. This has been hard, but I'm still trying to figure out this problem I've been having down there with ole' boy anyway. I've been to the doctors and they said that I was fine. but I know something is wrong, because whenever Kyndal really excites me, nothing happens down there. The only person that I seem to get aroused by is Sasha, and I've tried my best to stay away from her.

She's been on my back a lot lately about spending more time with her and the kids. I just don't get what she wants from me because I don't want her and she doesn't want me either. I was kind of mad at her for how rude she was to Kyndal when I introduced them a few months back. She said that there's no need to keep introducing her to women that aren't going to be around for long. I told her that she got this one wrong because I'm starting to make plans for a future with her.

Things are looking up for me. I recently found a job that pays more than my last job did. Kyndal helped revise my resume and even performed some practice interviews with me. I love this about her. She's so caring and resourceful as well as a true lady.

"Come on baby," she said, pulling my hand. "The car is here."

I pulled out my wallet to retrieve a tip for the valet. "Just follow Marcus," she instructed.

I looked in my rearview mirror and saw a red car flashing its headlights. It looked like Sasha's car, but I knew it couldn't be her. However, as I pulled out, so did the car.

"Baby, I hope you like the spot tonight," said Kyndal.

"I hope so too," I replied, still aware of the car following us. It looked like there was a woman driving but it was so dark I couldn't see.

Kyndal has really been trying to convert me, which isn't a bad thing. I was actually learning a lot about religion. My mother would really be proud, but she's still mad at me for not trying to make things work with Sasha. Although I haven't introduced her to Kyndal yet, I'm sure that she will love her.

"I hope that one guy sings tonight. He has a way of getting people to turn their lives over to God. It's as if his voice speaks directly to your soul and demands that you ask for Salvation."

"Oh, so you think tonight is the night that I'm going to get saved," I laughed.

"I didn't say that," she said. "I know you will do what's best for you when the time is right. However, it's not a bad thing, Kent."

"Whatever, Kyndal. I just don't know if I'm ready. I mean, I won't be able to do all of the nasty things I want to do to you if I'm saved," I laughed.

"Kent you're so silly," she said hitting me. "I'm going to leave that one alone. But remember, God accepts people as they are—nasty, dirty, flaws and all."

I looked in the rearview mirror to see the car still following me. I knew then that it was Sasha. Damn, I didn't feel like dealing with her tonight, especially with Kyndal and her friends.

I placed her hand in mine, she pulled it up to her lips and kissed it.

"To a good night," she said.

"To a great one!" I replied, looking back at the car behind me, hoping my mind was playing tricks on me.

Kyndal

When we arrived at Jubilee, it was starting to rain, so Kent said that he would drop me off at the front door while he parked the car. Marcus let Gabby out as well. We went inside to the hallway to wait for them.

"Girl, guess what?" asked Gabby. "Earlier tonight, I told Marcus that I loved him."

"Wow, what did he say?"

"He said he loves me too, always have and always will."

"I'm so happy for you, Gabby. See, you got your Awesome Man of God after all!"

"Yes I have. I'm so happy Kyndal. It seems that he really does love me."

"He does. Love is a great feeling."

"Yes, yes," she responded. "What about you and Kent? I saw the way you looked all surprised when he said he loved you earlier."

"It's just that I really care for him, but I wasn't sure if it was love. I really like him and I can feel the love growing, but I'm not sure."

"You're just scared, Kyndal. Kent is nice and I can tell that you really care for him. You two have some amazing chemistry together. Aside of him having all those damn kids and not having a stable career, I think you can overlook his flaws. Promise me you won't run this time."

"Wow, Gabby. Did you just say that you liked Kent?"

"Yes, I like him for you. I want to see you happy and it looks like he makes you feel this way. I didn't say that I liked the fact that he has all those damn kids."

We laughed and the men walked in looking a little frustrated.

"Baby is everything okay?" I asked Kent.

"Yes. Let's just get to our seats. I need a drink," he said.

I laughed. "Well I hope you enjoy your sparkling grape juice."

Marcus led Gabby to the table right in front of the stage, where we were seated the very first time we were here. We followed close behind.

"Hey friends," Gerald said as soon we sat down at the table next to them. Melissa smiled at me and I smiled back and waved.

Their wedding day was approaching. She visited my office last month to ask my advice on if she should tell Gerald about her life before she came back to church. I told her that she needed to be honest with him and at least tell him about having and losing a child because he should know that, but she disagreed. I told her to ask God what he wanted her to do and to listen closely for his response.

Kent flagged the waitress and told her to bring him the strongest drink they had and she said she would bring a glass of sparkling red grape juice instead of white. We laughed.

Once the show began, Kent seemed to relax a little. He laughed at some of the poetry and was amazed by the gospel rap. Once the singers began to sing, I thought I saw him bow his head a couple of times. When my favorite singer Michael got on stage and began to sing William McDowell's *I give myself away* I couldn't help but rejoice and give praise.

It wasn't until the song was almost over and he was asking those in the audience that needed salvation to ask for it that I saw Kent's hand rise. However, he didn't get up from his seat. He just sat there with one hand raised repeating the words of the song. I turned away from him because I wanted him to enjoy this moment alone.

I turned to Gabby who was crying herself.

"I'm ready Kyndal," she said lifting her hands. "I'm ready."

I held one of her hands while Marcus held the other. Once the song was over, many rejoiced, many kept praising God. Everyone stood to their feet. Kent seemed to be filled with the spirit. His head remained bowed, but his lips were moving.

Gerald took the stage and asked all believers to stand and give praise to God. He gave a testimony about how he was saved at the age of 17 after an attack on his life almost took him out. He said that he too was a victim of the streets. He told of how he once lived a life that he hadn't told anyone about, not even his family. However, he said that, when he was faced with death, he confessed to God that he would surrender his life to him if he just allowed him one more chance to live.

He screamed, "I surrendered and I thank God that I can you see now. Thank God!" everyone clapped.

The last singer took the stage and began to sing Mary Mary's "God in Me," which changed the mood of the crowd.

Once she was finished, Marcus got down on one knee and took Gabby's hand, "Gabrielle, earlier today, when you professed your love for me, that was the greatest feeling I've had since I been with you. That day, that you walked through those doors, I knew that my prayers were finally answered because God had sent me my angel. Today, I vow to make my angel my wife. Gabrielle, Will you marry me?"

"Yes," she said, crying. I came over and started hugging both of them before they could hug each other.

I turned to look at Kent, who was standing behind me smiling. A few of Marcus's friends that were sitting at the table next to us congratulated them too.

I walked over to Kent and said, "I'm so happy for them baby."

He agreed. "I'm also happy for you." I said to him. He smiled.

"Salvation is a great thing."

Thirty minutes later, we headed to the car. Kent held my hand as I leaned into him. "Baby," he said.

"I really do enjoy you and I love spending time with you. Thank you for tonight. No, better yet, thank God."

I smiled and looked up at him. Before I could kiss him, I saw a red car speeding our way.

"Baby…" I said as he pushed me aside. Before I could move completely away the car sped up and hit him.

"Kent!" I screamed. The lady in the car got out.

"I'm sorry. I'm sorry," she repeated. That's when I noticed that she was the mother of his children, Sasha.

Kent

All I could see were the headlights from Sasha's car coming towards me after I pushed Kyndal out of the way. After that I fell to the ground. I could hear people screaming around me, but I couldn't move.

"Oh God, please just let me get up." I tried to move my body, but nothing happened. I tried to lift my head, but I couldn't move. "Sasha," I screamed as she got out of her car and ran towards the crowd. No one heard me.

"I'm sorry, I'm sorry," she kept repeating.

Marcus knelt down beside me. "Can you hear me Kent?" I said 'yes', but he repeated it again. This time I screamed 'yes'. Still nothing.

"Call the police, now!" I heard someone scream.

"Kyndal," I yelled. I couldn't see her. "Why can't they hear me?"

"Kyndal?" I screamed again I saw Gabby was now holding her as she cried standing beside Marcus.

"Oh God No!" I screamed. "I'm right here," I yelled again. Still nothing.

I heard the EMS coming closer. "Okay I'm going to be fine. Nothing's wrong. They just can't hear me right now. Please God. Let me be okay. Please," I yelled after the EMS placed me in the ambulance.

They placed an oxygen mask over my face. I heard one of them say that my vitals were very low. They closed the door and rushed me to the hospital. "Oh God, this isn't looking good. They're gonna save me right? I was only hit by a car. I can't go out like this. I'm not ready. Why would she do this? They have to save me. Okay, all I have to do is show them that I can breathe. I'm breathing now. Check the machine again, man!"

The alerts started going off on the machine. "I think we're losing him!" one of the paramedics shouted.

"Hang on now," said the other one.

The doors opened and doctors came running towards the EMS. "Okay, I'm good now. They're going to save me, just as they do many people every day."

"Get him into ICU right now," I heard one of them say. "He's going to need blood right away. We have to stop the bleeding."

278

The next thing I knew, I was being flipped, poked and cut. I could see all the blood. I started to panic.

"Okay, God. I hope we're on good terms now. I know I haven't always lived the best life, but I haven't done enough wrong to deserve to die. Please God. Please. Don't let me go. Who's going to take care of my family? What about my kids? I'm too young. I'm only 31. I have a full life to live. I've been trying to do better. Please God, just give me another chance. I promise. I promise. I'm not sure what to promise, but I promise I'm going to do better from this day forward. I asked for salvation tonight and hopefully you heard me. Please God Please. Don't let me go like this."

All I could hear was the sound of the flat beep sound. We're losing him. They pumped on my chest. The flat beeping noise continued. "I think we lost him."

"God please, I'll give you my life. Just let me live. "

The doctors made two more attempts before I heard the flat beep go to a rapid beeping noise. "He's fine but we need another pint of blood stat."

"God has done it again," I heard one of them say.

"Every day," another one chanted. "If only they knew."

After giving me another pint of blood, the doctors left and a nurse came in to see if I could respond to her voice. I guess they still couldn't hear me, but the hand squeeze seemed to be sufficient.

Shortly after, I heard my mom, say "Thank you, Jesus," as she walked into the room.

"My baby," she said as she walked over to me. "My baby." She touched my face and then my father walked in.

"Hi Rose," he said to her. She didn't respond, still being her same stubborn self.

"How is he?" he asked. She still didn't respond.

Damn, Ma I almost died and you still can't get along with Pops. This is sad.

"Rose," he said. "I hope we're not going to have to go through this here. Our son almost died for Christ sake."

"How dare you even utter the word 'Christ'. Don't use His name in vain."

"Okay Rose, I'm not going to do this tonight. I'm here for my son, as I've always been."

"Hmph. That's because I made you be a father to him, but that didn't do him any good, did it? Running around with all types of different women and look where it's gotten him!"

"You ought to be ashamed of yourself right now Rose. Our son is lying here fighting for his life and you're still trying to fight with me because I didn't want to be with you. Rose, did you ever think that you were the reason he turned out the way he did? If you were there for him, showing him the love that he needed and wanted from you, maybe he would have turned out differently. But no, you wanted to so-call punish me by making me be a father. Please! If that's what they teach you at church and bible school, then I'm glad he wasn't raised by you."

Please just shut up the both you, I yelled. They didn't hear me.

"You didn't raise him, I did," she replied.

"Do what you do best? Take credit for the good. I wonder if God knows that you're an evil liar."

She rushed over towards him but the nurse interrupted them. "Excuse me, Miss. There's a lady outside in the waiting room that says she's his girlfriend. She asked to come in, but I told her family only. She said she was with him tonight."

"No, don't let her in," my mother replied. "Let me go see who it is."

"She's in the lobby," the nurse said and closed the door behind her.

"I hope it's Sasha," she said, walking towards the door. "Maybe she can tell me what happened to him."

Damn. I really felt bad knowing that it was Kyndal, not Sasha, waiting in the lobby. Kyndal hadn't met my mom yet. I hadn't even told my mom that I was seeing someone else because she was still pressing the issue of me and Sasha getting back together. If only they could hear me. "Pops!" I yelled.

He walked over towards me. "Son, I hope you're doing okay. Sorry about your Mom, she's never gonna change. You shouldn't have to hear us fight like this. Son get better. Love ya," he said walking away.

"Love you too Pops. I'm okay," I replied, as he walked away closing the door.

I wished I could be there with Kyndal right now. I feel bad that I put her in this situation and now she has to deal with my mom. Fucking Sasha! Why would she do this? I told her that I didn't want to be with her and she made it clear that she didn't want to be with me either. Damn, man. I know Kyndal probably won't stay with me after this. Sasha tried to take her life too.

I probably should have been more careful, knowing that she was there. I didn't expect her to wait around after we went in. She tried to make a scene in the parking lot before we walked in, but I told her it was best that she left. Although she seemed a little upset, I never would have thought she'd do something like this.

Damn Sasha. Damn!

Sasha

"I'm sorry, I'm sorry I didn't mean to hit him," I screamed but it seemed as though no one was listening. I heard someone call the police but I couldn't focus. Kent was lying there right in front of my car, bleeding like crazy. "I'm sorry," I repeated over and over. No one came to comfort me. Instead, they rushed towards him and his little girlfriend, who was now crying on the sidelines.

"I'm sorry," I repeated again. But I really didn't feel sorry. He embarrassed me in front of his friend earlier when I tried to talk to him. He didn't show me any respect when he asked me to leave. I am the mother of his children. I deserved a little more respect from him. When I asked him to come talk to me alone for a minute, he said that he couldn't because he had to get back to Kyndal.

"Oh really?" I said.

"Go home to the kids," was all he said.

That really pissed me off. He could've at least talked to me for a few minutes. As I sat in the parking lot, I debated on going inside and making a scene, but I couldn't move. I was heated as I sat in the car watching the door. It took them 2 ½ hours to come out of that place. When I saw them walking in the street, cuddling, I didn't know what to do, so I drove towards them. When he leaned in to kiss her, I pushed the gas, not caring what happened next. "Boom," was all I heard. It took me a few minutes to realize what I had just done. It was too late to think. Kent was lying in front of my car, bleeding profusely.

As the police sirens neared, I got nervous. I couldn't go to jail. I had to get home to the kids. I couldn't move the car and I couldn't run because the whole crowd was staring at me like I was the bad guy. Didn't they know he deserved it? He was a liar, a cheater and he should have stayed home with his family instead of running the streets with all those tramps all the time.

"She's right there," I heard someone say when the police arrived.

"Ma'm, is this your vehicle?" an officer asked.

"Yes," I replied nervously.

"Please follow me over to the squad car, I want to ask you a few questions."

"Sure," I replied, as we walked.

"Can you tell me what happened here tonight?"

I told him that I was driving and I didn't see them crossing the street and before I knew it, I hit him. He wrote my information down, then asked me if I could call someone to pick me up because the car would be towed.

I quickly pulled out my phone to call Christina. She got there in 15 minutes. When she asked me what happened, I told her the truth. She began shaking her head, saying that I should know better. I told her that I didn't want to talk about it, but she said I didn't have a choice. She suggested that we go to the hospital to check on Kent, which I refused. I didn't feel like dealing with any more of this tonight. I just needed to get some rest.

Kyndal

How dare this lady tell me that I need to go home and get some rest. I needed to know if Kent was going to be okay. When she told me that she was his mother, I expected her to be little more caring and understanding instead, she was very short with me, as if I was the one that hit him, not Sasha, the mother of his children, as I'd told her.

I waited in the lobby as she walked away. Twenty minutes later, I noticed an older man that looked just like Kent at the trash can. "Excuse me," I said to him.

"Yes," he replied.

"Do you know Kent?"

"Yes, he's my son. Who are you?"

"My name is Kyndal. I'm his friend. Is he doing alright?"

"I just spoke with the nurse and she told me that he was stable. However, he hasn't fully come to yet. She said he lost a lot of blood and had to get a transfusion. But he should be fine."

"Thank God," I replied softly. Lord knows I can't take another death on my watch just yet.

"Would you like to see him?" he asked.

"Yes," I replied. "But his mother told me to go home."

"I see," he said shaking his head. "You can come back with me if you like."

"I would love that," I replied, as I followed him back to Kent's room.

I wasn't surprised to see the breathing tubes, but I was still taken aback by how swollen the left side of his head was. I turned my head for a brief moment to contain myself.

"It looks bad, I know," his father noted.

I walked over to his bedside and rubbed his hand. I didn't know what to say or if I should say anything.

284

I didn't expect the night to go this way. We were having a good time. I probably should have told the police what happened, but I couldn't speak with them because I was still in shock. Sasha actually tried to kill us. Now that I think about it, she was trying to kill me.

It wasn't until that moment that I felt angry—angry at both of them. Kent had no right placing me in the middle of his baby mama drama. I removed my hand from his.

His father placed his hands on my shoulder. All the sadness I felt was leaving. I said a short prayer for him and left the room.

He would definitely be on my prayer list, but that was it. I didn't have any more room left in me for sympathies or tragedies.

"Its best that I remove myself early before it's too late," I said to myself.

Gabrielle

"Wow baby, what a night?" I said to Marcus as we entered my living room.

"Yes, what a night," he replied.

After leaving Kyndal at the hospital to speak with Kent's mother, we were finally arriving at home. It was 4:30 a.m.

"I hope he's okay," I said to Marcus, as I removed my clothes in the bedroom. He headed towards the bathroom.

"Baby, it's okay if you stay in here. I'm only undressing," I said to him.

"I know, but I still want us to keep our respect in line," he replied.

"Ok," I said, not wanting to do anything but jump in the bed. Five minutes later, Marcus joined me dressed in his T-shirt and boxers.

I was so sleepy, I didn't have enough energy to turn to him and give him a kiss goodnight.

"Baby," I said. "Can you come closer and kiss me good night?"

He softly kissed my cheek and then my forehead.

"I love you," I said before he moved away.

"I love you too," he replied.

This was one of many nights that I felt like saying this but just couldn't manage to get it out. I played with the ring on my finger and started thinking about how I'd managed to get here from where I'd just come from. It seemed like I was just under a dangerous attack and then out of nowhere, my knight in shining armor appeared.

"Gabby," he said. "Have you thought about what happened today at all?"

"Of course," I said smiling. "You're talking about the proposal right?"

"I'm talking about everything—love, life and death—and how they can all be here at one moment and then either gone or taken away from you the next. Think about it. Here we are, praising God and celebrating life, and then the next minute, you're crying and praying in hope of saving a life. Life is just too short. I mean, you just never know."

"I know honey, I know," I said, turning to face him.

"I'm thinking that we should just enjoy it while we're here. Tomorrow is really not promised."

I wasn't sure if he meant we should have sex right now or what, by the way he was looking at me. I remained silent because I didn't want to ruin it. But I kind of liked the whole idea of waiting until we were married to do it.

"Why don't we just do it baby?" he said.

"Do what?" I asked wanting to get a full understanding of what he meant. I really didn't want to do it now, but I would, if that's what he wanted. I'm just scared that he'll get it and leave me looking stupid like all the others, just when I thought I had something good.

"Let's just get married now baby?"

"Now?" I said shocked.

"Yes, we can do it in a couple weeks if you want to wait," he said lifting his head from the pillow. "I mean, I know you may have this big wedding day planned and I want you to have that. But let's just do it."

I was really surprised. I honestly didn't expect this from him. I hadn't expected him to propose so quickly and now he wanted to get married right away. I was happier than he knew. I'd never planned a big wedding because I never thought that I would even marry. That's what Kyndal wanted. He knows that I can't have kids, so there was no rush to get married, as we won't be starting a family. I guess, he really does want to be with me forever. Wow. Forever.

"Okay," I replied. "Okay."

Sasha

"Okay Christina, what do you think I should do? Tell on myself?" I screamed at her across the room.

"I think that's exactly what you should do, Sasha. You should be glad that he didn't die last night. What would you tell the kids? You killed their father, or better yet, that you were just so jealous and angry that he didn't want to be with you that you tried to kill him and his girlfriend."

"Get out of my house Christina!" I yelled.

"I'm not going anywhere. You need to call his mom and tell her what you did or I will."

"Get of my house damn it!"

"Look at you. You're not even the least bit sorry for what you did. I haven't seen you cry once since I picked you up last night. You never loved him Sasha, did you?"

I sat there for a moment, trying to convince myself that what she was saying was wrong. I wanted to cry I just couldn't. I loved Kent, but I wasn't in love with him.

"Didn't Aunt Lolly warn you about the dangers of using those love potions? Looks like yours turned out to be a disaster instead of true love!"

"Get out of my house Christina, right now! Get the hell out!"

She picked up her bag to leave. "I'm leaving, but I'm calling Mom to tell her about what happened last night. You need to get some help, Sasha, for real."

She slammed the door and I sat down on the couch. I wanted to go the hospital to see if Kent was okay, but I knew that I should probably stay away from him at this point. Although I hadn't received a call from his mother, I knew that she had probably heard about what happened.

Knock. Knock. "Come in Christina," I yelled at the door without getting up.

"It's not Christina," said Kent's mom as she came into the door.

"Ms. Rose! I mean, hi," I stuttered.

"Hi Sasha," she said softly. "Where are the kids?"

"They're over my mom's house."

"Have you been to the hospital yet?" she asked.

"Umm no, I was just getting ready to—"

"To do what?" she yelled, cutting me off. "Sasha, I really loved and respected you as a daughter. I would have never in a million years, thought you were capable of doing something like this to my son."

"I'm sorry," I said breaking down. "I didn't mean to."

"Oh you meant to do it honey, so don't lie to me. You're going to have to take that up with God. If I weren't a Christian, I would be on the other side of that couch right now. But because I know and love the Lord, I'm going to leave the punishment that you receive up to him. I can't believe that I was pressuring Kent to marry you—a woman that would take his life, all because he didn't want to share it with you."

"Ms. Rose, you just don't understand—" I started, but was cut off.

"Oh yes, I do. I've been where you are with Kent's father. However, I wanted to take his life in a different way. This is my son. My flesh and blood. I never would have thought," she said shaking her head.

"I'm sorry Ms. Rose, I truly am. If I could take back everything, I would."

"Well you better start by asking God to forgive you. The rest will be up to Him."

She pulled the door back open and left.

"It's too late for that. It's too late for everything," I said crying.

Kyndal

"Everything just happened so fast," I said to Dr. Anderson. "I mean, one minute, we're declaring our love for one another, and then, he's almost gone. But I still just can't get over the fact that it could've been me lying in that hospital bed."

"I can definitely understand where you're coming from, Kyndal. But what you have to understand is that it wasn't you. There's no reason for you to hang on to those thoughts. Instead, you should be celebrating the fact that you're alive."

"Celebrating, huh? And to think that I've been saved and rejoicing everyday up until this point. I know if God is looking down on me, he is hoping that I haven't given up on Him again, and I haven't. I just get confused sometimes, dealing with life."

"We all do," said Dr. Anderson

"You know what's funny? I'm usually the one to give suggestions on what to do in order to move forward. But look at me. I haven't even gone back to say my official goodbye to Kent."

"So he's doing okay?"

"Yes, I spoke with his father and he told me that he has fully recovered and, other than his leg being in a cast, he's going to be okay."

"That's great, Kyndal. Why don't you go see him? It seems to me that you care for him deeply. You said that, right before the accident, you declared your love for each other, right?"

"Yes, but I'm scared. I'm scared of all the things that he comes with. I'm scared that I really love him, but I don't know if I can take another failed relationship."

"Have you prayed about it?"

"I have and I keep getting this feeling that I'm supposed to be there for him, but I just can't."

"Kyndal, you've been through a lot over the last two years and I can understand your hesitation, but how can you move forward if you keep holding yourself back?"

"I know Dr. Anderson. I know all too well what I need to do. I just hope I have the courage to do it."

After leaving Dr. Andersons' office, I called Gabby. We made plans to meet for lunch to go over a few things for her "speed wedding".

"Hey Gabby, I'm running a little behind. I'll be there in 10 minutes."

"Okay," see you there.

I was so happy for my friend. All the things that she had wanted were finally coming through for her. I wasn't thrilled about having to plan a wedding in two and a half weeks but it would definitely take my mind off my situation with Kent.

When I arrived at the restaurant, Gabby was there, with another one our mutual friends, Sarah. They had already ordered food for us and had brochures and pictures set out on the table. We reviewed some of the information and made a few choices on décor and flower arrangements. After we left the restaurant, we headed to *La' Belle Brides*—my favorite bridal boutique. Gabby had already declared a Cinderella style dress but I had my heart set on her wearing something more modern. As she made a few choices to try on, I browsed through the racks for long trains and a more bodice style, just in case she changed her mind.

As I searched the racks, I couldn't help but think about being in this very same place two years prior. I had found the most beautiful gown. Gabby was here with me and we'd spent almost eight hours in the store, laughing about dresses.

After Gabby tried on the first two gowns, I asked her to try on a gown that I had selected. She said it wasn't my wedding but she would try it on just for me. The dress looked amazing on her. She tried to act as if she didn't love it at first, but immediately fell in love with it after looking at herself in the three-way mirror. Two hours later, my dress won and we were headed out.

"Kyndal," said Gabby on the drive home. "What's going on with you and Kent?"

"Umm, I haven't been back to see him since he has fully recovered."

"What?" she asked.

"I haven't been back to see him yet," I repeated.

"I heard what you said. I just can't believe you."

"I know. I just didn't want to deal with it."

"Damn Kyndal, I thought you were better than that. How can you be so in love with a person one moment, and then just leave him when he's down?"

"It wasn't like that, Gabby. That woman could have killed both of us that night. I've got too much on my plate already."

"Like what Kyndal? Work, church and work. You really need to get over yourself and your selfish ways. I bet he's going crazy, trying to figure out why you're not there with him. Now, I was never a big Kent fan because I've dealt with men like him in my past, but after seeing you two together and how much he really cares for you, I like him a lot. There's no telling what was going on in that girl's head. Maybe she just couldn't deal with him not wanting her anymore. Who knows? But you should at least give him a chance to explain."

"You're right. Maybe I'll go see him later today or tomorrow."

"Today Kyndal," she said, opening the door. "Tomorrow's not promised, remember that."

Kent

It's been two days since I've been lying awake in this hospital bed. The doctors said that I can go home tomorrow. They told me that my recovery from the head injury with no brain damage was miraculous. I just told them that I only have God to thank for that. They laughed as if it was a joke and I joined in because I knew the truth.

Most of my family has been here to see me, including Taylor, Angela and Missy with the kids. My mother has pretty much told the story to everyone, so I have a feeling that's part of the reason Sasha hasn't come to see me yet.

However, I'm really worried about Kyndal. Pops told me that she called daily to check on me, but never wanted to speak with me directly. I knew why and I couldn't blame her. I just hoped that it would somehow be different.

"Son, I'm going to have to leave for the day but I'll be back bright and early to pick you up," said my Mom.

"Okay Mom, thanks for everything."

To my surprise, she was being friendlier to my dad over the last two days. I don't know what happened to her, but I'm glad for that change.

Shortly, after my mom left, Sasha arrived without the kids.

"Hi Kent," she said as she walked in the doorway. She looked terrible. Her hair looked as if she hadn't combed it in days and her clothes were a mess.

"Sasha," I said looking in her direction.

"I hope I don't look too bad," she said shyly.

I didn't respond, partly because I didn't want to tell her the truth, but also because I didn't want to make her feel like everything was okay.

"Kent, I just came to tell you that I was sorry. These last few days have been the worst days of my life. I feel so bad for what I did to you. I just hope that you can forgive me," she said and started crying.

I stared at her because, as bad as I wanted not to forgive her, the love that I had for her wouldn't allow me to do that. She was the mother of my children and had been a great friend for many years. I could feel the hurt and the sincerity behind her words. Who was I to stay mad at her for all that she had done to me? God had given me a second chance. She deserved one too.

"Kent, I feel like I need to tell you everything before I go. I have always loved you. I wanted so much more for us. That's why I called my Aunt Lolly and asked her to give me the love potions that would make you love me back and stop cheating on me with other women."

"You did what?" I said angrily.

"I was hoping that everything would work out fine, but it didn't. In return, I became more vengeful and angry and you moved further away. I really didn't plan to hurt you that night, but something came over me after I saw you kiss her."

"Sasha, you could've killed us!" I yelled, turning my head away from her.

"I know and I'm sorry for that Kent. I'm sorry for everything. That's why I don't deserve to live," she said as she began to cry.

"Sasha, you should be sorry for what you done. But there's no need for you to talk like that," I said turning towards her.

"I don't Kent. That's why I came to say goodbye," she said crying harder. "I just don't deserve to live."

Kyndal walked into the room. She had tears coming down her face. She walked closer to my bed to where Sasha was standing and hugged her.

No one said anything for about 10 minutes, as Sasha broke down in Kyndal's arms.

"You deserve to live honey because God said so," said Kyndal. "Your kids need you and so does Kent. I'm here for you and we forgive you."

Sasha continued to cry, as they left the room. I was amazed by what had just happened in front of me. Kyndal was definitely a good woman, stronger than most I'd encountered. I just hoped that she would hopefully find a way to forgive me too.

Kyndal

I stood outside of Kent's room for about 15 minutes. I saw Sasha walk in and decided that it was best if I just stayed outside until she left because I didn't know how I would react towards either of them. After hearing her tell of all the things she did to get him to love her, my heart went out to her because I'd heard this same story so many times before. I cried, because a part of me felt bad for her, but also because I felt bad for myself. I thought about all the clients of my past being a reflection of myself. I'd done bad things to people all for the sake of love.

As I walked Sasha out of the hospital and drove her to her mother's house. I told her that she needed to seek God and ask him for forgiveness for all the things that she had done. I told her that from this day forward, she would have to dedicate her life to building a better relationship with her children and with God, so that she would be able to have all of the desires of her heart without having to choose other means to find love.

When she asked me why I was doing this for her.

I replied, "I was once dying to be loved. But God saved me and he'll save you too."

Epilogue

I stood at the top of the altar, waiting for Gabby to walk down the aisle. I had already started crying in the dressing room, as I watched her get dressed. She was definitely the most beautiful bride I'd ever seen. I watched as Marcus made his way down the aisle, smiling. Then came Gabby. I held my tears, as I'd promised her I wouldn't cry because she said she wanted beautiful pictures and we wouldn't have time to redo my make-up. When it was time for them to say 'I do', I almost said it with them.

I looked over into the crowd, where I saw Kent sitting beside my mom and Noah, dressed so handsomely. He smiled at me and mouthed "Beautiful." I smiled back at him.

After he was released from the hospital, I told him that we could continue seeing each other. This has taken a lot of prayer and asking for guidance on my part. But I'm proud of the man that he has become.

I know that this may be hard for many of you to believe, but I really think that I found true love. Kent's doing his part to show me and hasn't held anything back. Finally, I no longer feel the need to run away from love. I know that this time it's real because my heart says so.

For now, we're just taking it one day at a time, with God's help, of course.

Dying To Be Loved….Coming Soon

"I love you," I said to Marcus as he got out of the bed. This last week that we'd shared together in Italy had been absolutely wonderful.

The Le Boule Hotel was perfect for honeymooners and this room had so many places that we could make love. Speaking of making love Marcus and I …….

Ringg. Ringg.

"Gabby, it's me Kyndal."

"Hey," were the only words I managed to get in.

"I really can't believe it Gabby. I still can't believe that I waited this long for Kent and he …."

"Can't what?" I said to her right as Marcus walked into the room.

"Baby, I have to run out for a moment. I need to call a friend back home."

"Who?" I asked.

"Kent?" yelled Kyndal through the phone.

"Gerald?" answered Marcus.

"Oh," I replied.

"Why are you just saying oh," yelled Kyndal. "Did you hear what I just told you?"

"What?" I asked both of them.

"I said I'm going to the lobby baby. I'll be right back."

"Ok," I replied.

"Gabby what are you talking about?" yelled Kyndal. "I feel so stupid."

"Why?" I asked as Marcus closed the door.

"Hey man, sorry it took so long," said Marcus.

"That's okay. I just feel like my whole life is in shams right now. I can't believe she would do something like this and not tell me," said Gerald.

"Wow, man I would have never thought Melissa would be capable of that."

"Who are you telling? replied Gerald.

"I hope you're not still thinking of marrying her," said Marcus.

"It's almost like I don't have choice. I'd be disrespecting the family and not to mention that Pastor Graves has placed me on a higher level since I proposed."

"Damn man. I'd hate to be you right now. But there is no way I'd be marrying a whore. Who knows what all she did while she was out running the streets."

"I know because she said she told me everything and some of those things I still can't help but be angry about. But I have to do what's right by her family and the church."

"No man you need to think about this and do what's right for you? Do you really think it's okay to live a lie," said Marcus.

"No I don't man. But enough about me. How's the new wife?"

"She's great," I replied. "She's upstairs talking to Kyndal."

"Kyndal," said Gerald softly. "I miss her."

"You what?" asked Marcus.

"Nothing man," he replied. "She was a great friend."

"Alright now Gerald," Marcus replied. "You know its not too late to change your mind."

"I know but I have a lot to think about. I'm really going to have to keep my hears open and wait for the answer to come from the man above on this one. Enjoy your honeymoon, I'll catch you when you come back to the states."

I took the elevator back upstairs to the room. I hoped that Gabby was still lying in the bed waiting for me. When I opened the door she placed the phone back on the nightstand.

"Baby, you're not going to believe what happened between Kent and Kyndal."

"No you're not going to believe what happened between Gerald and Melissa."

"Well you go first," Gabby replied.

"No I think we should wait until after I have a little bit more of you," Marcus said while undressing.

"Yeah I think that can wait," I said crawling down to the edge of the bed……

HELP THE AUTHOR CHOOSE THE TITLE of the SEQUEL

DYING TO BE LOVED BY YOU

OR

DYING TO BE LOVED II: DAMAGED GOODS

Log on to take the poll @:

www.ericacoleman.com

TO MEET THE CHARACTERS OF DYING TO BE LOVED, VIEW SCENE PORTRAYALS, VOTE FOR YOUR FAVORITE CHARACTERS AND LEAVE FEEDBACK.
VISIT WWW.ERICACOLEMAN.COM
Join the facebook fanpage
@DYINGTOBELOVEDBYERICACOLEMAN

About The Author

Erica Monique Coleman was born and raised in Detroit, Michigan. Coleman graduated from Wayne State University with a Bachelors degree in Journalism. Coleman's creative talents as a writer, model, actor and spokesperson have enabled her to communicate and befriend large groups of men and women "who all have a story to tell." Writing has been her passion for many years, but her focus has mainly been on women's' life issues, as featured on her Blog titled, "Girl Let Me Tell You." She currently resides in Detroit, MI with her son whom she hopes will follow in her creative footsteps. *Dying To Be Loved* is her first novel with hopes of many more to follow.

A Word from the Author

I started writing this book on 1-11-11 after I declared that it was time that I release the hold on my gift and finally finish a book this year. I didn't know exactly how or what I was going to write about but I knew that I wanted to write something that would speak to readers. I declared on this day 1-11-11 that it shall be done.

However, as we all know life continues without us ever knowing what the end result will be. I held onto the prologue for about 3 months before I wrote chapter one. It wasn't until I experienced a little bit of sadness that I really started to write the book in late April. After two trying months, I continued to weather the storm refusing to give up.

In writing this book I became one with each individual character. In doing so, I was able to open myself up and allow the words to flow freely. As I almost reached the end, I let go and allowed God to take over my mind, body and spirit. In doing so, many new creative doors began to open for me. My word choices and creativity was becoming something unimaginable. Music played a huge part in this writing process as you may have noticed throughout the book.

However, I still didn't feel that I could end it. Therefore, I allowed myself to step away from it for three months with another promise that I would eventually finish.

During those three months my life changed. My way of thinking changed. I believe my whole disposition changed. I was taken on a spiritual journey that I still can't explain to anyone if I were asked to this very day. However, I am so thankful and grateful that I was enabled.

It wasn't until the end of September that I was able to finish the last chapters of the book in one week. God is so good.

I hope that in reading this that you will be taken on a journey. If you are dealing with any issues in life, I hope that you will find a way to face those things and let go so that you to will be able to move forward with your life.

God Bless

Moving Forward Publications

14404826R00161

Made in the USA
Charleston, SC
09 September 2012